VOLUME 2

FUJINO OMORI

ILLUSTRATION BY
KIYOTAKA HAIMURA

CHARACTER DESIGN BY
SUZUHITO YASUDA

YEN
ON

NEW YORK

IS IT WRONG TO TRY TO PICK UP GIRLS IN A DUNGEON?
ON THE SIDE: SWORD ORATORIA, Volume 2
FUJINO OMORI

Translation by Andrew Gaippe
Cover art by Kiyotaka Haimura

This book is a work of fiction. Names, characters, places, and incidents are the product of the author's imagination or are used fictitiously. Any resemblance to actual events, locales, or persons, living or dead, is coincidental.

DUNGEON NI DEAI WO MOTOMERU NO WA MACHIGATTEIRUDAROUKA GAIDEN SWORD ORATORIA vol. 2
Copyright © 2014 Fujino Omori
Illustration copyright © Kiyotaka Haimura
Original Character Design © Suzuhito Yasuda
All rights reserved.
Original Japanese edition published in 2014 by SB Creative Corp.
This English edition is published by arrangement with SB Creative Corp., Tokyo, in care of Tuttle-Mori Agency, Inc., Tokyo.

English translation © 2017 by Yen Press, LLC

Yen On
1290 Avenue of the Americas
New York, NY 10104

Visit us at yenpress.com
facebook.com/yenpress
twitter.com/yenpress
yenpress.tumblr.com
instagram.com/yenpress

First Yen On Edition: February 2017

Yen On is an imprint of Yen Press, LLC.
The Yen On name and logo are trademarks of Yen Press, LLC.

The publisher is not responsible for websites (or their content) that are not owned by the publisher.

Library of Congress Cataloging-in-Publication Data
Names: Ōmori, Fujino, author. | Haimura, Kiyotaka, 1973– illustrator. | Yasuda, Suzuhito, designer.
Title: Is it wrong to try to pick up girls in a dungeon? on the side: sword oratoria / story by Fujino Omori ; illustration by Kiyotaka Haimura ; original design by Suzuhito Yasuda.
Other titles: Danjon ni deai o motomeru no wa machigatteirudarouka gaiden sword oratoria. English.
Description: New York, NY : Yen On, 2016– | Series: Is it wrong to try to pick up girls in a dungeon? on the side: sword oratoria
Identifiers: LCCN 2016023729 | ISBN 9780316315333 (v. 1 : paperback) | ISBN 9780316318167 (v. 2 : paperback)
Subjects: | CYAC: Fantasy.
Classification: LCC PZ7.1.O54 Isg 2016 | DDC [Fic]—dc23
LC record available at https://lccn.loc.gov/2016023729

ISBNs: 978-0-316-31816-7 (paperback)
978-0-316-31817-4 (ebook)

3 5 7 9 10 8 6 4 2

LSC-C

Printed in the United States of America

VOLUME 2

FUJINO OMORI

ILLUSTRATION BY **KIYOTAKA HAIMURA**
CHARACTER DESIGN BY **SUZUHITO YASUDA**

IT BEGAN
IN A
BEDROOM

Гэта казка іншага сям'і.

Узнікненне ў спальні

It was a dark room.

A single magic-stone lamp on the wall was the only source of light. The corners of the room were masked in shadow. The air inside the chamber was damp and filled with the earthy scent of rocks. The only color in the room came from crystals among the silver and steel, and the rather fancy decorations adorning the walls and dangling from the ceiling glittered blue in the light.

However, the light itself was little more than a flickering candle. It barely illuminated the red rug on the floor, the wicker baskets along the walls, the wide shelving unit, or the crudely constructed bed in the center.

Two figures entered the room.

One of them was completely covered in full-plated body armor. The other was draped in a slightly dirty robe paired with a hood; the outfit covered the wearer from the face down. The two exchanged few words as they placed their belongings, starting with a backpack, in a dark corner before making their way to the wooden bed.

A man's face emerged from beneath an intimidating helmet, then he started removing his his armor one piece at a time, all the way down to the greaves that covered the tips of his toes. A fortress of flesh appeared from beneath his inner shirt, and the adventurer was already half naked. Leaving his underwear on for the time being, the man took a seat on the side of the bed and glanced at the hooded figure. The cloak was not all that tight around her body, and yet her figure was easily distinguishable when looking at her ample breasts and slim waist. It became even easier when she started to peel back layers of clothing to bare her skin.

"Oi, strip already. Don't kill the mood after coming this far."

"Hold on. Don't be greedy."

The woman's high-pitched voice was surprisingly calm as it

responded to the man's naked desire. Slender fingers came out from beneath the cloak and pulled back her hood. At the same time, she loosened the string holding her hair in place. Unraveling all at once, it tumbled down her back with a soft swoosh.

She was a captivating woman.

Her body was a mass of seductive curves that would instantly grab the attention of any man. Her supple breasts were inviting, and she had a pleasingly rounded backside that could arouse just about anyone's desire. Her thin waist was rather high, her arms and legs lithe and thin. Her calm voice and demeanor seemed to contradict the alluring pheromones that wafted from her soft skin.

The large man on the bed knew from the start how provocative the woman's body was, but as he watched the cloak fall away from her, her face took his breath away. The light from the lamps dimly lit her figure, causing the man to audibly gulp.

"Why do you hide such a beautiful face?"

"To keep men like you from hounding me."

The woman smiled as she responded to the dumbfounded man's question without missing a beat. Not a single thread of cloth was left on her body as she slid in close to the adventurer. Wrapping her soft body in his arms, the man pushed her down onto the bed.

The shadows of the two figures intertwined on the wall; the wooden bed groaned beneath them.

"About what we were talking about before…what kind of quest did you take on?"

The woman spoke just before the fireworks could get under way.

The man paused, thinking for a moment as the seductive woman lay on her back beneath him. He froze, his lips mere moments from falling onto hers. Collecting his thoughts, he finally spoke.

"It was a strange one: head down to the thirtieth floor, collect some weird thing, and come back…"

The man seemed to suddenly recall something as he looked up from his partner.

She silently raised her eyes toward the man's not-so-large, yet muscular body.

"Oops, that was supposed to be classified. Do me a favor: Pretend you didn't hear it."

"Is that right...?"

She met his eyes as she spoke, placing her hand on his cheek.

Her dainty hand skimmed his face, running her fingers down his chin and angling toward the neck in almost a caress.

Then, suddenly, she gripped his throat.

"?!"

Five fingers sank deep into the muscular man's neck. Armor off and guard completely down, the man could only frantically grab at the hand threatening to suffocate him. Surprise and fear filled his eyes, but his assailant's arm didn't budge in the slightest.

He was unable to put up a decent fight. The room suddenly filled with the echoes of cracking bone and ripping tendon. The man's eyes became bloodshot as his mouth opened and closed over and over again. Only the sounds of ragged breathing and choked desperation escaped his lips.

The woman watched him, her face betraying no emotion. Then—*snap!*

His neck having been broken, his head fell limply onto her chest.

"..."

The woman unceremoniously tossed him aside, nothing but a rag doll along the edge of the bed. His body crumpled onto the floor with a dull thud.

Dim light brushed her skin as she silently sat up, lifted her long legs, and climbed out of the bed. Ignoring the body at her feet, she walked straight toward the corner of the room.

Still naked, she bent down over the man's backpack, ripped it open, and rummaged inside with reckless abandon.

The sounds of sorting echoed throughout the room for a few moments...Before long, her search came to a halt.

"...Not here."

After she muttered her findings to the empty room, she stood still for a moment. She clicked her tongue in frustration.

She glared at the man's body, grinding her molars together in an effort to contain her anger. Then she stood up as her anger turned to rage.

Her steps were violent as she strode to the dead man's corpse, then—.

SPLAT!

The man's head was crushed beneath her foot, the spray of blood dyeing the room red.

THE
AVERAGE
DAY

Гэта казка іншага сям'і.

кожны дзень пейзаж

Pang! Pang! The echoes of metal on metal filled the air.

Relentless, high-pitched bangs came from all directions at once. A shower of sparks accompanied each one, momentary light flashing throughout the room with every impact.

Falling hammers, masculine smiths wiping away rivers of sweat, the grunts and groans of their labor—this was a workshop through and through. Bright red flames burned at fever pitch within four massive forges, one on each wall. The heat exuding from their openings was stifling.

A young prum girl, most likely a student of the trade, hurriedly worked her way through the animal people and dwarves with her arms full of firewood and extra tools.

"HUAAAAAAAAAAAAAAAA?! Damn you, Amazon! Rot in HELLLLLLLLLLLLLLLLLL!"

Five large men were hard at work in a corner of the workshop, repeatedly striking a large chunk of adamantite. Bringing down hammer after hammer that looked powerful enough to crush a large-category monster's head in one blow, they shaped the extremely stubborn metal to their will, eliminating the impurities.

All the smiths had acquired the Advanced Ability "Forge," which allowed them to instill special characteristics in their work. The head of each hammer glowed with a soft red light—not unlike Magic—as they breathed steadily and transformed the ore in front of them into a weapon that would become something far superior to the rest.

The most experienced High Smith among them led the charge, his loud, gruff voice not allowing the others to slow down.

Aiz made herself as small as possible as she listened to the grievances of the sleep-deprived smiths, most of which were directed at her best friend or at herself.

Walking very quietly and hoping to go unnoticed, the blond-haired girl came to a stop in front of a deity.

"To think, you destroyed it in only five days..."

The girl's shoulders trembled under the weight of Goibniu's dry, heavy words.

While the god was small in stature, similar to a dwarf, his wizened features were offset by his incredibly muscular physique. He looked the human girl in the eyes and let out a long sigh.

It was the morning after the Monsterphilia.

Aiz was here to retrieve her weapon of choice, Desperate, from *Goibniu Familia*'s home, the Three Hammers Forge. The repairs were finally complete. She stood at the counter in the very center of the long, rectangular workshop. It was still quite early in the morning, and yet the smiths of *Goibniu Familia* were already hard at work all around her. Every single one of them was covered in sweat. It didn't matter if they were putting hammer to steel on a workbench, tending to the forge fires, reviewing the orders for custom-made weapons posted on a bulletin board near the doorway, or whatever else they been assigned—everyone was busy.

Goibniu handed Aiz's favorite saber, Desperate, to her over the counter at the same time that Aiz returned the weapon loaned to her during the repairs—a rapier.

At least, what was left of it.

"You young'uns sure know how to make a smith miserable..."

"...I'm sorry."

Goibniu looked down at the *remains* on the counter between them as Aiz's shoulders sank. Knowing that the remark was aimed at her and Tiona, she did her best to apologize. However, her weak voice was barely audible over the organized chaos surrounding them.

The rapier had been at her side during the Monsterphilia and shattered during the battle against monsters loose in the town. Now it lay on the counter, nothing more than scraps, the only piece still recognizable its hilt. Even a child on the street, at first glance, would be able to tell it was beyond repair. It had been unable to withstand the strain of Aiz's fighting style, combined with the stress of her Magic. Its days as a weapon were over.

"*Loki Familia*, again?!" came the fed-up whispers and angry glances of the hardworking smiths all around them. While Aiz felt guilty for causing them so much trouble, she was also grateful for their skilled labor.

"…How much do I owe?"

"Forty million valis, or thereabouts."

——*Gong!* That number reverberated her head, its weight hitting her like a ton of bricks.

Aiz rubbed her temple as she collected her thoughts…and decided she had no choice but to prowl the Dungeon to pay back the debt.

Goibniu crossed his arms and mumbled under his breath. Aiz realized something that made her shoulders sink farther still as she looked at the deity's stern expression.

Her apology to the white-haired boy would have to wait.

The sound of a blade cut through the air.

The light *swish*es that followed the blade were proof of the immense speed and precision of each strike. Silver flashes of a saber tore through the crisp morning air.

The sun had still not risen from the eastern horizon, and yet Aiz was practicing her techniques in the central garden of *Loki Familia*'s home.

No one had ordered her. It had been her idea to add early-morning training to her daily routine when she was nine years old. Whether for daily review or to polish her swordsmanship skills, Aiz had practiced in this garden almost every day she was at home since then. This kind of practicing paled in comparison to the combat experience she gained in the Dungeon, but she never neglected it. She couldn't afford to neglect it. Like many of her fellow adventurers, Aiz was afraid of one thing: becoming unable to move forward.

She didn't move far from one particular patch of grass in the garden. After spending a week with the rapier, she needed some time to become reacquainted with the finer details of Desperate. She swung vertically, horizontally, and diagonally, over and over, her blade singing around her. Keeping footwork to a minimum, Aiz's sword cut through the air like a baton conducting her one-person symphony of silver slashes and echoes.

Rays of red light started to light up the sky before she knew it. The sun was rising.

A leaf fell from the branch of the tree in the garden. *"Hyun!"* A silver streak cut straight through it in midair, punctuating the end of her practice. Aiz watched the pieces fall as she returned her blade to its sheath.

"…?"

Her morning practice over, only now did Aiz realize she was being watched.

Spinning to find the observer, she immediately saw the elf Lefiya standing next to the doorway to one of the towers adjacent to the garden. She appeared entranced, her eyes wide.

The elf, holding a thick book, stood like a statue and only snapped back into the moment when she noticed Aiz was looking at her. A smile quickly appeared on her lips as she balanced the book against her chest and gave Aiz a round of applause.

"A-absolutely incredible, Miss Aiz! I was so caught up in the spectacle that I forgot to announce myself!"

"Umm…Thank you?"

Aiz tilted her head as she answered Lefiya's praise. She had never been complimented on practicing before and was unsure how to react.

Lefiya's cheeks turned light pink as she excitedly ran up to the girl, her dark blue eyes shimmering in the morning light. Overwhelming admiration filled her gaze.

"So it *is* true that you practice even this early in the morning… That's why you're so powerful…I *must* learn from your example!"

After witnessing how the "Sword Princess" trained, Lefiya felt as if she had discovered one of Aiz's secrets and vowed to apply herself to it.

Aiz couldn't help but smile at the young elf, the corners of her lips turning upward.

"Who instructed you in the art of swordsmanship? Being a magic user, I am a novice with blades. Even so, I can see the quality of your techniques..."

"...My father, I guess."

Aiz let her gaze wander as she came up with her answer.

"Your father...Speaking of which, where are your parents now...?"

Lefiya's question trailed off as a new voice rang out from a different direction.

"Lefiya. How much time does it take for you to retrieve one book from the archive?"

"L-Lady Riveria..."

Another elf descended a set of stairs and entered the garden: Riveria.

She came to a stop, pointed ears completely still even as her jade locks wavered in the morning breeze. One look at Aiz with her hand still on the hilt of her saber, and Riveria nodded, piecing together exactly what had happened. She sighed under her breath.

"You haven't the time to be distracted by Aiz's training. You have your own to attend to. We will continue until breakfast is served. Aiz, we shall talk later."

"M-Miss Aiiiz..."

With the book under her arm, Lefiya weakly called out to her friend as Riveria pulled her back into the tower. In response to the elf's mournful look, Aiz gave her a little wave in an attempt to cheer her on.

Riveria was training Lefiya in magic. Judging by the bags under her eyes, they'd been at it all night. Aiz had been in a similar position until just a few years ago—in her case, learning the finer details of being an adventurer. She knew exactly how strict Riveria's teaching style could be.

Memories of those days flashing through her mind, Aiz waved again in encouragement as Lefiya disappeared from sight.

Aiz left the garden and walked back into another tower, saber in hand.

After a quick shower, Aiz made her way through the long, narrow hallways of her home toward the cafeteria.

Quite a few people were already there, busily preparing breakfast or setting up the table for other members of the familia. The various aromas wafting out of the kitchen made her stomach grumble. She'd been up for hours but hadn't eaten anything. A quick peek through the kitchen window told her that today's breakfast was composed of vegetable soup and salad made with liberal amounts of vegetables, salted meat and vegetable sandwiches, and vegetable omelets. A substantial delivery from *Demeter Familia* had come in just the other day and was being put to good use. Their produce was always sweet and crisp, so Aiz always looked forward to the deliveries.

Unsure whether they would be able to finish everything, Aiz grabbed some plates and started to help set the table.

She'd finished placing a few dishes when suddenly...

"Whoa! Miss Aiz! When did you get here?"

"We appreciate the thought, but we can handle this!"

While thankful, other members of the familia wouldn't allow her to do such lowly work as setting a table. They took the dishes right out of her hands and asked her to wait. Because she was always treated like the princess of a castle, there was quite a bit of distance between Aiz and the lower-ranking members of the group.

She understood that lowly chores like setting the table were beneath the elites, but even so...after seeing how Tiona and the others were able to mingle with everyone else, it would be a lie to say she didn't feel lonely.

Her shoulders sank as she stood empty-handed in the cafeteria.

"M-Miss Tione, breakfast is our responsibility..."

"*I'm* gonna cook the general's breakfast, end of story! You can't stop me; now out of my way!"

Aiz looked back through the window and saw Tione trying to push her way through the crowded kitchen to get to a cooking station. Talking excitedly with their younger peers—at least that's how it looked to Aiz—Tione looked very impressive. She watched as the Amazon was gently and politely "convinced" to leave the kitchen.

"Uwh..."

"?"

Feeling that she couldn't be useful in the cafeteria, Aiz ducked out into the nearest hallway. Turning the first corner, she nearly ran into the werewolf, Bete. He startled at meeting her so suddenly, the corner of his mouth twitching until he was able to force an uncomfortable smile.

"......Y-yo."

Aiz tilted her head, a little confused as to why Bete was so awkward this morning. Then it came to her.

Not much time had passed since the incident with the white-haired boy at a bar called The Benevolent Mistress. Bete's attitude had angered her at the time, but he had shown a great deal of remorse after the fact and had barely talked to her since.

Bete had been drunk—and while Aiz's opinion of him had dropped slightly, the night in question didn't bother her much anymore.

So, she was about to answer him with a "Good morning," when...

"G'morning, Aiz!"

"Guh?!"

Thump. Bete was pushed out of the way as Tiona rushed up to Aiz and gave her a big hug.

Aiz bent backward to support the Amazon's sudden weight. At the same time, Tiona looked over her shoulder at Bete and stuck out her tongue.

Crick-crick. Ignoring the sounds of Bete grinding his teeth together, Tiona hopped down, grabbed Aiz's wrist, and led her away.

"Aiz, nothing good ever comes from talking to Bete. Let's go!"

"Oi! I can hear you, you shabby, reedy-lookin' woman!!"

"Don't call me thaaaaaat!!"

"Ah, umm..."

"—Such a ruckus at the crack o' dawn! Keep it quiet in the halls, would ya?!"

And so Aiz and the others were scolded by the dwarf Gareth Landrock until breakfast was served.

"Now then, General. I lovingly made your breakfast myself. Make sure to clean your plate."

Breakfast was getting under way at the cafeteria.

Hands and arms crisscrossed the table, grabbing bowls of hot soup and fluffy omelets before they disappeared. The leader of the familia, a prum named Finn, sat at the head of the table, but was mostly hidden behind the massive amount of food placed in front of him. A gargantuan fish, its head, fins, and scales still attached, had been roasted whole over an open flame; a wild breakfast fit for an Amazon.

The fish in question was often mistaken for a monster because of its ridiculous size and the twisted shape of its thick scales—a dodobass. A species easy to catch in the saltwater lake southwest of Orario, it was sold throughout the city. This particular fish was still rather young when it had been caught, but it was well over one meder in length. The prum just stared at the fish without saying a word.

Tione looked extremely proud of her work as she convinced Finn, under heavy duress, to start eating. It wasn't long before every other set of eyes around the table looked at him with pity.

"Aiz, what'cha gonna do today?"

"Well, um…"

The many conversations of fifty-plus people at the table echoed around the long cafeteria.

Tuning out the noise, Tiona took a big bite out of the sandwich Aiz gave her before asking her question.

"I broke a sword the other day, and have to pay for it…"

"Are you talking about the rapier you used during the Monsterphilia?" Lefiya asked from the other side. Aiz gave her a quick nod.

She recounted yesterday's conversation with the god Goibniu—and why it was necessary for her to earn that money in the Dungeon. She felt a little shy being the center of attention and fell silent once her story was finished.

"Okay, I'll come, too! Knowing you, you'll be down there for a week, right?"

"But, Tiona…"

"It's fine, it's fine! I'm getting Urga remade from scratch, and I need to get some money ready."

"If…if it will not be a bother, please let me help you as well!"

Tiona offered to join her with the excuse that she had debts of her own. Lefiya just didn't want to be left out. Aiz felt truly sorry that she'd gotten two of her friends involved in her own problem but couldn't turn them away.

After all, it made her genuinely happy that they had offered to help in the first place.

"…Okay. Please join me."

The blond's face relaxed as a small grin appeared on her lips. The other two girls smiled back right away.

"Home will be pretty empty with us gone. Maybe we should tell Finn first?"

"I agree. The next expedition is not for a while yet, but if we are planning on spending more than a few days in the Dungeon, I believe it would be a good idea to inform Loki and everyone."

Lefiya answered Tiona by saying that disappearing without notice would make the others needlessly worry about them.

The three girls started to discuss how long they would stay in the Dungeon and what they would need to prepare for their trip. Other members of the familia had finished breakfast and were starting to leave the cafeteria, returning to their rooms one by one.

Aiz watched the room empty out and suddenly realized that Loki was nowhere to be seen. It seemed strange to her that their normally lively and energetic goddess didn't stop by to say hello. She hadn't heard anything about Loki drinking so much the night before that she was bedridden by the resulting hangover again.

"You three, what've you been talking about?"

"Oh, Miss Tione."

"We're going to spend a week earning some money in the Dungeon. Wanna join us?"

Her breakfast with Finn over, Tione walked over to the group of girls sitting farther down the table.

Finn had refused to eat her lovingly prepared dodobass on the grounds that he could never hope to finish it. So she took it on herself to eat the rest of the meal that her "sweetheart" took a few bites from. Tione looked rather pleased with how things had turned out this morning, but her expression soured after hearing Tiona's plan for getting the money.

"A week? I don't want to spend that much time away from the general, so that's a no."

Tiona had had a feeling her sister would say that. A twinkle in her eye and a grin on her lips, she played her trump card.

"You know we were gonna invite Finn along, too?"

"Then I guess I have no choice but to give you a hand. Be grateful."

Aiz glanced at Lefiya as the two girls shared a grin at Tione's sudden willingness to help out.

Loki Familia's home, the Twilight Manor, was more like a housing project of several high towers gathered together in one spot. The largest, thickest tower stood in the center and was surrounded by the remaining six.

The shape and height of the six towers varied, but all of them were connected at the base—creating a ring around the independent central tower—and each was connected on the higher floors by stone bridges to make traveling from tower to tower more convenient. Three of them were devoted to the male members of the familia, and four to the female members. Shared spaces such as the archives and cafeteria were not centralized in one tower. Simply put, the place was loosely supervised chaos.

Finn's private quarters, and office, were located in the northernmost tower.

"Finn—we're coming in."

Tiona knocked twice and announced herself before opening the double doors and walking into his room. Aiz was close behind her, followed by Lefiya and Tione.

Finn's quarters and connected office space were wide and roomy—fitting for someone in charge of the familia. A bookcase covered an entire wall on one side, and a rug as colorful as a wreath of flowers decorated the floor. A tall grandfather clock stood against the back wall. The entire room had a calming, brown color-scheme, making the white marble fireplace stand out.

In the back of the room, Finn was seated behind a large desk that didn't fit his body size in the slightest.

"What's gotten into all of you, barging in here like this?"

"Ah, Lady Riveria...You were in here as well?"

Finn was focused on the task at hand, his eyes poring over a stack of paperwork. Riveria was standing at his shoulder.

The two of them had come straight to his quarters to work on the familia's finances right after breakfast. The familia's second-in-command held another stack of paperwork in her arms as she eyed the new arrivals.

"We'd like to talk to Finn about something."

"Hmm. Can it wait a few minutes? I'm almost at a stopping point."

Finn didn't even look up as he responded to Tiona.

His feathered pen was a blur as he signed his name over and over again before receiving another stack from Riveria.

Aiz used the time to have a look around his quarters. First, she was drawn toward the grandfather clock. She admired the inlaid crystals, probably magic stones, in the clock face that read 9:30 in the morning, and she listened to the clicking of the pendulum's swing. Next, the tapestry hanging above the fireplace, opposite the bookshelf, caught her attention.

It showed an armored woman who was surrounded prominently by spears and a slew of other weapons.

Gold and silver thread had been woven into fabric to create the image of a goddess.

The deity was known as Phiana, a *fictional* goddess that many prums believed in with all their heart and soul. She was represented by a group of knights from the Ancient Times.

Those knights were the first and last taste of glory for prums as a race—even Aiz knew their story. However, as soon as the living gods had descended from heaven, belief in Phiana had disappeared overnight. Prums lost the belief that unified them and soon faded into irrelevance.

Now, in a world where people of many different races received the Blessing from deities and forged their own stories of heroism, the number of famous prums was surprisingly low. Aiz had heard that Finn had come to Orario to champion his race and reinvigorate his kin.

In a move he himself would not deny was shameless, Finn had entered into a contract with Loki and received her Falna in the center of the world, the Labyrinth City, in hopes that his name would ring out.

Considering that a tapestry of Phiana was hanging proudly in his quarters, it was safe to assume that Finn had not lost faith in her. It also showed that Loki either was either quite generous or indifferent to the fact that the leader of her familia had faith in a goddess other than herself. Aiz also knew that Loki didn't ask to be worshiped, or anything close to it.

It was also quite possible that Loki allowed it because he was Finn.

Aiz looked over her shoulder toward the prum sitting in the back of the room. The familia's flag, the comical smile of the trickster—their familia's emblem—hung on the wall behind his desk. Her train of thought finally came to a stop.

"That should do it. Sorry to keep you waiting. What's on your minds?"

"You see, General, Tiona and these two would like to spend some time in the Dungeon and would like to know if you're interested in joining them…"

Tione stepped in front of the other girls the moment Finn looked up from his now-finished paperwork.

Finn had a quick and simple response: "Sure." He agreed not only to let them go into the Dungeon for an extended period of time, but to join them as well.

"I was just thinking about taking a jaunt into the Dungeon myself real soon anyway. It's nice to prowl at your own pace every now and then."

As the acting leader of the familia, he was in charge of organizing and overseeing every expedition they undertook. He smiled and said it would be fun to go in without any major plans or people to look after during his free time. "No backing out now, Finn!" Tiona said with a grin, knowing that his participation meant Tione would come by default.

"This might be a good chance to get out and stretch your legs, Riveria. You've been overloaded with busywork recently, so why not join us?"

"…That is absolutely true. I shall accompany you. I feel sorry for Gareth, but he will have to take charge in our absence."

With that, their party became six.

With the exception of Lefiya, each member was a top-class adventurer. The five of them were a very formidable group.

"Oh, keep this a secret from Bete! If someone tells him, he'll want to come. And if he comes, we'll never have a moment of peace."

That morning's conversation still fresh in her mind, Tiona's lips twitched threateningly as she looked at each of her allies in turn.

Her warning was greeted by strained smiles. At the same time, they knew that sending all their heavy hitters underground would cause its own problems, so there were no objections.

"How about meeting at Babel Tower once everyone's preparations are complete? Say, around noon?"

""Yeah!""

The Amazonian twins thrust their right arms in the air. Aiz did the same, with Lefiya following suit, albeit a bit more reserved.

Riveria chose to keep her mouth shut, closing her eyes and ignoring their childish excitement. And so everyone agreed to Finn's proposal.

Orario's Northwest Main Sreet, "Adventurers Way," was bustling with too many people to count.

The early-morning sun shone down from a blue sky, gleaming and sparkling on all types of armor as humans and demi-humans hurried to finish their preparations for entering the Dungeon. The shutters and heavy doors of every shop had been flung wide open in an attempt to welcome customers inside. The proprietor of a shadier shop farther down the backstreets was holding various kinds of suspicious-looking potions in one hand, trying to convince an inexperienced female adventurer to buy a few. Adventurers in a hurry constantly ran into one another, bumping shoulders and shouting insults back and forth, yelling at someone else from somewhere else about something or other.

The adventurers preparing to go to the Dungeon again today made this street come to life.

"Amid, high potions, please! The good stuff, and lots of them!"

"I'd like the same one as Tiona...Five please. And a magic potion, too."

"Yes, of course."

An emblem depicting a ball of light among medicinal herbs hung inside a building of clean, pure white stone.

Tiona and Aiz had found their way to one of the many counters. Standing on the other side of this one was Amid, a doll-like girl with long, light silver hair. A vast inventory of potions in different-colored vials lined the shelves behind her. Silver hair waving from side to side, she quickly collected the items they requested and placed them on the counter. The two girls' faces were reflected in the sky-blue and citrus-orange-colored liquids in front of them.

"Are you planning to spend a long time in the Dungeon starting today?"

"Yep. Tione, Lefiya…Finn and Riveria are coming, too."

"Amid, anything you want? We'll be going to at least the thirtieth floor, so if you tell us what to get we can pick something up for you!"

"May I make such a request? Since you offered…Could you retrieve some White Leaves for me?"

She asked Aiz and Tiona to get supplies for *Dian Cecht Familia*, which specialized in medicine and other healing items. Checking their memos one more time, the girls stocked up on everything they might need.

The Dungeon was not a forgiving place, and staying in top condition was extremely difficult. Therefore, a great deal of adventurers brought more items and weapons with them than necessary if they planned on staying there for an extended period of time. Their backpacks might be a bit bulky, but adventurers tended to believe that it was better to have something and not need it than to need something and not have it. It was the only way to prepare for the unexpected.

Accepting their friend Amid's request, the two girls bought a small mountain of items before leaving the shop.

"Lenoa. We are coming inside."

"Ahhh, Riveria, so you've come…What's this, the girl is with you today?"

"I-it has been a long time."

The elves had arrived at a shady-looking shop located off a side street branching from Northwest Main Street, after many turns, a descent down a staircase, and a warped wooden door.

The shop itself was decently spacious, but a bit dim. Magic-stone lamps designed to look like fireballs hung from the ceiling. The shelves built into the walls housed jars filled with snakes, frogs, scorpions, and other off-putting insects. Something seemed to be simmering in a black cauldron in the back of the shop, judging from the red steam rising from it. Lefiya's eyes jumped from item to item; she wasn't used to these surroundings. At the same time, an elderly lady behind the counter held a staff out to Riveria.

"Have the magic crystals been replaced?"

"Yes, all good to go. Got the special ones just like you asked for. But, my word, breaking four at once on one of those expeditions or whatever it is you do, it's unheard of..."

The shop owner's white hair stood out against her black robe. Her crooked nose twitching, the wrinkles around her mouth worked their way into a smile as she complained.

Riveria had asked her to make repairs to her silver-and-white staff. Taking it in both hands, she inspected it closely. As a high elf, her graceful features were enough to make goddesses jealous. Immaculate jade eyes made their way up the shaft of her weapon, counting a total of nine magic crystals before looking back at the old woman.

Staffs designed for magic users like this one wouldn't last long in hand-to-hand combat and couldn't be found at the run-of-the-mill weapon shops. They were designed to amplify the users' Magic power and increase the effectiveness of their Magic, completely different from weapons like swords that were designed to provide a cutting edge to an adventurer's Strength. Therefore, the creators of these staffs must also possess very powerful Magic. Very few people were capable of creating these weapons from scratch, and the ones with such an ability were referred to as "mages." To put it another way, they were smiths for staffs.

Mages used wood from the holy trees that comprised many elvish forests as well as special kinds of metal and ores to create items that enhanced a magic user's abilities. They also could create magic crystals that didn't exist naturally in the world. Coming in many brilliant colors, the crystals dramatically increased the effects of spells. The difference between a staff with these crystals and one without was like night and day. The head of the staff that Lefiya carried with her was equipped with four azure magic crystals.

Rows upon rows of short staves and long wooden staffs, said to be a mage's heart and soul, lined one of the walls of this shop, which was already filled with many mysterious and questionable items. Looking around to see if there was anything else important, Lefiya happened to catch a glimpse of a strange book on a shelf high above the counter.

"Umm…Correct me if I am wrong, but is that a grimoire?!"

"Ahh, well spotted, child. That it is."

Lefiya blinked her eyes in disbelief as the shop owner slowly nodded. Incredibly thick, the book cover was littered with unusual letters and insignias. The rare grimoire held a miracle within its pages: the ability to force a reader to learn a Magic spell. Out of all the people in the world, it was possible to count the few who were able to make them.

"You do not seriously expect me to believe that you created it, Lenoa?"

"Ee-hee-hee-hee, oh no no. I'm not that powerful of a mage. I have an acquaintance in Altina who was nice enough to spare me one."

Lenoa's response suggested that she wasn't divulging the whole story.

A well-made grimoire not only taught its reader new Magic, it could also increase the magic slots in their Status. The absolute maximum number of slots was three; there was no way to add a fourth. However, those with two slots would gain a third, and those with one would gain a second. This one item could dramatically increase an adventurer's Magic ability instantaneously. For that reason, a single grimoire was valued more than even top-of-the-line weapons.

This particular one was up for sale but had had its price reassigned several times as the older ones were crossed out a written over. Even so, the enormous figure on the price tag sent shivers up Lefiya's spine.

"Well, for the *two of you*, who can use more than four spells, this thing ain't more than a shiny paperweight, I bet."

Looking like an old witch who would never reveal her birthplace or familia allegiance, the store owner eyed Lefiya and Riveria with her crooked nose held high and a smirk on her lips.

"There are some in Altina who have their eyes on you."

"M-me as well? Not just Lady Riveria?!"

"Come, child, did you think no one would notice such a flashy title as 'Thousand'? EE-he-he-he, don't travel alone at night."

"Enough with meaningless threats, Lenoa. Lefiya, do not take her seriously. We are leaving."

"You don't play along at all, do you, Riveria?…Hee-hee, thanks for the business."

The shop owner watched them go out the door with a mysterious smile on her face. Pulling Lefiya, still gulping with shock, by the wrist, Riveria left the shop behind.

Finn and Tione arrived at the white marble lobby of Guild headquarters.

Working their way through the Pantheon's massive crowds of adventurers that could rival the throng on the main street outside, they made their way to a large bulletin board.

"It's good to accept a normal quest every once in a while. We're going there anyway, so why not do our adventuring our way? Plus we need money, right?"

"Yes. Aiz and Tiona both have to pay for their weapons. Aiz has to foot a ridiculous bill, too, but that idiot sister of mine just *had* to order a weapon loaded with adamantite…"

"So then, we need a lot of simple quests that pay well…Sounds like we should stick with monster-type quests."

Finn and Tione searched the bulletin board for any quest that lined up with their plans. The board itself had so many sheets of paper pinned to it that it was difficult to see the original color underneath. Each sheet of paper detailed a quest available for adventurers to undertake, ranging from collecting special drop items to protecting merchant caravans. Even though not all the quests involved the Dungeon, they had many options to choose from.

"Hey, this one looks interesting."

"Which one?"

"'Song that echoes through the Dungeon…Please find the source of the song I heard in the Deep Levels'…Oh? Apparently it's not a monster's roar, more like a sweet melody. Captivating enough to make this guy fall in love, by the sound of it. He wants to know if it's a person, a monster, or the Dungeon itself…The client claims he thinks about it so much he can't sleep at night."

"That's no good, General. It's obviously a wild-goose chase. The reward isn't that good and we don't have time to waste on it."

"Where's your sense of adventure?"

Finn's shoulders slumped at Tione's less-than-enthusiastic response. There was nothing that adventurers loved more than a mystery that made their hearts yearn for an answer—or at least, that's what Finn claimed. The prum flashed a youthful, toothy grin.

The two of them spent some time finding quests of interest and took them off the bulletin board. Next they went to the Guild's reception counter to fill out the paperwork, and the quests were officially theirs. Once they completed the mission, they could return to this window with the contract and proof of completion—or the requested items—and claim the rewards left by the quest's client.

In addition, an adventurer's reputation with the Guild increased every time they completed a quest. Complete enough of them, and the Guild was likely to raise their familia's rank. Of course, not all quests were equal. Carrying out the difficult missions was the best way for Dungeon-prowling familias to gain a good reputation in the Guild's eyes.

Finn and Tione thanked the reception clerk for his time as soon as the contracts were complete. Then the two left the Guild and made their way to meet up with the others at Babel.

"Oh, it's Finn and Tione."

"We're the last ones? Sorry to keep you waiting."

The four girls had gathered in the shade of a tree that stood about ten meders from the white skyscraper towering over the center of Orario's expansive Central Park.

Three sets of eyes turned to see Finn, carrying a spear over his shoulder, and Tione with a large backpack slung over hers. Kicking one of the broad leaves, Tiona excitedly picked up her own massive weapon as the last of their party arrived.

Riveria and Lefiya had magic staffs at the ready, and Aiz adjusted Desperate's sheath at her waist.

"Looks like everyone's ready to go. Shall we?"

"Yes. It has been too long since we have prowled the Dungeon together."

"Eh-hee-hee~. I've been itching to get in there all morning!"

"Would you look after yourself, for once?"

Finn and Riveria exchanged words just before Tione got tired of Tiona's giddy excitement. Lefiya smiled at the two Amazons before turning to face Aiz.

"I will do my utmost to be useful."

"Thanks, Lefiya...I'll work hard, too."

Aiz flashed a faint smile before joining the others looking up at the sky.

The white skyscraper seemed to pierce the heavens overhead. They spent a few moments taking in the sublime tower before bells rang out from the east. It was now exactly noon.

With the metallic ring echoing through the city, the battle party made their way through Babel Tower's front gate.

"..."

In the highest room of the Twilight Manor's central tower.

Loki sat quietly among the many types of glass bottles and unique items scattered around her room, sifting through news pamphlets one at a time.

Sold by merchants and even a few familias, each of them had several articles written in Koine. Many strategies went into selling these papers—some came with minute illustrations, others had attention-grabbing titles or humorous wit in their narratives. Anything to appeal to potential customers.

Loki's eyes lit up as they passed through some recent gossip and found an article pertaining to the monsters escaping into the city—the incident during the Monsterphilia.

"Dahh~...Nothin' new in this one, either."

Loki stayed in her chair as she tossed the news back onto the table. In addition to the several other pamphlets that she had just read, there were a few larger illustrated papers spread out on it. Most of them depicted the events of the Monsterphilia.

Ganesha Familia's negligence, a spy's plot to attack the city, some god who just wanted to see what would happen—each one had their own theories as to how the monsters escaped, but Loki was looking for something a bit more specific: information about the carnivorous plant monsters. None of the papers even mentioned them.

"Hmph," grunted Loki in frustration as she leaned back in the chair and put her hands behind her head. Gaze rising from the table to the ceiling as if she was deep in thought, she slowly stood up.

She left her room and ascended the spiral staircase that connected it to the rest of her home, then she went across one of the stone bridges into another tower.

She glanced inside every room she passed to see who was around. Unable to find anyone, she ended up in the main lounge that functioned as a reception room. It was also a favorite relaxing spot for many members of her familia.

"Oh, just you, Bete? Where's Aizuu and the rest?"

"...The Dungeon, where else? Even dragged Finn down with 'em. Won't be back for a while, by the sound of it."

The werewolf had his feet up, sprawled out on a sofa in a small room just off the hallway that was often used for consultation. He had glanced at Loki coming in and spat out a blunt answer without bothering to get up.

"So ya got left out?"

"Like hell I did!"

Bete snarled as he sat up. Muttering something like "Don't be stupid" under his breath, his now-free tail slapped against the sofa with a loud thump. She had hit the nail right on the head.

"There, there, now," she said in a soft, soothing voice.

Changing the subject, she asked him what his plans were for the day. "...Ain't doing jack," he said after a few moments of silence.

"...Say, Bete. Sorry, but would ya mind stickin' with me for the day?"

"Huh? And do what?" asked Bete, eyebrows sinking into a suspicious glare.

"There's *somethin'* I wanna look into."

INCIDENT

Гэта казка іншага сям'і.

ўваходжанне

Aiz's battle party entered the Dungeon through Babel Tower at noon as planned.

Goblins and kobolds attacked them within moments of entering the first floor, but they were quickly dealt with. With Aiz and Tiona acting as scouts and the front line of their formation, it didn't take long for monsters to realize they didn't stand a chance. In fact, the path in front of the two girls was practically clear from that point on. Other adventurers also noticed their presence and were careful not to get too close.

They breezed through the upper levels and proceeded all the way down to the seventeenth floor.

"Ahhh, I feel like myself again with Urga in my hands."

"Miss Tiona, has your weapon been remade?"

"Yep, this is her! Urga, the second! Still hot off the anvil~!"

Tiona casually spun the hulking double-bladed sword Urga around in her right hand as she responded to Lefiya's question. She had picked up the made-to-order weapon from *Goibniu Familia* just before their excursion began. She looked like a kid who had just left a candy store with the biggest lollipop imaginable.

It was a little bit thicker than Urga the first, and most likely sharper, too. It required a ridiculous amount of time and resources for the High Smiths to create, more than even Aiz's Desperate. Tione used the fruits of their efforts to recklessly dive at an oncoming liger fang, slicing through the beast like a knife through butter.

"*Goibniu Familia*'s smiths must've worked half to death..."

Tione sighed to herself as she pulled the magic stone out from what was left of the monster's body. Although Lefiya had been assigned the role of supporter for this journey, Tione joined her in collecting the stones and drop items, placing them into long, tubular backpacks.

Finn and Riveria enjoyed the show as Aiz made quick work of another liger fang. The blond swordsman then collected its magic stone and a drop item, liger fang fur, by herself. She had to aggressively engage monsters in combat in order to earn enough money to pay off the rapier, but the real money was waiting in the Dungeon's lower levels and Deep Levels.

In general, as one ventured deeper into the Dungeon, they would find stronger and stronger foes. And as the monsters got more powerful, the loot after defeating them would also become more valuable. That's why, for the strongest adventurers like Aiz, it was much more efficient to get to the lower levels as quickly as possible.

The path to 40 million valis was going to be a long one. Aiz treated this as a warm-up as she cleared the way to the deep levels for the rest of the battle party.

"The Goliath's not here. Someone take care of it?"

"Hmm, most likely the adventurers of Rivira slew it. Bad for business if no customers can get through."

The battle party had arrived at the very back of the seventeenth floor, a cavern that was large enough to allow large groups to pass through it all at once. Tiona and Finn couldn't see the floor boss—a category of monster known as Monster Rex—that could slow down the advance of adventurers indefinitely. Instead, comparatively smaller monsters like Minotaurs roamed the open space unhindered.

Aiz and the others advanced straight through the boss-less cavern. Tione and Finn jumped into the fray to help finish off a few aggressive Minotaurs. Even though Lefiya was not very good at close-quarters combat, she managed to get in a few hits using staff-fighting techniques she had obtained thanks to Riveria's instructions.

The group pressed forward until they arrived at a tunnel at the end of the cavern—the entrance to the next floor.

"All right~. Break time~!"

Tiona, the first out of the sloping, curvy tunnel, stretched her arms as high she could. As the rest of the party emerged, they were greeted by warm light shining down from the ceiling of the eighteenth floor. There were only a few trees in their immediate vicinity, but a lush forest spread out in front of them.

Light and clean air like this was completely out of place in the middle of the Dungeon, which was crawling with monsters. It was hard to believe they were deep underground in this safe point, similar to the one that was on the fiftieth floor, where *Loki Familia* had made camp on their previous expedition.

"No matter how many times I come here, this floor is always beautiful."

"Yes, it is…"

Elves were known for their love of nature, especially forests. Lefiya's cheeks flushed a light pink as she spoke and Aiz nodded in response.

The group made their way into the forest, beautiful moss-covered trees and intertwining streams reflected in their eyes.

"I believe…it is the 'afternoon' now."

Riveria shielded her eyes with her left hand as she looked up through the foliage.

Thousands upon thousands of crystals covered every inch of the ceiling just beyond the shady, wide leaves of the forest's thinning canopy.

A large group of white crystals in the center of the ceiling shone like the sun. They were surrounded by a vast sea of other minerals emanating soft blue light that spread out in all directions. Each formation emitted a glow that looked like mums in bloom, and all of it coalesced to create a "sky" deep underground. It was a mystery of the Dungeon that took many an adventurer's breath away.

This sky changed with the passage of time, creating "morning," "afternoon," and "night." However, the intervals were not equal and varied slightly from the ones on the surface, meaning that there were times when the cycles were almost identical and times when they were totally different.

©Kiyotaka Haimura

It was safe to say that these crystals were the eighteenth floor's most distinctive feature. They not only covered the ceiling, but also sprouted from anywhere and everywhere on the ground, trees, and rocks. Even the crevice in the floor running along Aiz and the others' path was filled with indigo blue crystals.

"Hey, hey. Any thoughts? We gonna go straight through to the nineteenth floor?"

"We're stopping at Rivira first. If we don't sell the stones and items we've already collected, our inventory will be completely filled in no time."

The Amazonian sisters exchanged a few words as the battle party proceeded from the southern forest and toward the "town" in the western portion of this floor.

The eighteenth floor was the first safe point adventurers came across in the Dungeon. The scenery was so beautiful that it was often called the "Under Resort."

Continuing north out of the forest, the first thing that came into view was an open prairie dotted with crystals of various sizes and shapes.

In the very center of the floor was a colossal tree, standing proudly in the middle of the vast, blue-green plain. It was called the Central Tree, and some of its roots created the tunnel that led to the nineteenth floor.

The northern region was a marshy wetland, while the large forest stretched from the south toward the east. A break in the plain lay to the west, a midnight-blue lake with a large island in the middle. This magnificent scene of nature, wrapped in a beautiful azure "sky" and decorated with magnificent crystals, was a sight that one could not find outside the Dungeon. This view had quite the reputation—great enough that wealthy people on the surface would hire adventurers to take them there so they could see it with their own eyes.

The eighteenth floor itself was shaped like a big dome with steep cliffs forming the edges. It created the sense that one was inside a miniature display.

Aiz's party made their way to the edge of the lake and crossed a massive tree that had been cut down to make a bridge to reach the island. Each of them enjoyed the scenery as they made the climb toward their destination.

"I can barely remember the last time I came here!" Tiona said as she made her way to the top of the island that looked as though it had once been part of the main continent and somehow wound up in the Dungeon. The town of Rivira was constructed on the top of its steep cliffs.

Two connected wooden pillars and flags over the main path bore the words TOWN OF RIVIRA.

Simply put, it was a relay town for resupply, rest, and transportation of goods, operated by upper-class adventurers who were strong enough to make it down here as they pleased.

It was originally part of the Guild's plan to make exploring previously unknown floors easier for all adventurers, intended to serve as a frontline base. However, constant waves of monsters coming in from other floors required a considerable commitment of manpower—including hired adventurers who were Level 3 or higher—and of course, everyone needed to be paid. The cost of keeping the station up and running far exceeded the benefits, so the Guild scrapped the plan. Adventurers, however, had had other ideas and moved in to create the Dungeon town of Rivira.

"Um, I have always been curious about this, but…The number engraved into the wood, 'three hundred and forty-four,' does that mean…?"

"It does. That number represents the number of times Rivira has been rebuilt. This is the three hundred and thirty-fourth version… which indicates that Rivira has been destroyed three hundred and thirty-three times before."

"Th-three hundred and thirty-three…"

Lefiya couldn't take her eyes off the numbers even as she followed the group through the wooden archway while Riveria explained.

Monsters were never born inside a safe point, but this was the Dungeon. No one knew when an Irregular would appear. Rivira was wiped out whenever one of those unexpected monsters reared its ugly head.

In the event one did show up, all adventurers would evacuate the town and return to the surface rather than stand their ground.

As soon as the storm passed, they would immediately return to rebuild.

That was the main difference between the Guild, which had been forced to maintain a constant defense, and the adventurers running the town now. Rivira had come to represent the tenacity of the shadiest adventurers. Some referred to it as "the world's most beautiful rogue town" in a mixture of contempt and praise.

"Well, let's go inside already. I wanna lie down, not stand out here all day."

Tione urged the rest of the party to pick up the pace. They entered the main street moments later.

The town was built on the east side of the island, atop a two-hundred-meder cliff that looked out onto the lake. They used the natural formations of crystal and rock to ring the town with a rough wall. While not the prettiest of sights, it was sturdy enough and tall enough to repel most monster attacks.

After walking through the arch, Aiz and the others immediately saw lines of tents, wooden huts, and small shops that would pass for street stands anywhere else. Many had been built into the side of rock walls with cheap materials in order to reduce expenditure—and for ease of reconstruction. So many corners had been cut that hardly any of the structures in town could really be called a building.

Despite the simplicity of this town, little more than a village, pillar-like crystals and small clusters of minerals reflected the rays shining down from above, making the light dance on everything. Along with the deep blue lake below and its beautiful vantage point overlooking the entire floor, it became much more stunning than the average town.

Passing by taverns that had been established in naturally occurring caves, Lefiya inquired as to their plan moving forward.

"We'll exchange our magic stones and drop items for money, and then...?"

"Where should we stay? Should we make camp in the forest like we always do?"

"Hmm, maybe we should stay at an inn this time? We didn't bring any camping supplies with us, after all."

"But General...Spending a week here is going to cost a considerable amount of money! This is Rivira, you know..."

Apart from the weapon and item shops, there was also a place to sell hard-earned loot. It went without saying that a town composed solely of adventurers would only do business with adventurers. At the same time, prices were so high it was almost scary to ask.

Simple packs of rations and pre-owned longswords carried price tags with more than four zeros. It was enough to make the average customer feel like they were being scammed and want to scream in frustration. But there was a reason that all these goods were all at least twice as expensive as they were outside the Dungeon: the sellers knew their customers didn't have any other choice. That was the harsh truth behind adventurers selling to their own kind. They knew how valuable water was in a desert.

Of course, the lodging business was no different.

"Tione, don't be so stingy! It's okay to live it up a little every now and then."

"Who you calling stingy?! You're just careless with money!"

Finn smiled as he listened to Tiona and Tione trade verbal blows before making a suggestion.

"Why don't we stay at an inn? I'll pay for everyone. I know a few of you need to save up some money."

"...Sorry, Finn."

The members of *Loki Familia* had always passed through Rivira without stopping to avoid paying an arm and a leg for accommodations. Thanks to their leader's generous offer, the group decided to spend the night this time.

Knowing that Finn was referring to her, Aiz was quick to apologize.

"Times like this are the only ones I get to spend money. So don't worry," Finn responded with a lighthearted smile.

"…"

"Riveria…?"

Aiz thanked Finn just before looking up and noticing that Riveria had been silent all this time.

The elf's eyes were drifting between the beautiful white and blue crystals scattered throughout the town. She opened her mouth to speak.

"It's the town. Something feels off."

"Now that you mention it, the streets are much emptier than normal…"

Lefiya took a look around as she echoed Riveria's concern.

They could count the number of people on the main street with one hand. The lack of travelers passing through the gate wasn't cause for concern, but when the main square was just as sparse, they couldn't help but feel something was wrong.

Many adventurers used Rivira as a base of operations for traveling below the nineteenth floor for the simple reasons that monsters were never born at the safe point and that it was the only "town" inside the Dungeon. Equipped with shops, taverns, and places to sell loot or buy luxury goods, the town's very existence meant they didn't have to return to the surface for anything. It wasn't perfect, but many adventurers were thankful it was here.

Normally, the Dungeon town was bustling with people taking a break from the labyrinthine hallways and the dangers that awaited them on other floors. But now, it was practically deserted.

In a plaza carved into a rock outcropping, surrounded by a small fence made from rusty old swords and spear shafts, Aiz met the gazes of Tiona, Tione, and Lefiya.

"Well, um…What now?" Tiona asked.

"First things first; let's visit a shop. Talking to a local is the best way to gather information," Finn answered. Spear balanced over his shoulder, the prum led the group away from the observation point and down the main street.

Taking a closer look, they could see that many shop owners had up and left their stores. Eventually, they found a place that would buy their magic stones. The shop wasn't much more than a tent, with a few pieces of wood for a counter, but the group made their way toward it.

"You open for business?"

"Huh? Ahh, *Loki Familia*, huh? You customers?"

The Amazonian owner looked bored out of her mind as Finn approached her. "That we are," he responded.

Only the counter divided the inside of the "store" from the outside. An inventory of monster teeth that resembled elephant tusks, bottles filled with precious stones, and other items bought from adventurers were lined up inside the tent behind the owner.

As Lefiya and Tione handed over the loot, Finn began questioning the Amazon under the guise of small talk.

"The town seems different than I'm used to. Something happen?"

"…Ahh, so you guys just came in, then."

The owner looked up from meticulously counting the magic stones and cringed.

"*There was a murder.* An adventurer's body was discovered in town."

Finn's eyes went wide. None of them could hide their shock and surprise.

Even without being asked, the Amazon scratched the side of her face and recounted what she knew.

"They found it just a little bit ago. It's a small town, so word travels fast. Now most people are up there gawkin'. No one's died around here since that time two drunken idiots had one hell of a brawl and offed each other. That was quite a while ago, so this is big news."

The Amazon, wearing little more than a dancer would onstage, picked at one of the braids in her hair and sighed to herself.

Finn decided to ask another question. "Are you sure someone killed this adventurer?"

"I ain't got a clue. All I know is what I heard as the droves hurried by. The details are beyond me."

"Do you know where the body was found?" Riveria asked.

"Up the cliff from here, at Willy's Inn. There's bound to be a crowd of people up there by now. It'd be impossible to miss, so why not go and see for yourself?"

The owner fell silent after that and focused solely on calculating the value of the items on the counter. Writing the number on a piece of paper, she placed it in front of the group. After the discount she had taken for the information, the figure was surprisingly low.

Aiz and the others sold all their loot and left the tent behind without complaining.

"…What should we do, General?" Tione asked.

"Since we're going to stay here, we can't exactly pretend this isn't our problem. Let's go check it out," Finn replied, beginning to walk.

They followed the shop owner's instructions, ascending the cliff past all the other shops crowded at the edge.

Willy's Inn was located at the top of the slope and opened toward the lake on one of the highest points on the island. Considering that Rivira was built on the flattest parts of the cliff face, visitors to the town had to deal with the steep gradient. Surrounded by sea-blue crystals and green foliage, the band climbed a stairway of wooden logs that had been installed by the town residents.

Now that they were away from the center of town, they saw a large group of adventurers.

All crammed into a rather narrow passageway, every one of them had gathered at the entrance to a cave. A billboard attached directly to the cliff wall read WILLY'S INN in big, bold Koine letters.

This place matched their information perfectly.

"Ah damn, how the hell are we going to get through all of them…?"

"Is it really possible to go inside?"

The mass of demi-humans created a living wall that had no obvious weak points. All their voices created a continuous din inside the passageway. Tiona and Lefiya strained their necks, trying to get a look inside, but Finn kept walking forward.

"I'll go have a look. All of you, please wait here."

The savvy prum made use of his small frame, quickly disappearing into the mob and vanishing from sight. "Ohh!" Tiona and Lefiya were thoroughly impressed, but there was one who couldn't accept his decision: Tione.

"General, wait for me!—Hey, all of you! Out of the way!"

"Holy sh—! *Loki Familia*...?!"

Tione's threatening yells got their attention. One look at her clenched fists and the fire in her eyes, and the crowd hastily made a path for her right to the front.

Feeling embarrassed for causing a scene, Aiz and the others quickly dashed through the opening and caught up with Tione. A few strong adventurers, serving as lookouts, stood in front of the main entrance. Apparently, Finn had made quite an impression on them, and they allowed the girls to pass without attempting to get in their way.

Willy's Inn was a natural cave that wound its way deep into the rock. The cavern itself was surprisingly wide and tall, spacious enough that the five girls could easily walk side by side. None of them felt the claustrophobia that normally accompanied entering a dark space like this.

A counter was set up just inside the entrance, a reception desk of sorts. The walls were decorated with high-quality magic lights styled to look like lit candles. Three decorative daggers were hung on the walls like paintings. A rug with very thick fur was spread underneath their feet, most likely a drop item obtained from a monster that lived farther below in the Dungeon.

The group knew, just by looking at the spacious entrance, that Willy's Inn was one of Rivira's best accommodations. The girls made their way past the stone walls and the glinting blue crystals that grew in their cracks as they caught up with Finn and went deeper into the inn.

There were several wide holes on both sides of the path, with drapes hanging over them—the dark red cloth served as doorways to the guest rooms. Taking a glance behind one of the drapes, Aiz could see a bed and a few other amenities.

It didn't take the group long to find a room that was being guarded by three adventurers. They were let inside after exchanging a few words with the guards.

"…!"

Words left Aiz the moment she stepped past the drape.

The room in the heart of the cave was dyed a deep red. The headless body of a man lay sprawled out on the floor, accenting the tragic scene.

The body's lower half was still clothed, the burgeoning muscles on his upper body giving contour to his dark, wheat-colored skin. The positions of his arms and legs spoke to the pain and suffering of his final moments. What was left of his head had been crushed underfoot, the remains looking like smashed fruit above his neck. There was no way to tell what his features had been before the incident. Small bits of flesh and brain tissue floated in the pool of blood that surrounded his body.

"Don't look, Lefiya."

Aiz refused to explain as she used her body to block the elf's view of the room. After convincing the confused girl to stay back, she once again went inside to take a better look around.

The rug that had originally been red was now dotted with dark black blotches. A wicker basket, a bookshelf, and the bed had all been splattered with blood as well. Magic-stone lamps that had been brought in to the rectangular room illuminated every bit of the aftermath of the atrocity.

The crystals adorning the room looked as if they were weeping tears of blood.

"Gory…"

Tiona's nose scrunched up as she made her remark. Two men who were already inside the room turned around as they suddenly realized they weren't alone.

One of the two adventurers kneeling beside the body and inspecting the crime scene frowned at the moment that Aiz and Tiona came into view.

"Hehh? You two, you can't be in here! It's off-limits! The hell are my lookouts doing?!"

"Hey, there, Bors. Sorry, but we're coming in."

Finn addressed the angry human as if they'd met several times before.

He was a hulking man with muscles to match. His threatening aura, strong enough to make anyone who saw him flinch, was topped off by a black eye patch. His upper body was protected by a sleeveless battle cloth that accentuated his wide shoulders and massive biceps.

Bors Elder.

An upper-class adventurer, he ran one of the main exchange shops in Rivira. He was the kind of guy who would say, "What's mine is mine, and what's yours is also mine," right to another adventurer's face without hesitation. He was, without a doubt, the most powerful resident in Rivira.

Among the adventurers that gathered in Rivira, people with close ties to the Guild or legal power of any kind simply didn't exist. The ones who ran businesses down here had grown tired of jumping through all the hoops of rules and regulations on the surface. The only thing they needed to become successful was the ability to keep others quiet. Power was king in this "rogue town."

At Level 3, Bors was the strongest adventurer in Rivira, and therefore the person in charge in times of emergency by default. Holding this position also meant that he often interacted with the leaders of familias that stopped by to use the town's facilities.

He had already stepped in and taken charge of this situation. Finn approached him, both hands up in an effort to be as unthreatening as possible.

"We're planning on staying here for a while. In order to focus on our own matters, we'd like to help settle this one as quickly as possible. That work for you, Bors?"

"Heh, you sure talk the talk, Finn. Doesn't matter if it's you guys or *Freya Familia*, you always show up acting all high and mighty just because you're strong."

"He should look in the mirror, don't you think?" Tione muttered arrogantly under her breath as she listened to their conversation. A bead of sweat rolled down Lefiya's neck as soon as the Amazon's words reached her ears. "P-please be calm!" she said in a hushed voice, desperately trying to prevent a scene.

"So then, what happened here? Any clues to this adventurer's allegiance or the one who did him in?"

"Ahh...The guy pushing up daisies wore full plate armor and brought some chick wearing a robe in here. His helmet covered his face, so I have no idea who he was. But the chick is gone, so there's no doubt she's the killer...Ain't that right, Willy?"

"Yeah, those are the only two I let in, Bors."

The other man in the room, next to Bors, was an animal person: the owner, Willy. He was of medium height and build, but his hair was an absolute mess. Stripes of red war paint on his face ran down both cheeks.

The owner of the inn added to his story.

"The two showed up last night. Both of 'em kept their faces hidden and asked me to rent out the whole place."

"Two people wanted the entire inn to themselves...? Oh."

"Yeah, exactly. My inn doesn't have doors or anything like that, so voices tend to travel. Anyone could have one hell of peep show, if they wanted to."

Finn was thinking out loud when Willy jumped in to confirm his suspicions. Lefiya's mind started racing as she, too, connected the dots, causing her entire face to blush bright red.

"I could tell that was his plan from how giddy the man's voice was. I couldn't care less and had them pay up front...I walked away, half wishin' he'd go to hell, only to have him end up like this. Gave me some pause."

The tone of Willy's voice was like he was discussing the day's events over drinks, but salty lines of dried sweat covered his face. Rubbing the back of his neck with a shaky hand, he knew he had messed up. A long sigh escaped his lips.

Riveria, clearly mourning the loss of life, walked over to the body and placed the cloth over the remains of the man's head. Finn took his eyes off her and asked another question.

"Did you happen to catch a glimpse of the woman's face?"

"Her hood was so low, couldn't even see her eyes. Same with the guy, couldn't see either of their faces…Ah, but you know, I could tell one thing. Even with the robe, that lady had one fine body. One look at her and I was on the verge of grabbing at her without thinking."

"Ohh, actually, I caught a glimpse of her in town, too…Damn fine. Didn't see her face, but no doubt about that."

Bors corroborated Willy's statement, the two of them energetically describing her figure like an object of envy.

As their breathing came harder, Tiona and the other women in the room stared at them with unamused, ice-cold gazes.

"…But you know, this is your place, isn't it? How could you not know something happened in one of your rooms? Aren't you at the counter out front all the time?"

"Gimme a break. Knowing that a woman like that was in the back, hearing her voice would've driven me crazy. Since I couldn't be the one back there with her, I put up the 'no vacancy' sign and hit up the bar right away."

Willy shrugged his shoulders as he answered Tiona.

Claiming he wouldn't have made it through the night without alcohol, he said he spent the time with a bottle. Other adventurers who were at the bar were able to verify his story, giving him an alibi.

Willy hadn't come back to the inn until early morning. By then, the man was dead and the robed woman nowhere to be found. That much was certain.

It wasn't hard to figure out what the man had had in mind just before his death, based on the clothes on the floor and his minimal attire. Most likely, he had been caught up in the moment and slain with his guard down.

Tione, who had been looking around the room out of boredom, came back to the group and made eye contact with Bors.

"By the looks of it, no one saw the robed woman leave this place, did they?"

"That's right, not a soul. Got a few of my underlings out gathering info, but everyone's come up empty-handed so far."

"Did either of them provide their familia's emblem at the time of transaction?" Speaking for the first time, Riveria approached Willy from beside Tione.

"Sorry, but no. He just dropped this enormous bag of magic stones on the counter and said he didn't need change. There didn't seem to be a need to ask for more."

Willy's head drooped in apology.

It was extremely uncommon for adventurers to bring large amounts of money into the Dungeon—there was no use for the bulky extra weight in battle. Therefore, the purchase of weapons, items, and accommodation was carried out using familia emblems. The business owners prepared documents similar to IOUs that became valid when an adventurer signed his name and stamped their emblem onto it. A shop representative would then go to the surface at a later date and collect the money from said familia.

If Willy had conducted business as usual, they would have the names and the familia of either the victim or the perpetrator on hand. However, the transaction had been completed with a trade. There was no paperwork, no proof. The man who died must have been a solo adventurer—no one at this point had come to Rivira looking for a lost ally, and no one in town claimed to know him. And with no face to go by, it was highly unlikely anyone ever would. No one knew who he was.

"No matter. We're going to get the guy's body to tell us what we need to know—Oi, where's that Status Thief?!"

Bors yelled out into the hallway. Almost immediately, the hurried footsteps of a human echoed toward them.

The newcomer stopped in front of the entrance before entering with a short animal person who had been stationed outside the room. He had a bottle clutched in his right hand—glass the same color as magic stones and filled with a clear liquid—and handed it to the shorter man. Bors then unceremoniously flipped the corpse onto its stomach with a dull flop as the animal person, his mouth and neck hidden by a long scarf, approached it.

Pop! The animal person pulled the cork out of the bottle and set to work. Pouring the liquid onto the body's back, he slid his fingers across the dead man's skin in a precise pattern.

"If I remember right, Status Thief is…"

"An item that forces our Statuses to appear. It is needed because we cannot release a deity's 'lock' on our own."

Riveria stood next to Lefiya, providing context to everyone who stood over the corpse. Her eyebrows sank to a scowl as she watched the man's fingers move.

Only those who had the Advanced Ability "Enigma" were able to produce this item that was created from the ichor in a deity's blood. Its main ingredient made the substance illegal. Status Thief would never be bought or sold at a store on the street, but it was occasionally on the market underground. It was better to assume that the item could be found in Rivira.

Being that it only had one purpose and that the number of chemists who could create it was extremely limited, the number of bottles on hand at any one time was quite low. And of course, they were incredibly expensive.

It was normally used to reveal the true identity of assassins and other criminals. Statuses always displayed an adventurer's full name as well as the name of their god or goddess.

"Where does someone pick up a skill like that?"

"It's not as if adventurers only started doing anything for money last week, you know."

Tione's eyes closed halfway in annoyance at her sister's amazement as the two Amazons watched the animal person's fingers pick up speed over where the slain adventurer's Status was hidden.

Using the item to help loosen the "lock" and tracing complex patterns and movements to "pick" it open, the man didn't take long to bring forth a large jumble of characters and letters that resembled an epitaph on the corpse's back.

"Bors, it's done."

"Ah, good work."

The short animal person stepped out of the way as Bors leaned in for a closer look. "Son of a b—," he muttered and slapped his forehead. "Totally slipped my mind. Can't read hieroglyphs…Oi, you there! Go find one or two really smart-lookin' elves and bring them back here!" Bors yelled to another adventurer stationed outside the room.

"Wait. I can read divine hieroglyphs."

"Me, too."

Riveria and Aiz were quick to speak up.

Bors's un-patched right eye went wide in surprise. Shrugging his shoulders, he stepped out of the way. The two women came forward to get a good look at the Status.

Riveria knelt beside the body while Aiz stayed on her feet. Everyone in the room was focused on them as two sets of eyes, one jade and one gold, worked their way through the glyphs.

Riveria slowly opened her lips after a few moments.

"His name was Hashana Dorlia, a former member of…"

"…*Ganesha Familia*."

The moment that Aiz finished Riveria's sentence—a deafening silence filled the room.

Every noise was gone in the blink of an eye.

A sense of panic was quick to overtake the stillness.

"*Ganesha Familia*?!"

"Oi, you sure?!"

Aiz and Riveria kept their eyes focused on the body even while screams of fright filled the room. Finn and the Amazonian sisters were quick to notice the intensity in their gazes.

The victim had belonged to a powerful familia—one strong enough to compete with the top dogs like *Loki Familia*. That knowledge was enough to make Willy's blood run cold. He wasn't the only one.

Bors quivered as he lost his sense of calm, and he yelled a fact that could not be ignored:

"This ain't no joke—wasn't the Strong Fist Warrior Hashana a Level Four?!"

Aiz and Riveria had revealed the death of a powerful adventurer.

Everyone's train of thought arrived at the same conclusion—the robed woman was powerful enough to take down at least a Level 4.

What's worse, this incredibly powerful murderer could still be among them. A cold shudder ran through the room.

CHAPTER 3

GEKAI DETECTIVE LOKI

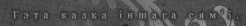

Гэта казка іншага сям'і.

Ніжняя мяжа дэтэктыў Локі

The sun shone brightly at its zenith.

The hustle and bustle of daily life in Orario carried on underneath a clear blue sky. The Shopping District was alive with the voices and footsteps of its many visitors, but even the surrounding areas were so full of people that it was difficult to see the stone pavement below. Many had given up trying to reach their destinations on foot and flagged down one of the numerous horse-drawn taxis to traverse the large city.

Loki and Bete, however, made their way through all the humans and demi-humans as they walked down East Main Street.

"Lookie there! Jyaga Maru Kun! Bete, wanna split a few with me?"

"I ain't eatin' any. Now, would you stop makin' detours already?"

Bete's patience was reaching its limit when the two of them turned off the main road and Loki happened to spot a street stall selling the fried potato puffs known as Jyaga Maru Kun. The werewolf clicked his tongue in frustration as Loki went off to place an order, anyway.

They started walking side by side as soon as the goddess returned, one of the jam-flavored puffs already in her mouth. Bete was attracting a lot of attention from people on the street and inside shops with open windows. Every set of eyes locked on him was female.

His long, muscular legs moved his 180-celch frame forward. The young man exuded a wild aura that was compounded by a tattoo on his cheek. Despite that, his face was perfectly symmetrical and very attractive. Apparently, many people considered an animal person's signature ears on top of their head and swishing tail to be rather cute.

Bete could feel the yearning stares of two female animal people on the other side of the street. He met their gazes with his own amber glare.

The two young women jumped in surprise before nearly tripping over their own feet.

"Ahh, such a waste. An' those two were pretty cute...Be~te, ya gotta be nice to the ladies, ya hear?" Finishing her snack, Loki licked her fingers as she watched the events unfold.

"I hate weak women most of all."

Bete didn't bother watching the girls disappear and spat out his retort.

"Eh~, no way. Ya don' get that squeezin' feelin' in your heart when a damsel in distress looks at ya for help? No urge to be her shield?"

"Hah! Makes me wanna puke. If you can't protect yourself, go crawl in a hole somewhere and don't bother coming out."

"So cold...Yer a real contradiction, aint'cha, Bete."

"Oi, what's that supposed to mean?!"

"It's, well, ya know—ya bein' head over heels for Aiz an' all!"

"Like hell I am!"

Bete growled as his face turned bright red.

"Hee-hee-hee," laughed Loki, clearly enjoying the exchange.

The werewolf's efforts to hide his emotions, and even his threatening posture, could not withstand the giggling goddess.

"Ahh, screw you...Oi, how many times are we gonna walk around the same block? Didn't you wanna look into something?"

Bete pulled back his lips, baring his teeth as he asked Loki for a straight answer.

He didn't have much of a choice when his goddess came to him at home and asked for his help "searching." However, they'd made several laps around the buildings that lined East Main Street without doing much at all, up to this point.

Loki had stuck her head into a few out-of-the-way empty buildings and tried talking to shop owners and passersby, but frustration was starting to get the better of Bete. Even his ash-gray tail was starting to twitch with annoyance.

"Hnnn~," muttered Loki as she looked around on tiptoes, holding a cloth sack over her shoulder. "To be frank with ya, I've been doin' some diggin' on my own since yesterday...Now I'm makin' sure I didn't overlook nothin'."

Two days had passed since the Monsterphilia, and Loki was investigating East Main Street.

After her meeting with Freya, Loki had gotten a hunch that a third someone—someone with a hidden agenda—had released the man-eating flowers at the same time the Goddess of Beauty set other monsters free.

Considering that Lefiya had sustained considerable injuries when she and a few others had been drawn into the fray, Loki had more than enough of a reason to get involved.

She had focused her investigation on East Main Street exclusively, but had yet to come across any promising leads.

The plant monsters had burrowed up from beneath the street. Unfortunately, all the holes had been plugged and everything seemed back to normal in the surrounding area.

"So you're saying the 'lookin' into' you're doing is to find where those monsters came from? What a pain…Don't Ganesha's guys or the Guild know anything?"

"Thought about asking 'em, but they were attendin' to festival cleanup and gettin' people back on their feet. Wasn't the right time."

Loki looked up at the Coliseum while conversing with Bete. The imposing structure towered over everything else in the area.

In fact, many facilities owned and operated by the Guild were located on or around East Main Street, including the Coliseum. Most events hosted in Orario were held in one of the many Guild-operated facilities built in this area. That meant there was an abundance of hotels and inns close by to accommodate travelers visiting from out of town.

Turning off East Main Street, the two went into an area dominated by expensive hotels standing higher than three stories tall. The farther in they went, the more the beautiful red brick buildings gave way to the cheaper, wooden inns. Suddenly, Loki came to a stop.

There was a slight opening between four buildings at the end of the narrow alleyway.

It led to a square clearing with only a few old dusty crates in the corner and a small shack made of stone built opposite to the alleyway's entrance.

"We've crisscrossed the town quite a bit already...so this is all that's left."

With that, Loki made her way to the shack's heavy wooden door. Expecting it to be locked, the goddess was genuinely surprised that there was no resistance when she grabbed the rust-covered handle and pulled...*Creak*, the hinges moaned as the door slowly opened.

There was nothing inside the shack, except for the entrance to a set of spiraling stairs that went straight down. Loki showed no hesitation and went right inside. *Tap, tap.* Her footsteps echoed off the stone walls surrounding the stairwell.

Loki and Bete descended into the thickening darkness, following the spiral around and around—until they emerged into the city's sewer system.

Dim light from sputtering magic-stone lamps provided vague outlines of the surroundings as the sound of flowing water reached their ears. The darkness farther down the sewer tunnel was so thick they couldn't see where it ended.

"I knew I shoulda forced this onto Raul..."

Feeling that this was going to be more trouble than it was worth, Bete voiced his frustration under his breath.

"Now, now, you'll get a nice treat after we're done."

Loki stuck her hand into the cloth sack and withdrew a magic-stone lantern. She clicked it on, and the details of their surroundings immediately came to light.

"It's just gonna be some kind of liquor, right?" said Bete with a cocked eyebrow. Loki laughed at his accurate prediction as the two of them started walking down the tunnel.

"Tiona and Tione did some pokin' around down here the day of the Monsterphilia, but I just wanna be sure. They might've missed a few things chasin' after those monsters."

"Those two only got air between the ears. Can't even imagine how much they missed."

They continued down the rather narrow tunnel, the sound of

running water growing steadily louder until they found the main drainage vessel.

Constructed completely out of stone, the tubelike tunnel was about six meders wide. The water flowed down the center while footpaths lined the edges. Loki and Bete followed the path along the right side.

WHOOSSSSH. The rushing sound was so loud that it drowned out the possibility of conversation. Other tunnels fed into the main one from many directions, amplifying the echoes.

At the same time, while the air was mustier down here than on the surface, the stench of sewage...was missing.

Loki's light illuminated several thin, purple crystalline columns at the end of one of the smaller tunnels. In the shape of a grate, this magic-stone product of Orario wasn't designed to alter the flow.

Instead, it served as a barrier to contamination, and only allowed the current through after purifying it. Put simply, it was a filter. The liquid rushing through the main tunnel was so clear it was hard to believe it had ever been dirty.

These purifiers had been set up at the end of every channel feeding into this one, preventing the smell from ever reaching suffocating levels. This way, the brackish lake to the southwest would never be contaminated by draining sewage.

Loki marveled at the creativity of the people of Gekai, coming up with useful inventions like this.

"Ya know, with all these twisty-turny paths and the feel of this place...it's a little bit like the Dungeon, wouldn't ya say?"

"Hah! Don't make me laugh."

Bete, who spent his days in the real Dungeon, scoffed at Loki's remark. This man-made "dungeon" was not even worth comparing to the real thing.

Along the wall were openings that branched off into side paths, or sometimes staircases, and there were even raised bridges that connected to the other side of the tunnel. Bete felt no pressure from traveling through the dark sewers and was very careful to keep Loki safe from danger, albeit while voicing complaints. A raider fish, a monster native to the open ocean that must have found its way in through the brackish lake, jumped out of the stream to feast on potential prey. However, one swift kick, courtesy of Bete, slew it before it even got close to the goddess. The whole incident was over before Loki even realized she was in danger. "Ouuu," she said with puckered lips, impressed by the strike she hadn't even seen.

The lantern-style magic-stone lamp in her hand cast light in all directions. Two long shadows trailed across the stone walls. Bete's silhouette resembled that of a wolf on the prowl, complete with ears and tail, stretching as far as the light shone down the tunnel behind them.

"Oh?"

Something came into view after the two of them had spent a decent amount of time exploring the main channel.

An iron door, the likes of which they'd never seen before, appeared at the edge of the lantern's glow.

It had obviously been there for quite a long time. Opening down the middle, the two sides were made from heavy iron and sealed shut by a large padlock on the front.

"The heck is this?"

"A sewer…from the old days."

Loki spotted a plate on the wall. Holding the light up close to it, she managed to read the faint letters on it. Apparently the sewer had been built before the modern system was installed and ignored ever since the new one was completed.

Even so, Loki thought it was a bizarre design and questioned the intelligence of the architect as she brought the light closer to the iron door.

As more details came into view, Loki noticed that the jet-black rock showed signs of being used—opened and closed many times by human hands.

"Well, ain't this fishy…"

Her thin eyes opened a little wider as she whispered to herself.

It would be perfectly logical that Guild employees came through here periodically, but that meant there was something interesting behind the door. Loki wasn't going to walk away from this without knowing one way or the other.

She summoned Bete to her side with a simple glance. The werewolf was by no means enthusiastic, but he took the padlock in both hands and started to pull. *Crick, crick, crick.* The padlock groaned right away before breaking with a metallic pop.

Splitting the lock into two pieces, he tossed them aside and opened the iron doors with ease.

To their surprise, wall-mounted magic-stone lamps lit up the old sewer that supposedly wasn't in use.

"Hold on, why's there water in here?"

Passing through the door and ascending a small staircase, they realized that the path was flooded. There were no dry bridges like the ones they had followed to get here. Bete curled his lips back as he watched the surface of the black river running through the tunnel.

Loki lowered her lantern to just above the surface of the water so she could see its depth. Suddenly, she looked up at her adorable family member.

"Bete, gimme a ride!"

"Come again?"

"I don't wanna get my shoes wet! So, piggyback!"

"Are you frickin' serious? It ain't that deep, so shut up and walk!"

"But~! You have to carry me! I want a piggyback! I can't go on without a piggyback!"

Watching his goddess throw a temper tantrum, Bete muttered, "Dammit, woman," under his breath with his tail twitching up a storm. "Fine, just shut up already!" He gave in, covering the wolf ears on top of his head to protect them against Loki's whiny voice, and knelt in front of her.

Looking down at his wide shoulders as if her own personal chariot had arrived, Loki grinned and squealed like a child as she jumped on.

"Now then, onward, Bete! I'm expectin' a smooth ride!"

"Any complaints and I'm tossin' you in."

Doing his best to hold down the rage flowing through his veins, Bete stood up smoothly with Loki draped on his back.

"Whoa!" shouted Loki with innocent glee, suddenly seeing everything from a higher vantage point. It was hard for Bete to believe that a deusdea could be so pure.

She looked left and right, thoroughly enjoying the view as Bete trudged his way through the flowing water.

"Neh-hee-hee, do ya feel like yer carryin' some cute little lady? Too bad, 'tis me!"

"Shut it."

"Tell me, tell me! What's it feel like?! Me on yer back instead of Aizuu—how do ya feel?!"

"Wanna go for a swim...?"

Bete's lips twitched as Loki leaned over his left and right shoulders back and forth, trying to get a better look at his face. Veins bulged on the werewolf's forehead as he fought back the urge to throw off the extra "luggage" and her perverted smile right then and there.

Bete pressed forward, water sloshing around his legs as he did his best to ignore Loki's constant questions. Half of his metallic boots were hidden by the dark water flowing by his shins. Compared to the well-organized layout of the modern system they had just passed through, the old sewer was far more complicated and felt more like the labyrinth farther below.

"Wonder if the Guild was lookin' around this far in after the festival?"

"The air still smells like people. This water's muckin' things up, so I can't tell much more than that..."

Loki raised the lamp and kept her head on a swivel, looking for anything strange. Bete took a long whiff of the air after she made her comment.

Using the superior sense of smell that all werewolves had, Bete was able to tell that someone had been in this part of the old sewer recently. He explained that it was too faint to figure out how many people there were as he turned to face the direction of the smell.

"Hnn," whispered Loki, her left arm wrapped around his neck while the right held the lantern high to light up the path.

She casually swung her legs back and forth while Bete made his way up the tunnel against the current...until a "hole" appeared in the wall.

"Well, somethin' really let loose..."

The stone wall was crumbling around the edges of a wide, jagged opening. With water pouring from the lower rim, this seemed to be the origin of the liquid flowing through the old sewer system.

Loki tilted her head as she gazed upon the opening. Judging by the outward-facing border, whatever caused it had most likely come from the other side.

"This the jackpot...?"

Loki grinned. Her searching had finally paid off with a promising lead. And then...

Flick! Like a beast raising its head, Bete's wolf ears suddenly stood on end.

"Get off."

One look at the side of Bete's face told Loki she had no room to argue, and she complied.

Bete was so focused on the dark area on the other side of the hole that he barely heard Loki's feet hit the water next to him.

"Those damn Amazons...where the hell were they lookin'?"

His mood worsening by the moment, Bete led the way inside.

"It's all *still here,*" he spat, with Loki not far behind.

Loki followed the werewolf even deeper into the cavity. It had been carved by something large—whatever it was, it had passed through many different tunnels on its journey, all of which were now inundated with water. Bete showed no hesitation as he went even farther into the darkness. Soon, he spotted a wide staircase in the distance.

The cold sensation of water around his ankles gone, his footsteps echoed against a hard surface as the straight path opened up before him.

"Is this...a reservoir?"

Loki held her lantern aloft as she looked around the area.

. It was a long, rectangular chamber filled with a forest of columns. Each of the equally spaced structures was supporting the ceiling overhead. They had to be at least ten meders high. The vast hollow space shrouded in darkness was indeed worthy of being called a reservoir.

Since the Dungeon was beneath the city and the brackish lake was connected to the sewer network, Loki reasoned that they must now be underneath the southwest portion of the city, quite a ways from Central Park. Evidence of the water level still remained on the walls and columns, as if this reservoir hadn't held water for a long time. This space could have practically been used to dry-dock a boat. The magic-stone lamps on the ceiling were just barely strong enough to emit a thin, weak light.

Loki's ears picked up a faint, slithering sound in the distance.

Spinning to face it, she immediately saw Bete with his back toward her and something large moving in the darkness.

A yellowish-green body emerged from the darkness a moment later.

The flowered predator appeared, resembling an overgrown vine intertwined with the columns, and was soon was joined by another, and another.

Sensing that they were not alone, the snakelike creatures worked their way through the darkness toward the intruders. Their bodies writhed, releasing puffs of pollen as their bud-like heads split open.

Their fangs bared, flashing in the darkness from the other side of the colorful, ominous pollen cloud, the monsters reared up their bodies and looked down on Loki and Bete from just below the ceiling.

"Loki, get back and stay there."

Bete, who was already braced for combat, didn't even look at his goddess as he spoke.

His amber gaze was locked solely on the monsters. Leaning forward, he kicked off the floor and raced into battle at the same moment the closest monster's roar echoed throughout the chamber.

"OooOOOOOOOoooOOOOOOOOOO!"

The plant monster charged, its roar the pitch of a broken bell.

Three in all, the monsters advanced in unison like a muddy green tide. Not to be outdone, Bete charged forward to meet them. One hard step with his left leg launched him off the stone floor.

Setting his sights solely on the closest monster, he swung his long right leg forward.

"You freakin' stink, all of you!"

"?!"

Bete's right foot connected cleanly with the monster's head like an athlete kicking a ball. The creature's long body arced backward into the air as echoes of the dull impact filled the chamber.

It was pure strength; no tricks or special techniques were involved. Bete repelled the monster's charge with a limb that paled in comparison to its gigantic, snakelike frame. *Crack!* The metal boot that covered Bete's right foot had struck one of the monster's fangs. Pieces of the tooth fell from its mouth.

Bete easily dodged the incoming attacks that came from his left and right, counterattacking as they passed. He refused to let the plant beasts get anywhere near Loki. Their bodies fell far off to the side.

Along with power, the ash-colored werewolf was known for his speed and precision. Even among *Loki Familia*, he was considered the best at reading his opponents and retaliating against their next move before it could even happen. Each of the beasts seemed to be two or three seconds behind him as each attack was neutralized in quick succession.

His speed to overwhelm, his precision to keep the opponent at bay, and his uncanny ability to start vicious brawls in an instant were what inspired his nickname: "Crazed Wolf, Vanargand."

Setting up for a final blow, Bete jumped toward a monster that had fallen to his right. Every muscle in his body worked in unison to bring his right leg down onto the monster's exposed neck like the blade of a guillotine.

"Huhaa?"

However, his killing strike didn't go through anything.

He was expecting the creature's bud-like head to roll across the floor. Instead, a single petal fell. That was the only sign that he'd made contact at all.

A sound of surprise and disbelief escaped his throat as pain shot up the nerves in his legs from behind the metal boot. "Tsk!" Anger coursed through him at the thickness of the creature's hide. The monster shook its head a few times to recover, then released its own rage-filled roar.

"The hell you need that solid a body for…?!"

Bete voiced his frustration as his other two enemies joined their ally and attacked as one.

It was strange for Bete to agree with Tiona about anything, yet they had the same opinion about this monster. Lips twitching at the thought, he moved to engage all three at once. Each of the beasts released several vines, launching them like spears from all angles. Bete made use of all the space available to dodge them, as well as take cover behind stone pillars when necessary.

Not even Aiz Wallenstein could match the werewolf in terms of pure speed, and Bete was using everything he could muster as he fought the creatures to a stalemate.

"Mhmm, they're movin' so fast I can't tell what's even happenin'."

Back at the entrance to the reservoir, Loki watched the battle from the shadow of a stone pillar.

The moment that she saw an ash-gray flash that was probably Bete, one of the monsters went flying. She couldn't comprehend anything that was happening, so she kept her vermilion gaze on the monsters not currently in combat, in an attempt to study them.

It was impossible to tell at the Monsterphilia because the flower monsters had never fully emerged from the ground, but the ends of their "tails" were thick and bulbous. Numerous tendrils sprouted from the bases of their bodies like the roots of a tree, along with things that seemed like root hairs.

They probably dig those thingies into the Dungeon to feed, she thought to herself…before suddenly noticing a strange shadow above her head.

It came from the ceiling—a single stem wrapping itself around the pillar that served as her hiding place.

Twitch. She felt a shiver run down her spine. Her suspicions were confirmed the moment a speck of pollen fell on her shoulder.

That ain't good. Loki knew she was in trouble. Dashing from her hiding place, she looked up…

And saw exactly what she had expected: another one of the plant monsters staring at her with its fanged mouth wide open.

"AAAAAAAAaaaaaaAAAAAA!!"

"Ehgawd!"

An intimidating roar hammered her from above. Green stalks raced forward like whips in an attempt to grab her, but only hit empty air.

Loki's screams didn't sound as afraid as they probably should have, even as she sprinted at full speed.

"Uoohhh! I'm done for! It's gonna catch me~!"

Loki raced through the chamber, her quick and light-footed movements reminiscent of a fugitive on the run from the law. However, with her all-powerful Arcanum abilities sealed, an actual mortal criminal would have been faster. There was no way she could escape the ravenous monster.

With a great deal of luck and good timing, Loki jumped to the side and behind pillars as the vines raced past her head. However, the monster's open jaws slithered closer every second.

"There was another one?!"

Confidence disappeared from Bete's face for the first time. Putting his battle with the other monsters on hold, he kicked off the ground in a desperate attempt to reach his goddess in time. However—it was already too late.

The monster's gaping mouth was mere seconds away from swallowing the deity whole. Bete's face was blank as he reached out to his goddess at full speed. At that moment—

Loki thrust her hand into the bag she carried over her shoulder and pulled out a handful of dark crystals. She scattered them across the floor with one quick flick of her wrist.

"Lookie there!"

Dark purple magic stones now sparkled all over the floor off to her right.

Not just any magic stones, but high-quality magic stones. Even the monster could tell at a glance, immediately changing course with a hungry look in its eyes.

Bete watched in amazement as the monster sharply veered away from behind his goddess.

"Pure magic energy, magic stones, livin' people...These monsters seem to pick targets in that order."

Loki whispered to herself as she watched the monster willingly slither away from her with her thin, discerning eyes.

She had heard about it from Lefiya, who had firsthand experience during the battle at the Monsterphilia. Therefore, she had prepared quite a few magic stones to use as decoys during the investigation— just in case.

If they're drawn to magic, then magic stones should work, too. Her hypothesis had been right.

"Look, Bete, it took a hike!"

"Sheesh...Just don't get eaten, got that?!"

Bete didn't have long enough to actually sigh at his goddess. Catching a glimpse of another monster coming up behind him out of the corner of his eye, he unleashed an arcing roundhouse kick over his right shoulder.

Picking up momentum, he spun even faster as his left leg slammed into the approaching creature's head. Thrown backward through the air in a wide arc, the monster hit the other two creatures, sending them all to the floor.

"We make one heckuva combo, Bete! Breathin' as one!"

"Like I care. Stop trying to piss me off, stupid woman!"

Bete snarled a retort as Loki ran toward him. The goddess couldn't help but grin, knowing her follower wouldn't openly admit he was worried about her.

The werewolf broke off eye contact to keep from feeling even more uncomfortable.

"These things sure are a pain in the ass...Can't even make a dent in 'em."

"Now that ya mention it, the Amazon twins couldn't do nothin' with their bare hands, either. That skin's pretty thick, ya know?"

"Why didn't you say that sooner?"

Bete furrowed his eyebrows, irritated that his goddess brought up this information as an afterthought.

The two turned together to look deeper into the dried reservoir. The monsters were beginning to untangle themselves.

Neither let their guard down as Loki explained that Lefiya's Magic and Aiz's sharp slashes had worked well on these creatures last time.

"...Hate to use this, but might as well," Bete mumbled as he reached behind his waist with his right hand.

The sound of sliding metal softly echoed in the chamber. He withdrew a knife from its sheath that appeared as if scarlet flames burned from within—a magic sword.

He leaned down so that he could align the blade with one of his faintly silver boots.

Frosvirt, his "Superior" metallic boots, had the ability to absorb magical energy. The scarlet flames burning in the blade of Bete's knife died down almost instantly as their energy poured into his right boot.

"Just curious, but what did that run ya?"

"One mil."

"Uwaoh, a one-million-valis attack! That's gonna be somethin' to see!"

A pale yellow jewel in the middle of his right boot shone in the darkness until all the energy from the magic sword had been absorbed. *Crack!* The blade shattered and fell to the floor the moment the last of the scarlet flames disappeared. The jewel then instantly turned scarlet. As if on cue, the boot erupted in searing, crimson flames.

Whoosh! New echoes filled the chamber as Bete stood ready, an inferno embracing his right foot.

"—I'll send 'em flyin'."

Bete's wild nature appeared in a toothy grin on his lips.

He stepped once toward the nearly untangled mass of monsters. Then, slowly, he took another step and another. As the red-hot flames seared half of his footprints in the stone floor, suddenly, he picked up speed.

The creatures howled like so many broken bells as he approached. All that did was make him smile, the tattoo across his cheek flexing with the muscles beneath. Finally, he kicked off the floor.

Jumping clear out of his enemies' line of sight, he eyed them from above as he snorted. His arc came to an end at a stone pillar, and he kicked off of it with his left leg over to another pillar and another. He changed his angle of attack three times before finally charging the monsters from their blind spot. Bete swung his flaring right foot out to the side and brought it crashing down with all his might.

"————————————————!!"

A searing flare bloomed upon impact with the closest monster's head.

The flash was enough to make anyone want to shield their eyes. Frosvirt's physical power combined with the energy from the magic sword to enhance Bete's already enormous strength. Flames roared as the creature's head was cleanly severed from its body. It instantly dissolved into ash before it could even feel any pain.

As Bete landed on the floor, the first monster to notice him leaped into the air for a counterattack.

"Burn!!"

Bete somersaulted into the beast's oncoming strike.

Deep-red shadows danced across the chamber walls and pillars as Bete's burning leg swept across the beast's entire body, setting it alight. *Whoosh!* Roars of the ensuing inferno filled the chamber while Bete jumped out of the way.

Flipping in midair, he watched upside down as what was left of the creature dissolved to ash. The corner of his lips pulled back into an unmistakable grin.

"Bete, get one of the stones!"

"Ah-hah? Just had to ruin my fun..."

The werewolf heard Loki's order just as he finished off the second monster. He selected his next target to carry it out.

He knew from his previous encounters with the carnivorous plants that their magic stones were located deep in their throats. Closing the distance in the blink of an eye, he held back his full strength and delivered a dizzying blow just under what would pass for the monster's chin.

The upward strike flung the creature backward, with flower petals falling in its wake. It was still very much alive, shrieking until it landed on the stone floor, where it writhed in pain. Bete stomped on its still-smoking lower jaw to pin it in place. Grabbing its upper jaw with his left hand, he ruthlessly forced its mouth wide open—wide enough to snap the joints.

The creature's hot breath bellowed up from beneath him. Bete wasted no time in thrusting his right hand deep into its mouth to snatch the stone out.

"*Nasty!*" he growled to himself, wrinkling his nose as he dodged an attack from the remaining monster.

Tucking the magic stone into his shirt, Bete turned to face his final opponent and charged.

"You're the last one!"

He advanced at full speed, but the fanged plant had other ideas. It launched a wave of tendrils at the werewolf in an attempt to forestall the frontal attack.

The yellowish-green whips reflecting in his eyes, Bete turned, dodged, and wove his way through them. The monster's body seemed to cringe as the last of its spear-like stems passed by the werewolf without hitting its target.

He closed the remaining distance with the ferocity of a hungry predator, kicked off the floor, and soared.

©Kiyotaka Haimura

Bete thrust his burning foot forward in midair, tearing through the darkness like a flaming arrow.

"Burn in Heeeeeeeeeeeeeeeeeeeeeeeell!!"

The resulting kick caused an explosion that engulfed the creature's head. What was left of its body came blasting out of a cloud of smoke, as though it had been shot from a cannon.

It hit the closest pillar head-on, but didn't stop there. Two, then three pillars were destroyed before a fourth one finally withstood the impact. A small avalanche of stone joined the lifeless corpse on its way down.

The headless creature's body was covered in the rubble before finally turning to ash and disappearing entirely.

"Hell of a show, there…"

Loki's murmur echoed through the silence as the dust cleared.

The scarlet light disappeared from Bete's right foot a few moments later as the remaining embers went out completely.

The fight over, a stunning silver gleam returned to the metal boots as he stood still in the old reservoir.

"Got some evidence, but nothin' that'll get me closer to the bad guy."

"Had to use a magic sword, wasn't even close to worth it."

Flip, flip. Loki tossed the magic stone between her hands as she and Bete made their way back through the sewers.

Their battle with the hungry plants over, they were retracing their steps to return to the surface. Looking around the dried-up reservoir yielded no results, and since Bete didn't have a spare magic sword, they felt it was a good time to call it a day. It was too dangerous to proceed without the proper equipment.

Already clear of the older sewers, Loki took a closer look at the magic stone as the two of them walked down the main waterline.

It had a brilliantly colored core. It was obvious that this was different from normal, dark purple magic stones. "Hmm," Loki whispered to herself, without realizing, as she eyed the ominously shimmering crystal in her hand.

"Now that I think about it, it's the same as the one Tione ripped from that a monster on floor fifty."

"Floor fifty…You mean the new breed that y'all ran into on the expedition?"

"Yeah, that filthy-lookin' caterpillar monster."

Bete commented on the similarity of the two magic stones as Loki intently examined the one in her hand.

It wasn't long before the two of them arrived at a familiar spiral staircase. Going up the many loops and arriving back in the stone shack, Loki and Bete enjoyed their first breaths of fresh air after hours underground.

Turning toward the sun shining brightly in the blue sky: "Haaaa!" Loki took a deep breath and stretched her arms high above her head. Bete showed no signs of fatigue, only cracking his neck with each hand as his shoulders finally relaxed.

"Shall we head home?" said Loki casually, and the two of them left the shack behind.

Out of the narrow backstreets and on toward row upon row of high-class hotels, the street steadily became wider and busier as they went. It wasn't long before they were surrounded by the voices of townspeople.

Then, just as they were making their way back toward the center of the city—

They encountered a deity as they rounded a corner.

"Oh? That you, Dionysus?"

"…Loki?"

Loki came to a stop in front of the familiar face.

His beautiful golden locks stretched down to his neck, framing an enchanting smile that could make anyone, male or female, melt on the spot. His glass-colored eyes met Loki's. Indeed, it was the god she'd had a short conversation with at Ganesha's Banquet of the Gods only a few days ago.

Of course he wasn't dressed in his finest attire, but he still carried the aura of royalty and wore an expensive outfit. An elf woman with beautiful black hair stood at his side, most likely a member of his familia.

"Yo," said Loki, surprised by their chance meeting.

"Hold it."

Loki came to a sudden stop. "Hmm?" she said as she turned to face her own follower. His gaze was fierce, staring icy daggers at Dionysus.

"It's them."

"…What's them?"

Loki questioned as Bete jerked his chin in their direction. He opened his mouth to speak, eyes unblinking.

"The unusual stench in the sewer—*it's theirs*."

Loki's usually narrow eyes went wide, while the other two's expressions froze in shock.

An endless stream of voices traveled all around the cliffs and up the blue crystal pillars.

But the nervous interest of all the adventurers outside was nothing compared to the all-out confusion threatening to overtake an inn built into the rock face.

The location was the Dungeon eighteenth floor, at Willy's Inn in the town of Rivira.

No one could take their eyes off the Status engraved into the back of the headless corpse in the middle of the room. Onlookers, including Aiz Wallenstein, wore various expressions of shock.

"…W-was this man truly killed with only brute force? There could have been, I don't know, poison or something…"

"As in, the attacker strangled him once he couldn't move?"

Tione responded to Lefiya's question with another question. The obviously uncomfortable elf nodded awkwardly in response.

Her view of the body was obscured behind Aiz and Tiona. However, her dark blue eyes could still see his lifeless limbs, and that was enough to make her tremble.

"The Advanced Ability 'Immunity' is listed under his Skills, so no, I don't think so…"

"Someone of Hashana's prowess would hardly be affected by even the most potent toxins, even in high doses. It is unlikely he fell victim to that."

Aiz and Riveria continued their analysis of the hieroglyphs on the dead man's back.

One combination of the divine characters spelled out "Immunity" in one of his Skill brackets—it protected him against different types of status effects, including poison. What's more, the skill had reached "G."

A G-level Immunity would have granted him protection from almost everything under the sun. Even a poison created by an expert chemist would have a difficult time slowing him down.

"We know that she caught him off guard, but a female adventurer strong enough to strangle a Level Four…?"

"…What about one of *Ishtar Familia*'s Berbera?"

Tiona responded to Finn's verbal train of thought.

Bringing up the group of ferociously seductive, lithe courtesans made Finn pause and think. "Hmm," he mumbled without looking away from the corpse on the floor. "If that were true, then this would be a simple open-and-shut case. But there's something more here, just begging to be discovered."

"That's right. This is too out in the open," Tione added.

One of the guards in the room suddenly pointed at Aiz and the others, his entire body shaking as if he were one step away from losing his mind.

"L-listen to what you just said!! The lot of you show up here, actin' like you only just got to town. How do we know one of you ain't behind this?!"

Bors and the rest of his group snapped to attention, his words ringing in their ears.

Top-class adventurers, people so strong they could silence a crying child with a glance, were now the top suspects. Indeed, there were several female adventurers in the room who were physically powerful enough to kill a second-tier adventurer like Hashana.

"Huuh?" Tiona voiced her disbelief while Tione denied his claim with a look. Riveria closed an eye, more perturbed than threatened. Lefiya, however, was on the verge of a panic attack.

Aiz wasn't sure what to do, either, nervously shifting her weight.

"If one of them is the culprit…"

"Yeah, Finn couldn't'a done it."

A ring of adventurers surrounded *Loki Familia*. Willy was too scared to finish the sentence as he backed away, but Bors nodded and finished it for him. Prums were small, but more importantly, Finn was male. That automatically removed him from the list of suspects. With that, every set of eyes in the ring moved across each of the women. They were looking for someone who matched the description of the lady with a body curvy enough to be identified beneath a hooded robe.

First Aiz and Lefiya, then the room examined Riveria and Tiona.

Not much in the way of a bustline…That was especially true for Tiona. Showing quite a bit of skin as it was, all the men in the circle nodded as one.

"Not her."

"No, definitely not."

"Hey!"

Tiona stepped forward, fists raised and itching for a fight—until Aiz grabbed her under the armpits to keep the Amazon at bay.

Tiona continued voicing her grievances, but the ring of adventurers turned their attention to Tione.

"…A body like that could lure any man she wanted into a trap, don'cha think?"

Plump breasts with shapely cleavage, a small waist, and a round, soft behind, in addition to supple thighs, made her an extremely attractive woman with curves in all the right places.

Tione could feel every set of eyes wrapping around her body from all angles the moment Bors said those words. The men seemed much more interested in her than her younger sister.

"—Agh?"

Tione wasn't about to let that slide.

A spark of fury ignited within her; her eyes burned with enough anger to char anything that got too close as she exploded into a tirade.

"My chastity belongs to the general and no one else!!

"Da' hell do any of you know about it?!

"Seriously, anyone bring something dirty anywhere close to my legs, it'll get ripped off and shredded to a thousand pieces!"

A surge of insults and threats poured from her mouth.

She brought her body up to its full height, acting much like a dragon, ready to lash out. She took a step forward, cracking the stone floor beneath her foot.

This time it was Tiona who jumped in to keep her older sister under control. However, every man in the ring had just experienced the true meaning of terror. Every single one of them had their knees together in a desperate attempt to protect their manhoods.

"…Um, Bors. As you can see, none of these girls would use their body in that way. It's just not in their nature."

"Y-yeah…Sorry for suspectin' you. M-my bad."

The normally gruff and masculine Bors had both hands clamped tightly over his crotch, pitifully nodding as he struggled to put words together.

Finn had grown tired of the situation, rolling his eyes at the spectacle. So he took a deep breath to clear his thoughts and took another look around the room.

"I'd like to do a little investigating. Might have to touch a few things, is that okay?"

"Sure, do what you want."

Bors surrendered his authority over the crime scene without any fuss, realizing that it was now beyond his ability. Finn thanked him and asked for Riveria's help in checking the area around the body.

Everyone in the room, including Aiz and the Amazons, gathered in a corner to give the two some space. First, Finn took a closer look at Hashana's remains.

"The cause of death was blunt force to the head…No, these wounds suggest the neck was broken first."

"So you surmise that the killer snapped his neck and killed him before crushing his head?"

"Looks that way to me."

Finn responded to Riveria's inquiry while taking a closer look at what was left of the man's chin and neck area.

Rolling the body onto its back and replacing the cloth that covered the gruesome sight, he noticed that the rest of the man's body showed no signs of a struggle. It must have been over in an instant.

"There had to have been a reason…Or maybe…"

Finn raised his gaze from the body and onto a backpack in a corner of the room.

Walking past blood-splattered armor, he made his way over to the pack to see if there were any clues left behind. Immediately, he could tell that someone had nearly torn it apart while looking through it.

"The robed woman might've been after something special Hashana was carrying at the time."

"Ohhh, now *there's* a simple answer. And because of that, the poor guy got lured into a honey trap and ended up dead."

"Looking at the condition of this bag…I would say the attacker was not acting in desperation, but something closer to irritation."

Finn, Bors, and Riveria shared their opinions. Aiz walked away from the group of observers to take a look for herself.

The fabric was torn in many places, literally nothing more than threads holding the seams together. The bag's contents were strewn about the room, potions and other items lying scattered across the floor. Someone searching for an item in a panic would have likely thrown everything in the same direction. This seemed more like the result of the killer venting her frustration.

"So she couldn't find her objective and decided to take it out on the corpse…That would make sense."

"Sounds like something Tione would do."

"I would never do anything like this!!"

Tione howled at her sister, refusing to be compared to the murderess.

Finn ignored their steadily escalating bickering and started looking for any leads that might still be waiting to be found among the items.

"What have we here?"

His sharp eyes managed to spot a bloodstained piece of paper among the shattered potion bottles and broken drop items.

He picked it up as Aiz, Tiona, and Lefiya came to his side.

"What's that?"

"A request form...for a quest?"

He unfolded the piece of paper, but the thick bloodstains made it nearly impossible to read any of the information written on it.

Finn squinted his eyes and held the red paper up to the light in an attempt to read what was still legible.

"Floor thirty...Alone, collect...Secretly..."

The group around Finn used the new information to form their own ideas about the quest's original intent.

A few moments passed before Finn took a guess, but they all were thinking the same thing.

Quietly, he mumbled as if talking to himself.

"Hashana accepted the quest, and the killer was after the thing that he went to the thirtieth floor to retrieve...?"

Silence pervaded the room.

Still kneeling where he had found the paper, Finn got to his feet. Then he looked up at Bors, who was standing beside him.

"Any idea what kind of equipment Hashana usually wore?"

"Let me think...That guy was pretty famous, but he almost never showed up in Rivira...Willy, any ideas?"

"Well, if my memory serves me...he always had a helmet on. Looked a lot like Ganesha's. You could never really see his face. But I don't think he ever wore full-plated armor before this—no, I'm sure of it."

Finn pondered their responses, fingers resting on his chin. A long

"Hmmmmm" escaped from his lips. The prum's eyes were back on the dark wheat-colored corpse.

Riveria took a step forward and opened her mouth to speak.

"I believe that Hashana concealed his identity in order to carry out the quest. It is highly unlikely that he mentioned this to anyone in his familia."

Riveria's emerald gaze was locked squarely on the blood-splattered armor on the floor.

There was a strong possibility that Hashana had acquired this armor for the sole purpose of fulfilling the client's request. *Ganesha Familia*'s emblem was nowhere to be seen on any of the plates.

Considering how fast information spread, the fact that none of his former allies were taking any action at this point proved that Hashana was working alone—he'd accepted the mission directly from the client.

"...Bors, would you seal off the town, for a bit? I don't want anyone still here to leave Rivira."

Everyone's gazes snapped to Finn the moment he made his request.

Bors's face wrinkled up around his eye patch as he scratched his boulder-like chin.

"You think the killer is still walking around here like nothing happened? If it were me, I would've hightailed it out of here while the gettin' was good."

"A powerful adventurer like Hashana was given a quest in secret...Whatever the culprit was looking for, it needed a powerful protector. At the very least, it was worth committing murder to acquire. If said item wasn't recovered, the killer can't exactly go back empty-handed.

"That and," added Finn as he licked the base of his right thumb, "I'm sure she's still here...Got a strong hunch, anyway."

Bors look down meekly at the confident blue eyes staring up at him. "All right, then," he said with a nod.

Waving his thick arms in the air, Bors issued orders to his fellow residents in the room.

"Close the north and south gates. Then, gather everyone in town in one spot. Restrain anyone who won't to listen to ya—they might be the one we're after. Willy, explain the situation to adventurers that just arrived and separate them from the main group."

"O-on it."

Tiona, Tione, Lefiya, and Aiz watched all of Bors's subordinates trip over themselves and each other in their rush out the door.

"Well, we walked into something big."

"Yeah…"

"We're already in this deep. Looks like it'll be a fight to honor Hashana's memory. We owe it to him to find the killer."

"Y-yes."

Aiz gave short responses to the Amazonian twins, her eyes focused on the now forever-silent body.

Taking their words to heart, she resolutely raised her face and joined the others as they left the room behind.

The town of Rivira was being shaken to the core.

The air crackled with tension.

The temperature was mild, the heat of the afternoon sun warming the street. However, the area around Loki felt ice-cold. Four people stood face-to-face, exchanging glances of surprise and suspicion.

Bete's declaration hung in the air for several seconds before anyone made a move.

Seeing the wolf glare at her god, the young elf jumped in front to protect Dionysus.

"Stand down, Filvis. You're no match for him."

"But, still…Lord Dionysus."

The elf called Filvis didn't move from the spot, keeping herself directly between them.

She was a pure young elf. Face perfectly symmetrical and delicate, her eyes were like a set of unmarred red jewels framed by silky pale skin. Her outfit was mostly white, complete with a cape around her shoulders and a high collar that concealed her neck. Elves were known for exposing as little skin as possible, and she was no exception.

Arrow-straight glossy black hair fell nearly to her waist. Carrying herself with dignity, dressed in white, she had the look and feel of a young priestess.

What a fine-lookin' young lady, Loki thought to herself as she watched Dionysus place his hand on the girl's shoulder and step in front of her.

"We shall make no attempt to run or hide. Would you be willing to hear us out, Loki?"

"…Why not. Let's find some place to go."

It was the deity's willingness to cooperate and the sincerity in his glass-colored eyes that convinced Loki to take him up on the offer.

They found what they were looking for in a red brick hotel facing the street nearby: a lounge with a window. Handing the owner some extra money was enough to convince him to let them make use of it.

"If possible, I'd like to keep this conversation between us," requested Dionysus. Of course he didn't want strangers overhearing what he had to say, but he also wanted to keep their "children" in the dark. Loki accepted.

"Oi, you sure about this?"

"Eh, it's fine. I'll signal ya if things go sour, Bete. You'll come to my rescue, won'cha?"

Bete whispered into the goddess's ear and she responded in kind. While he wasn't all that thrilled with her answer, he went outside the hotel and stood right in front of the lounge window, ready to spring into action at a moment's notice.

The two deities found a private booth away from the other seats in the lounge. Loki took the closest seat and looked Dionysus right in the eyes.

"All right, spill the beans."

She leaned forward, her elbows on the table between them.

Loki was determined to hear any and all information concerning the Monsterphilia and the hungry plants that Dionysus had to offer.

"Of course," said the deity with a nod. "To start with, I would like to resolve the misunderstanding. I am not the one behind these incidents, as you seem to believe, Loki."

The goddess was eyeing him like an interrogator. Dionysus's opening statement made her raise an eyebrow, but she said nothing. He took that as his cue to keep talking.

"Just to confirm, the information you seek all pertains to the plant monsters, am I right?"

"Damn right. And ya showed up while I was seekin' it."

"Is that right." Dionysus gave a quick sigh. "Now where to begin…"

The god broke eye contact, choosing to look at the table while he collected his thoughts.

As Bete and Filvis stood side by side, facing the street just outside the window, several moments passed before Dionysus slowly opened his mouth.

"I'm looking for those monsters. Well, I was."

Looking Loki in the eyes once again, he continued.

"One month ago, several of my children were slain."

"!!"

Dionysus added that she would understand if she looked for evidence at the Guild.

"The killer's method was simple: approach from the front, grab the neck, then break it. Three of my followers died instantly."

"…And their Levels were…?"

"Two were Level One, and the last was Level Two."

If what the god said was true, that meant the killer had to be strong enough to kill an upper-class adventurer without a second thought.

Loki turned her ear to listen more closely.

"I was unable to take the deaths of my children lying down, so I launched my own investigation. During that time, I found evidence that led me to believe my children saw something they shouldn't have, and were subsequently erased."

"And that would be…?"

"This."

Dionysus reached into his jacket and withdrew a brilliantly colored magic stone.

Loki watched in silence as the god placed the stone on the table.

"The one that I found a month ago was much smaller, a fraction of a shard at best. I recovered this one on the day of the Monsterphilia, from one of the creatures that your Sword Princess slew during combat. I was lucky to get my hands on it before the Guild."

"…That's one dangerous bridge yer crossin'."

Had he been discovered, Dionysus would have aroused suspicion and possibly been mistaken for the perpetrator.

Dionysus smiled wryly at the mixture of awe and respect on Loki's face.

"Their bodies, as well as the stone fragment, were discovered in a desolate alleyway in the eastern part of the city, very close to where we are now. And then, a particularly large event was held here just a few days ago."

"The Monsterphilia?"

"Yes. It may have been a coincidence, but I thought the two could be related. Thinking that something might happen, I set up a watch, and then I waited."

Just as he had suspected, something had happened.

While Freya's game of cat and mouse had caused quite a stir, the green monsters with brilliant magic stones in their throats had appeared, just as Dionysus had anticipated.

"The reason that you found us during your investigation, and that our smell was present in the sewer system, is that we, too, were on the trail of those monsters…While it's painful for me to admit, they were too strong for my children to overcome, and I was unable to reach any solid conclusions."

Dionysus's shoulders sank, confessing his disappointment. His side of the story complete, the deity fell silent.

He answered every single one of Loki's follow-up questions. It turned out that the strange door to the old sewer system was also his doing. At his request, Filvis had removed the old door by force and replaced it with a similar one.

Loki couldn't help but admire his character, the confidence to take evidence right out from under the Guild's nose, as well as to answer any question without hesitation despite his delicate looks. Dionysus must have figured out what Loki was thinking because a small smile began to form on his face.

"Cut that out, will ya? Givin' me the creeps," said the goddess, waving her hand a few times across her face. "...Anywho, for the time bein', I'll take yer word. I'll know for sure once I get to the bottom of this."

"Sorry about this. And thank you, Loki."

A long sigh escaped from Dionysus's lips. Relief flooded through him the moment their misunderstanding had been cleared up.

"To tell you the truth, I was trying to discern the familia of my children's killer at Ganesha's Banquet the other night. It was my intent to provoke the gods I suspected at the party and see what rose to the surface."

Oh yeah, Loki thought to herself after hearing Dionysus's admission. Memories of that night came flooding back.

"Are you going to cause a ruckus again?"—Yes, he had asked her that very question.

So he was trying to provoke her then judge her reaction?

*This bastard...*Loki growled to herself and nearly gritted her teeth.

"...But the strength to suffocate a Level Two adventurer without breakin' a sweat, that's somethin' else. That's gotta mean the killer's around Level Three or Four, yeah?"

"Yes, I believe so as well."

"The list of suspects gets a heck of a lot shorter if we only look at familias with adventurers over Level Three."

That was the reason Dionysus had targeted Loki during his investigation.

With high-level adventurers like Aiz Wallenstein in her court, he had no reason not to suspect *Loki Familia*.

"Not quite. There are some, like Hermes, who don't report children who have ranked up. Ignoring any of them would be careless."

"The dandy's up to that kinda stuff...?"

"Indeed. A child's lie may be plain as day, but gods can never be sure if the words of their own kind ring true."

Dionysus emphasized that a considerable number of deities had no problem with bending a few rules. He straightened his shoulders for the first time since the meeting began and boldly declared:

"As far as I'm concerned, every god and goddess in Orario is a suspect, and an enemy of my children."

The blond deity's unwavering gaze met Loki's. He was absolutely serious.

"Ohh?" said Loki, opening her thin eyes a little wider under his glass-colored stare.

A grin appeared on her lips.

"So, what d'ya think of me?" she asked him casually.

"...Much more innocent than I thought before."

"C'mon, go ahead an' make that *completely* innocent, why don'cha?"

Dionysus's smile returned, irritating Loki to no end.

"At the very least, I trust you more than any other god in Orario."

I wonder about that, Loki thought to herself. "Still no idea what the bad guy was after, but I got the feeling this ain't over. Monsters in the sewer an' all."

"Yes, I'm inclined to agree."

"Ya said ya already did some pokin' around? Anything catch yer eye?"

Dionysus's smile disappeared the moment Loki asked her question. A frown grew on his face, his gaze sharpening.

He leaned over the table and dropped his voice to make sure he wasn't overheard.

"How do you believe those monsters made it to the surface in the first place, Loki?"

"...Well, you'd think Ganesha's kids woulda brought 'em up for the Monsterphilia."

Several types of monsters had been captured in the Dungeon and taken to the Coliseum in the days leading up to the festival.

Ganesha's followers were the only ones who could do so without appearing suspicious or being investigated by the Guild.

"But we're talkin' 'bout Ganesha here. He loves kids. Him, doin' somethin' he knew would put 'em in danger? Wouldn't happen."

She could see the dark-skinned deity in the back of her mind, wearing his usual elephant mask and making his usual strange declarations.

Ganesha's love for the children of Gekai bordered on blind stupidity. Of all the deities living in the city, he was by far the least likely suspect. Loki took it a step further and said that investigating him at all would be a waste of time.

"It's more likely that someone like a certain airheaded vixen swiped the monsters from the shadows, or one of Ganesha's kids is pullin' the strings…"

Dionysus cut her off, shaking his head.

"That's not it, Loki. You're starting from false premises."

The deity leaned in even closer, their faces aligned and gazes locked.

"Who was it that ordered *Ganesha Familia* to retrieve monsters from the Dungeon? Going back even further, who was it that came up with the Monsterphilia in the first place?"

Loki's eyes shot open.

"Ya sayin' the Guild's *behind everything?"*

Dionysus's silence was his confirmation.

"That's crazy…" Loki mumbled, gazing at the deity's face and shaking her head.

"They've protected Orario's peace, the Guild. Yer pointin' yer finger at Ouranos? You'd be threatenin' the whole city."

"Even so, they *are* at the top of my list. At the very least, I have a good reason to suspect the Guild."

It was true that the Monsterphilia had been first proposed by the Guild. It hadn't been born from the gods' eccentric impulses.

The festival itself was still rather new and had only been organized relatively recently. When it was first brought to Denatus—the meeting of gods and goddesses—the Guild didn't explain much about it, only that it would be "interesting." But that was enough to get their plan approved.

Only now did Loki understand why Dionysus put himself in so much danger to retrieve the magic stone before the Guild could. He had already suspected them and needed to make the first move.

Loki sat quietly in her chair.

Keeping her mouth closed, she only eyed the deity with caution. It was Dionysus who finally broke the silence.

"I have a suggestion."

"…?"

"Would you be willing to investigate the Guild for me?"

His words hit her like a stone wall. It took almost a full minute for her to respond.

"Wanna run that by me again?"

"Should the Guild have someone at or above Level Three at their disposal…If Ouranos has warriors under his command, it's too dangerous for my own familia to get too close. On the other hand, as the leader of one of the strongest familias in Orario, you don't have that problem, Loki."

"Oi, quit horsin' around! Who would actually do somethin' that idiotic?!"

Dionysus was unaffected by Loki's angry outburst, letting her words brush past him like the afternoon breeze.

His eyes narrowed again, a faint look of sadness on his face.

"You can't pretend that none of this ever happened, either—can you, Loki?"

—*This bastard.*

Loki grabbed hold of the deity's collar, raising her right hand high, filled with the urge to drive her palm into Dionysus's perfectly shaped cheek.

He was right. Now that Aiz and her other beautiful children were involved, she couldn't just sit silently on the sidelines. And now that she had a solid lead, she couldn't just let it drop.

But above all, she hated the satisfied smile on Dionysus's face. His grin widened, white teeth glistening.

"…Ya planned on draggin' me into this from the very start, didn't ya?"

"Of course not. This is complete coincidence, I assure you."

Loki clicked her tongue. She couldn't help but feel like she had walked right into a trap, and now the weight of her role was clamped tightly to her shoulders.

While Dionysus denied Loki's accusation, he did admit to one thing.

"But yes, I was looking for some assistance."

Loki no longer tried to hide her contempt for the brazen god.

One look at her eyes and Dionysus flashed another grin. As Loki's grip on his collar loosened, the god slowly rose to his feet.

"Of course, I will be continuing my own investigation. But please, give it some thought. You'll be the first to know if I find anything else." With that, Dionysus left the lounge.

Loki watched him with a glare intense enough to burn a hole in his back. "Dammit..." she mumbled to herself through gritted teeth as she sat up in the chair. Putting both hands behind her head, she looked up at the ceiling and gathered her thoughts.

Completely forgetting the time, she didn't even notice when Filvis disappeared from the window.

She didn't snap out of the trance until Bete came to the lounge to check on her.

"Oi, finished yet?"

Loki didn't move, or even look at him. A heavy moment passed before she brought her hands back down to her sides and, full of resolve, jumped to her feet.

"Sorry 'bout this, Bete, but could ya stick with me a little longer?"

The werewolf was caught off guard by his goddess's serious manner. Sighing to himself, he obeyed without argument. The two left the hotel and turned onto East Main Street. Arriving in Central Park, they set their sights to the Northwest.

As soon as they arrived on Northwest Main Street, affectionately known as Adventurers Way, the solemn Pantheon—the white marble building that served as Guild headquarters—came into view.

"Bete, wait for me here."

"Again...?"

"If I ain't back in an hour, somethin' probably happened to me and ya can charge in all ya want. Countin' on ya."

Giving Bete orders to stay put once again, Loki walked halfway across the Guild headquarters' grounds and came to a stop.

Now it was important not to draw unwanted attention. Going in alone was best. After all, she didn't want to get kicked out before they heard what she had to say.

She needed to get to the Guild's very core, to a certain god who sat in the inner circle.

"Well, then, wonder what I'm gonna find…"

After a moment to admire the superb architecture and craftsmanship of the building, Loki started walking once again.

An open blue sky high above her head, she brushed shoulders of adventurers as they walked by and passed through the front doors of the Pantheon.

The town of Rivira was humming with unrest after Bors gave the order to seal the exits.

Many people watched as groups of powerful dwarves pushed boulders into the north and south gates.

The town of pristine white and blue crystals had been transformed into a prison.

"That didn't take long."

"Because I threatened anyone who didn't show up with being put on our blacklist and gettin' thrown out of all our shops. Anyone afraid of losing the privilege of using our facilities will follow orders, even if they don't like it."

"That, and they're afraid to be alone, I bet."

"Yeah," said Bors, nodding at Finn's assessment. The two of them looked over the crowd. Each face showed different levels of unease and fear as the mass of people shifted nervously from side to side.

They knew what was going on. Bors had already informed them of

Hashana's murder. It was an understandable reaction to finding out that a powerful adventurer with no qualms about taking a life could be hiding among them.

Everyone had gathered in Crystal Square. Not only was it the center of town, but the wide clearing also had an amazing view of the surrounding area. Two gigantic crystals, one white and one blue, stood like twins in the middle of the clearing. Hashana's blood-splattered full-plated armor and a few of his other belongings had been placed at the foot of the crystals.

Hundreds of adventurers stood in front of the many tents and makeshift shops that surrounded the square.

"This'd be real easy if we found a top-class adventurer other than you guys mixed in with the rest..."

"She probably wanted a scene from the get-go. Either she's in disguise or has an unreported Level...I'm certain she's taken steps to avoid sticking out."

"So we're not dealin' with an idiot."

Finn and Bors stood at their perch under the shadow of the twin crystals and continued looking through the crowd.

Rough estimates of the number of adventurers and shop owners in Crystal Square were around five hundred. Considering that many adventurers used Rivira as a base for their own Dungeon prowling, it wasn't a particularly low number, but not all that high, either.

"It's going to take forever to check everyone..."

"True, but...we can narrow it down quite a bit."

Tiona was overwhelmed by the sheer number of adventurers they would have to question, but her eyes went wide with Aiz's response. "What do you mean?"

"It was a woman who killed Hashana..."

"Oh, I see! We only have to talk to the female adventurers!"

"You should've been able to figure that out by yourself..." Tione was dumbfounded by her sister's reaction to what she considered to be obvious.

"To refine our investigation further still, said woman needs to have a body that men desire," Riveria added.

"This'll be a piece of cake!" said Tiona with her fist in the air. Lefiya looked on, not noticing the strained smile forming on her face.

"This would go a whole lot faster if we could see their Status or at least their Levels. But that would violate the rules in place to protect our privacy."

"Not to mention that we would draw the resentment of every familia in Orario."

Lefiya added to Riveria's comment.

They watched from their perch atop a low boulder as men and women were divided into two groups. About two hundred of the adventurers in the square were female, most of whom were Amazons. It almost looked like a witch hunt from the Ancient Times, with all the men surrounding the female suspects.

One of the Amazons puffed out her chest and declared she was guilty of nothing. A young cat person crossed her arms to express her anger and frustration, tail swishing back and forth.

It was the "afternoon" on the eighteenth floor of the Dungeon.

A large hourglass had been placed at the front of the square—it didn't tell time so much as show when the next "night" would fall. There wasn't much sand left in the top as the group made their preparations.

The "sky" shone bright blue overhead as they started to focus on finding someone with the criminal's body type.

"I believe it would be easiest to start the investigation by physically examining the suspects and their baggage."

"Hee-hee-hee, well, if you insist..."

Bors laughed like a dirty old man at Finn's suggestion and turned to face the crowd of women.

"You heard him, ladies? We need to check every inch of your bodies—so off with the clothes!!"

"HELL YEAHHHHHHHHHHHHHHHHHHHHHHHHHHHHHHHHHHH HHHHHHHHHHHHH!!"

Bors's demand sent all the men into a frenzy.

"As if!" "Burn in hell!" The women wouldn't have anything to do with it. Glaring at the men waving their hands in the air and over-flowing with enthusiasm, all the female adventurers voiced their refusal in no uncertain terms.

"Enough with the foolish assumptions. We will conduct the investigation, not them."

"Okay, then." "All right." "Where's his masculine solidarity?" "U-understood."

Ignoring the moans of disappointment coming from the male adventurers, Riveria stepped forward to begin the process. She called out to Aiz and the others to follow her into position.

Complaints from the men filled Crystal Square as the members of Aiz's battle party lined up shoulder to shoulder and waited for the female adventurers to come to them.

"Now then, please line up, here..."

Lefiya paused in her instructions.

Looking around, she noticed that none of the female adventurers were coming to her, or any of the other girls for that matter. Instead, there was a mad rush to line up in front of Finn. The queue was already snaking its way around the square.

"Finn, hurry up and inspect me!" "Please!" "Every inch of me!!"

"........."

Finn didn't know how to react as an avalanche of women threatened to overrun his position.

"Braver" Finn Deimne.

As a top-class adventurer, he also held the title of being the first or second most popular man among the ladies in Orario.

"Damn those *sluts*...!!"

"Wait, Tione!"

"Let go of me! Can't you see how those perverts have their eyes set on the general?!"

The sight of a small army of women overwhelming Finn infuriated Tione.

Tiona jumped in at the last moment, holding her older sister back in a desperate attempt to stop her. "Look in the mirror, would you?!" she retorted.

"Finn's getting pushed down!"

"Oh no, they're trying to take him home!"

"—URGHAAAAAAAAAAAAAAAAAAAAAAAAAAAAAAAA AAAAAAAHHH!!"

The prum was in danger of being carried away by the mob, and the jealous roars of the male adventurers echoed through the air.

Tione was ready to snap. Breaking free of her sister's hold, she charged headlong into the chaos that had descended on Crystal Square.

"Um, ehh…"

"Ahh, I don't even know what's happening anymore…"

It would be impossible to find the killer in this mess. Aiz and Lefiya watched quietly, both feeling a headache coming on.

Riveria and Tiona did their best to intervene but were unable to get the pandemonium under control.

"…?"

Aiz couldn't bear to watch anymore and looked away from Finn. At that moment, she happened to catch a glimpse of someone toward the back of the mob.

A chienthrope girl with a midsized bag slung over her shoulder.

Most of her skin was the color of wheat, the one exception being her face. It was pale green, as though she might be sick at any moment.

"Miss Aiz?"

Lefiya noticed the blond girl had spotted something. The elf followed her line of sight and found the suspicious dog person.

She stood out like a sore thumb among the frenzied women, her eyes darting between the twin crystals in sheer terror.

She took a step back, then another. The mob engulfed her for a moment before she used the commotion as cover to make her escape.

"—Let's go."

"Y-yes!"

They could hardly afford to ignore her at this point.

Aiz and Lefiya exchanged a quick nod before taking off in hot pursuit.

"Such a pain..."

She sighed and muttered to herself, disappointed in this turn of events as she watched the women fight over a prum.

Killing him might've been rash...but he saw too much, and he had to be silenced after. Enyo's gonna be pissed.

She could still feel Hashana's last breath and his neck snapping under her fingers.

She cracked the knuckles in her right hand while feeling more and more trapped, with nowhere to go.

"Now then, what to do...Freedom of movement is a thing of the past...And *it* might not be in this town anymore...Although my gut tells me otherwise..."

More talking under her breath.

Watching the events taking place in the square like a hawk, she hid among the crowd and started to plan her next move.

And I've got to worry about "Aria" on top of all this...Such a pain...

Growing more irritated by the moment, she briefly considered killing everyone in the square. The moment that that thought crossed her mind—her eyes caught quick flashes of movement.

An animal person breaking away from the mob, with a blond-haired knight and the elf magic user on her tail.

Sensing an aura of desperation from all the girls, both chasers and pursued, she watched the three of them disappear from the square.

"..."

Ker-thump. She dug her heel into the ground and changed direction. Making her way through the mob as quickly and quietly as she could while ignoring the suspicious glances coming from all directions, she took off after the girls.

Far above, the water-blue crystals on the ceiling sparkled like the sky.

Slowly but surely, that sparkle dimmed as "night" fell over the town.

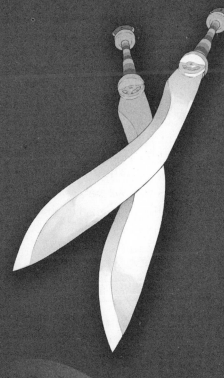

ORB

Гэта казка іншага сям'і.

каштоўнасць

Loki stepped through the front door of the Guild headquarters and into the main lobby.

It was late afternoon, before the sun had started to set in earnest. There weren't many adventurers in the Guild at the moment, especially when compared to peak hours. Several of the beautiful receptionists stood behind the counter, every one of them enthusiastically imparting advice. "Oh, aww..." Loki said to herself, moved by the scene before continuing to glance around the lobby.

She was quick to spot even more adventurers standing in front of the quest bulletin board and a few more waiting their turn in the consultation box. However, the Guild employees standing at attention at various points around the lobby were far more prominent. All of them were dressed in black suits, and one of them had taken notice of Loki's presence. So the goddess made the first move, smiling and waving. The tension instantly dropped from the woman in uniform as she smiled and gave a picture-perfect bow in return.

Loki made her way casually through the lobby, pretending that she had only come there to kill time.

"Oh, Misha. Workin' hard, I see."

"Ah, Lady Loki."

Loki had seen a face she recognized and immediately walked up to the counter to say hello.

The human girl greeted her with a friendly wave. The cheeks of her round, baby face pulled back into a smile.

Misha Frot worked at the Guild as one of the receptionists. The two of them had met only a few days prior at the Monsterphilia. They had shared information and cooperated to respond to the crisis in the city.

The girl was rather short, standing at 150 celch. Her peach-pink hair and innocent eyes gave her a cute aura. Considering that each receptionist was beautiful in her own right, a baby-faced employee like Misha was unusual.

"Is there something I can do for you?"

"That there is. Somethin' I wanna ask ya."

The goddess propped her elbows up on the counter and leaned toward the girl who sometimes didn't speak quite clearly.

Loki grinned and asked her question.

"Ouranos around?"

Misha froze the moment she heard that name.

The lobby was business as usual. However, the space around Misha and Loki fell still, as if it had become its own little world.

After a few heartbeats, the wide-eyed receptionist panicked.

"L-L-Lord Ouranos, is it? Well, um, ehh…!"

"No, no, Misha. This is *your* job; everyone else is busy. Ya gotta do it yourself."

Misha's head was on a swivel, looking back and forth for someone to help her. Loki gently took her hand and softly gave her advice.

The other receptionists were away from the counter. In fact, Misha was the only one at their station. A few Guild employees were watching from afar, but all they saw was a womanizing goddess making a pass at a cute girl. Misha was on her own.

The receptionist looked at the goddess as if she were being strangled by a snake.

"…I-I'll contact my boss. P-p-please wait…"

"That'll just end up leaving us with red tape, so don't bother. Come on, Misha. Can't ya answer one little question?"

Loki tightened her grip on Misha's hand as the girl looked for an excuse to get away. Pulling the girl back to the counter, Loki started tracing Misha's fingers with her thumb.

"Wh-wh-what would that be…?" she asked meekly, shaking like a scared puppy. Loki look down at those watery eyes, her grin the same as always.

"Is Ouranos at the usual spot?"

"……"

Try as she might, a simple yes or no wouldn't come out of the cutely childish receptionist's mouth. Running out of options, she quickly broke off eye contact.

Loki grinned from ear to ear as she read the girl like a book.

"Thank you, Misha. I'll treat ya to a drink sometime."

"L-Lady Loki?!"

The goddess waved good-bye and left the counter.

That's when she made her move.

Circling around a counter, she entered a hallway that she knew was supposed to be restricted to all but employees of the Guild. She zipped through the hall on light feet, wind in her ears as she passed by Guild workers carrying stacks of paperwork one after the other.

Caught by surprise, the clerks couldn't recover in time to say anything to the swift goddess. She left in her wake a trail of people in black suits with their mouths open.

"If memory serves me right, this should be the right way…"

A secondary office was crammed full of desks, a library, archives; Loki glanced into every room as she rushed down the hallway.

Trying to remember the layout from the last time she was there, Loki made a few more turns before finding a long red carpet with golden trim. "Oh?" she said while raising an eyebrow. Quickening her pace, she practically ran down another long hallway.

The rug extended down the middle of the corridor, and both sides were lined with pillars. She could see the stairwell leading down at the end of it.

"—Please stop, Goddess Loki!!"

"Hm…Company?"

The echoes of many hurried footsteps stopped Loki just before she set foot on the stairwell.

A middle-aged elf led a large group of Guild employees in a desperate attempt to stop her.

His suit might have been of far better quality than the others', but the size of his gut put enough pressure on the fabric to make the seams groan. Beads of sweat dripped down onto his loose double chin. The graying hair on his balding head swished back and forth as the elf wiped his chin with the palm of his hand. Even his pointed ears were shriveled with age.

He wasn't all that short, but the extra weight he carried made him look more compact than he was. Even his legs looked puffy and short underneath his black slacks.

A dignified image of beauty usually came to mind whenever an average person thought of the elven race. He was about as far from that ideal as possible.

"Yo! Royman! Long time, no see! How ya been?"

"G-Goddess Loki, this is a sacred path that leads to the Temple of Ouranos. P-please, leave here!"

Loki greeted him like an old friend, waving as the he and his subordinates lined up shoulder to shoulder in front of her.

"*Haaah...haaah...*" The pudgy elf gasping for breath with his hands on his knees was none other than the most powerful man in the Guild, Royman Mardeel.

Elves were known for their long life spans. In fact, Royman had been working at the Guild for over a century and had been promoted to his current position a little more than ten years ago. Now over 150 years old, he oversaw everything that happened in the city and gave the final yes or no for every major decision. At the same time, he enjoyed the perks afforded to him by this position and had been living in the lap of luxury for some time.

His bulging, flabby body looked more like a rich merchant's rather than an elf's. "Return to the front at once!" he repeated, recovering from his fatigue with steady, deep breaths. Instead, Loki turned on her friendly charm and walked right up to him.

"Well, I'll be! Put on more weight, have ya? Lookit how squishy you are!"

"What is the meaning of grabbing me like this...?!"

Loki had her right arm wrapped around his shoulders and a roll of his belly fat clenched in her left hand.

She looked thoroughly entertained as she pushed and pulled it back and forth, causing waves to lap across his gut. All the while,

Royman's eyes were twitching with restraint. He tried to push her away many times, but the grinning goddess wouldn't budge.

Royman Mardeel was hated by every elf in Orario.

Forgetting the pride and prestige of his race, he had become shameless. His kin considered him to have been poisoned by money and his lavish lifestyle, fattening up in the process. It wasn't uncommon for him to be referred to as the "Guild's Pig." Even Riveria considered him to be the "shame of her race."

Loki watched Royman's face turned red, veins popping in frustration, and thought to herself, *Kids really are cute.*

Her opinion of the man under her arm was the complete opposite of elves like Riveria.

Even the wise elves could fall from grace. The children were foolish, and that made them lovable—every time Loki saw Royman, she was reminded just how much she loved the buffoons in particular.

And that was exactly why the mortal world of Gekai was so entertaining.

"Goddess Loki, I shall repeat myself. This is a restricted area; no one is allowed to come through here. Even your position as a goddess *does not* override that…!"

"No need to be such a stick-in-the-mud. I just got a question for Ouranos, ain't that okay?"

"No, absolutely not!"

Even as Loki toyed with the elf on the fancy red carpet, she looked around the hallway. None of Royman's subordinates had the courage to interfere in an argument between their boss and the goddess, so they just stood there with looks of uncertainty on their faces.

If Loki was serious about investigating the Guild, Royman would be on her list of suspects by default, but… *Eh, he ain't behind it*, Loki thought. He'd been living the good life and thoroughly enjoying it; it was highly unlikely that he would do anything to jeopardize his position. Now the subordinates who advised him, on the other hand—they would be worth looking into.

However, her current goal was to get to the core of the Guild—to the one who was waiting at the bottom of that stairwell.

Now, what to do, what to do...

She had needed to reach the bottom of that staircase before being found.

Being a deity meant nothing the moment she tried to descend the stairwell. Now that her intentions had been discovered, Guild employees would physically force her back and probably throw her out altogether if necessary. That's how important the Guild was to the people of Gekai. Not to mention that Royman himself was afraid of anyone else having direct contact with the god below.

Wobble, wobble. Loki played with the aging elf's belly fat as she considered her next move.

"—It is no matter. Royman, let her through."

That's when it happened.

A majestic voice echoed up from below, reverberating between the many pillars and around the red carpet.

"But, Ouranos...!"

"I said it is no matter. All of you, leave us."

Royman tried to protest but quickly fell silent with the second response.

He nervously glanced back and forth between the stairwell and Loki. Head drooping, Royman led the others away, his feet dragging in the slow march all the way to the exit.

Loki watched him until his round and hunching silhouette completely disappeared. Now alone, she turned on her heel and walked toward the stairs.

The owner of the majestic voice stayed silent, proof enough that he was allowing Loki to approach. The red carpet dampened her footsteps as she made her way into the dim area at the end of the hallway.

"..."

Click, click. Loki's shoes echoed against the stone floor as soon as the carpet ended.

When she finally reached the bottom of the stairwell, sputtering magic-stone lamps were the only things that lit the way forward. Loki kept her hand on the wall for balance as she descended.

—The origin of the Guild dated back almost a thousand years.

This was the place where the civilized peoples had fought against continuous waves of monsters that emerged from a giant hole in the ground during the Ancient Times.

They had needed a lid—something to keep the monsters from coming out of the hole. An alliance of many races was formed for the main purpose of containing the monsters. Unfortunately, all their plans kept failing.

The more progress they made on the "lid," the more monsters would emerge, utterly destroying it when it was mere days from completion. Countless lives were lost every time. Even the mightiest heroes fell, one after the other.

Finally, when the allied races managed to construct the tower over the hole and thought their mission was a success, it collapsed before their eyes just like all the other "lids." Everyone had been on the brink of despair—when streaks of white lights descended from the heavens.

The deities had arrived.

They appeared all over Gekai, a world overrun with monsters. When the confused people asked them why they had come, most of the divine beings said, "To be entertained." There was one among them, however, who was different.

He enthusiastically joined forces with the people of Gekai in their effort to complete the "lid" over the hole.

Indeed, he was the first one to bestow Falna onto the "children."

With the cooperation of other gods and goddesses, he was the one who made it possible to complete the central tower that would become Orario's "lid" and the city's centerpiece, and who saved the world from the ravenous monsters that issued forth from the hole.

He came to be worshiped as Orario's founding deity. The remains of the alliance were reassembled under him as one large organization. Thus, the Guild had been born.

Even in the modern age, he was worshiped by many—Ouranos.

"…Yo, haven't really kept in touch."

The base of the stairs opened up into a stone chamber that looked to be as old as the Guild itself—a temple.

© Kiyotaka Haimura

The ground was covered by large slabs of stone, giving it the feel of a hidden room beneath a place of worship. Magic lamps were nowhere to be seen; rather, the dim chamber was illuminated by four torches on poles, their flames making shadows dance on the plain stone walls.

Directly in the middle of the square created by the torches was the altar.

It took the form of a large, stone throne—and on it sat an imposing, elderly deity. His blue eyes reflected the flame light from beneath his hood as he stared down at Loki.

"What is it, Loki?"

The air seemed to shake with every syllable.

A hooded robe concealed most of the deity's two-meder-tall frame. Wrinkles covered his well-defined facial features while white whiskers grew from his chin. A few locks of his hair, the same color as his thin beard, were visible underneath the hood. He wore a calm expression, sitting like a statue without the slightest waver.

Robust arms draped on the armrests of his throne, he loomed over Loki like an imposing mountain. He was the spitting image of the heavenly ruler that many people of the Ancient Times had envisioned before they met any deities face-to-face.

Even among the gods, his height was imposing. It granted the elderly deity such a strong presence that the people of Gekai bowed to him without even thinking why. His aura was just that powerful.

"What, I can't just pop in and say hi...? Well, there is somethin'."

Loki walked between two of the torches and all the way up to the altar.

"That last festival was a real mess. Problems poppin' up left and right, everyone pointin' fingers. How ya holdin' up?"

"I have left daily management of the city to Royman. It is not under my jurisdiction."

After laying the foundation of Orario, Ouranos had taken a stance of "reigning without governing," and hadn't budged since.

Leaving the day-to-day problems in the hands of the Guild, he spent his days in this chamber. He had chosen not to bestow its employees with a Blessing in order to avoid the power struggle that would inevitably ensue. Therefore, the Guild itself became more of a governing body.

He had renounced any claim to power. *Ouranos Familia* simply didn't exist.

As long as he didn't have any personal soldiers, the Guild lacked the ability to use force.

"Poor Royman. Forced to do every painstakin' little thing by an old man."

Another reason that Royman was afraid of outsiders talking to Ouranos was because of the Guild's current configuration.

He might wield more power than any other mortal in Orario, but even he couldn't go against his god's wishes. Should Ouranos have a change of heart, restructuring the Guild was more than a mere possibility. Those currently in power wanted to make sure that no meddlesome words ever made it to the ears of their god, so they cut off his temple from the outside world, declaring it sacred. This spot became physically and spiritually distant from the average citizen.

"What are you implying?"

At the same time, it was also true that this was a holy place that shouldn't be disturbed.

The reason that Ouranos didn't try to leave, and that the Guild kept their god cooped up in the temple, was that he continuously sent prayers to the Dungeon.

Ouranos's prayers were powerful—powerful enough that his divine aura prevented the Dungeon from spawning unfathomable amounts of monsters all at once. This unseen force kept the monsters belowground. In this way, he was preventing the tragedies of the Ancient Times from occurring again.

At the very least, that's what the Guild believed.

Royman and other high-ranking officials feared a change in the Dungeon most of all.

As for Loki, she thought it was insane for them to force *a god* to pray.

"So much happened at this year's festival, but some really gross, never-before-seen monsters were the worst. Who brought 'em up here, and who ordered 'em to do it...? Wish I knew."

"..."

Loki's interrogation had begun. However, Ouranos only sat in silence.

Firmly seated on his throne, the deity didn't so much as lift a finger.

Loki cut to the heart of the incident, determined to find the mastermind lurking in the shadows by directly asking the one who held the Guild in the palm of his hand.

"Who's pullin' the plant monsters' strings? The Guild?"

Crackle. A burst of sparks exploded from the torch nearby.

A flash of light fell upon the hooded robe as the sparks fell to the floor. Ouranos opened his mouth to speak.

"It is not as you say."

Blue eyes met Loki's vermilion ones.

"But it is somethin' huh?"

Loki whispered to herself, standing just far enough away not to be heard.

The majestic face beneath the hood maintained its serene expression throughout their conversation. Loki stared into his deep blue eyes for a moment before finally saying, "That so?"

"Sorry to bother ya. Keep doin' what you're doin'."

Loki spun on her heel, showing her back to Ouranos.

Her footsteps echoing among the muffled roar of the torches, Loki started walking toward the exit.

While there were still some unanswered questions, she was fairly certain that Ouranos wasn't the one behind the monster attacks.

Loki made up her mind while still reserving her final verdict. She wasn't sure of the whole scope, but she knew that the deity had been implying something on purpose during their brief conversation. Also, there was something about his steady gaze that made her want to believe him.

Someone's been watchin' me the whole time, but...eh, don't care.

Either Dionysus's hunch was off, or perhaps someone within the Guild was moving independently of Ouranos's will.

Either way, Loki was satisfied with the fruits of her investigation.

Coming to a stop at the foot of the stairs, she took a quick look over her shoulder.

The god illuminated by flames maintained his silence. His imposing frame hadn't even shifted on the throne.

The crystal-filled "sky" of the Dungeon's eighteenth floor was changing from "afternoon" to "night."

The millions of white crystals growing out of the ceiling stopped emitting light one after the other. The blue crystals scattered among them also grew dimmer. The blanket of soft, white light that covered the forest and plains became visibly weaker with each passing moment. The dark shroud of night took its place.

The town of Rivira, on the island in the middle of a large lake in the west, was overtaken by the darkness as well.

"Haaah…haaah…!"

A young animal person made her way between intricate rock formations as the area around her grew dim. Crystals sprouting from the ground glinted around her feet.

She fought for breath, even as she frantically looked over her shoulder. She caught a glimpse of her pursuers, a female knight with golden hair glinting in the darkness and an elfess with darker yellow hair carrying a magic staff. Her eyes shuddered as their reflections grew in her irises. She nearly tripped over a crystal in her path and faced forward again in her desperate attempt to get away.

She ran northwest, away from Crystal Square in the center of Rivira. At this rate, she would reach the city wall outside an isolated corner of town.

Bounding down slopes and staircases, she used her innate reflexes as an animal person to gracefully kick off stones and crystals that jutted out from the cliff face. The pouch over her right shoulder swung to the side as she tried to confirm that she was still being followed. Sure enough, she still saw the movement behind her.

But she could only see an out-of-breath elf with a staff in her arms. The other one was gone.

The animal person frowned, getting suspicious. So she made a sharp turn around the next corner and raced forward.

She entered a narrow passageway that was framed by the cliff face and a wall of large blue crystals. It was as if a valley had opened up to create an isolated one-way path.

She ran down the long and mostly flat route—only for the blond knight, Aiz Wallenstein, to appear right in front of her.

"Eh?!"

The blonde stood in the middle of the path, barring the exit. The animal person was in shock.

Aiz had instructed the elf, Lefiya, to keep up the pursuit and looped around in front at breakneck speed in order to cut her off.

Aiz slowly walked toward the girl from the front; Lefiya ran up from behind. The two had their target caught in a pincer. With nowhere to escape, the girl collapsed to her knees in the middle of the narrow path.

"*Haah…haa…*We caught her. That was amazing, Miss Aiz."

"Not really. It was thanks to you, Lefiya."

The two caught their breath and nodded to each other before looking down at the girl sitting between them.

She was a chienthrope with long black hair and two floppy dog ears coming out of the top of her head. Her skin was a healthy wheat color, and the streamlined muscles on her thin arms and legs looked just as powerful as an animal person's should.

She was wearing a thin, one-piece battle cloth and long boots that laced all the way up to her knees. On the other hand, she didn't have a scrap of armor anywhere.

"It might be a good idea…for the others to ask the questions, rather than us."

"I agree. Let's go back to the square."

Their suspect apprehended, Aiz and Lefiya didn't take their eyes off her as they attempted to bring her back—but.

"No!"

Floppy ears pulled all the way back as the girl looked up at her captors, tears streaming from her eyes, and made her plea.

"Please, no, anywhere but there! If I show my face there again, I-I…!"

"U-umm…!"

"Wh-what…what are you doing?!"

The chienthrope latched herself firmly onto Aiz, arms wrapped tightly around her waist as she looked straight up at her.

Aiz wasn't sure how to react, but Lefiya dropped her staff and immediately tried to pull the girl off her ally. "Please, please, please…!" The girl pleaded once again and buried her face in Aiz's stomach. Despite Lefiya's best efforts, she wouldn't budge.

The panic and desperation in her voice made the human and the elf exchange confused glances.

"Wh-what shall we do?"

"…Take her somewhere without any people."

"Are you sure that is okay?"

"Yes. She seems too frightened right now…We'll listen to what she has to say after she calms down."

Aiz returned her gaze to the terrified captive and made her suggestion.

Realizing that they would get nowhere like this, Lefiya nodded in agreement. Each girl took one of the chienthrope's hands and led her out of the passageway.

They guided her toward a storage lot closer to the town wall toward the northwest.

Hundreds of cargo boxes used to bring large amounts of items in and out of the Dungeon were being stored here. Looking around, they saw no shortage of pickaxes, shovels, and lumber scattered among them. Most likely, all the items used to build Rivira were stored here. Since everyone was at Crystal Square, the storage lot was eerily silent.

Each cargo box was taller than any of the girls. They had been lined up in rows or stacked on top of each other in a way that made the storage lot look like a fortress.

Aiz and Lefiya brought the girl all the way into the back of the lot and found a place that was protected by the boxes on all sides. Then, they turned to face her.

"Are you okay now?"

"...Yea."

Lefiya turned on a portable magic-stone lamp she had picked up on the way in.

Light illuminated the containers around them as the chienthrope slowly nodded in response to Aiz's question.

"And your name is?"

"Lulune...Lulune Louie."

"And your Level and familia?"

"Third tier, Level Two. I'm with *Hermes Familia*..."

Lulune slowly calmed down and caught her breath as she answered Aiz's and Lefiya's questions, cooperating without making a fuss. She had a face that would have looked friendly under any other circumstances, but she still shook visibly in the dim light.

Aiz looked her square in the eye and got right to the point.

"Why...why did you run away from the square?"

"...Because I thought someone was going to kill me."

"Why did you think that?"

Aiz pressed even further to get answers out of the quiet girl.

"Because you're carrying something that belonged to Hashana?"

That question got Lefiya's attention, too. Her eyes as wide as the chienthrope's, the two girls followed Aiz's line of sight to the pouch on her shoulder.

Both of Lulune's hands reflexively went to the medium-sized bag. She nodded after a few moments, almost like she was confessing, without releasing her white-knuckle grip on the strap.

"Why would you be carrying anything that belonged to him...? Did you...did you steal it?"

"N-no! I just...accepted a quest."

Both Aiz and Lefiya jumped when they heard the word "quest." Images of Hashana's blood-soaked form flooded into Aiz's mind as she looked at the girl in front of her.

Aiz asked the next logical question.

"What did it say?"

"To come here and pick up a package, then bring it to the surface...to the client."

"In other words, make a delivery?"

Lulune nodded again.

"I was supposed to meet a guy with the package at a predetermined bar. I didn't know who it was, but they told me what he would be wearing. When I saw an adventurer in full-plated armor, I knew it was him right away."

All she had to do after that was make contact and say the password.

The adventurer in full plate armor—Hashana—would have immediately realized that she was the one he had to give the package to, passing the item to her on the spot. It must have been finished in the blink of an eye, over so quickly that the robed woman didn't know about it.

Then, free from the stress of his quest, Hashana let his guard down and lost his life to the woman who invited him to the inn.

"Employing two adventurers for different roles, from different familias even..."

One quest had been issued to retrieve the package; another had been issued to deliver it to the surface. Whoever their client was, he or she paid extreme attention to detail. Even if the retriever were followed, having the exchange point among the hundreds of upper-class adventurers in the always busy Rivira would have made it difficult for the package to be tracked.

Lefiya couldn't help but be impressed with the lengths the mysterious client had gone to in protecting this delivery.

"Who is the client?"

"I don't know...Really, I don't. A little while ago, I was walking down a deserted street in the middle of the night and this really weird person just came out of nowhere..."

Lulune's eyebrows rose slightly as she recalled what had happened.

"They had on a thick black robe. I couldn't even tell if it was a man or woman. Of course I thought it was suspicious when they handed me the quest form...But the reward, oh man, that reward...And they paid most of it up front."

Lulune looked away in embarrassment, rubbing her neck with her right hand.

It wasn't hard for Aiz to envision the girl in front of her accepting a large amount of money from someone in a black robe, her tail happily swishing back and forth.

"Huh, wait a minute...Miss Lulune? You said you are Level Two, yes? From what you said, you accepted this quest on your own... Isn't it a little too dangerous for you to come to Rivira by yourself?"

Rivira was located on the eighteenth floor of the Dungeon—an adventurer's Basic Abilities needed to be between G and D to reliably reach the middle levels safely.

Therefore, a third-tier adventurer would have to be extremely capable to make it this far into the Dungeon solo, without any party members to protect them. Which meant that she had to be above a certain threshold to guarantee a safe arrival in Rivira.

Add in how careful the mysterious client was, and it was highly unlikely they would entrust a Level 2 adventurer with a matter this important.

A twinge of fear crossed Lulune's face the moment Lefiya asked her question. It took her a moment to form a response.

"W-well...Lord Hermes asked me to keep the rank-up a secret, so...S-sorry, I, um, I'm actually Level Three."

"""..."""

Aiz and Lefiya didn't know what to say. Lulune did her best to look as small as possible as she backed away from the two girls. She was more than likely one or two years older than them, but right now, she looked like a child being scolded by her mother.

However, this brought something else to light.

The mysterious client had access to information that enabled him or her to figure out Lulune was Level 3.

"...I should've just gone back to the surface rather than hang out down here. I recognized the armor in the square, so I knew it was the guy I got the package from. Once I heard he'd been killed...The killer was probably after what was in his bag, and I..."

Aiz had witnessed the moment in Crystal Square when Lulune connected the dots and started to panic.

The chienthrope's voice became quieter with each word. The girl didn't look up from the ground as she spoke. Aiz and Lefiya didn't say a word, only making eye contact with each other.

"Miss Aiz, our general really should hear this..."

"—NO!"

Lefiya had only meant to point out the limits of what they could do, but her choice of words sent a tremor of fear down Lulune's spine and she cried out.

"Large groups of people are scary! Hashana's killer is still in there somewhere! If they figure out that I've got the goods, this time I'll be the one that...!"

Lulune clutched the pouch tightly to her chest and unleashed an impassioned plea.

Lefiya froze, unsure what to do. Aiz looked closely at the girl's face in profile before lowering her gaze to the pouch.

"Give the package to us," she said.

Lulune's eyes shot open at the request.

Aiz looked at the blank expression on the girl's face, her golden eyes radiating unwavering determination.

Lulune started to crumble under Aiz's imposing stare. However, thoughts of collecting the rest of her reward were still alive and well in the back of her mind. She wavered, hesitating to answer for several moments.

She weighed the value of her safety against more money than she ever thought she'd have, but in the end, her life won. She set her jaw and nodded reluctantly.

"I was told not to ask about it, or to show anyone, but..."

She put the pouch onto the ground and opened the lid flap.

Reaching into a hidden compartment within the pouch, Lulune extracted a smaller bag shut tight with a pull string.

Beads of nervous sweat running down her face, she pulled the round bag off of the contents inside.

"...!"

"Wh-what in the world is this...?"

Lulune placed a crystal orb into Aiz's outstretched hands.

The orb itself was light green. A clear outer shell encased a green liquid—and a fetus of something unsettling.

The eyes on the fetus's face were disproportionately large to the rest of his body. They looked up at Aiz and Lefiya, unblinking. The head of the fetus had long hair that curled down to its shoulders, making it look female. *Ba-dum, ba-dum.* While the infant creature itself was silent, Aiz could feel its faint heartbeat through the shell.

"A drop item? Or perhaps a new form of monster?"

Lefiya voiced several more questions, but Aiz couldn't take her eyes off the orb.

This feeling...

She suddenly felt strange.

Her heart sped up, matching the pulse coming from the creature in her hands.

Aiz could feel the blood racing through her veins, getting faster and faster every moment her eyes met its gaze.

What is this...?

She had no earthly idea what this crystal orb in the palm of her hands could possibly be.

A high-pitched whine rang in her ears. At the same time, she could have sworn hundreds of worms were tunneling around under her skin. Aiz was nauseous within moments.

She fell to her knees the second dizziness overtook her.

"Miss Aiz?!"

She felt the orb slip from her hands and roll across the ground.

Lefiya kept Aiz upright, supporting her with her right hand as Aiz took many deep breaths in quick succession.

Lulune was frozen on the verge of tears.

"...!"

Lefiya quickly deduced that the cause of Aiz's breakdown had to be the orb. Snatching it up off the ground, she brought it away from the blond girl.

"Haah...haah..." Aiz's shoulders rose and fell with each breath. However, each breath was quieter than the last and she began to recover.

Silence once again fell on the clearing between cargo boxes, lit up by the magic-stone lamp.

Lefiya and Lulune watched quietly as the blond girl sitting on the ground finally opened her eyes, her hand still on her breastplate.

Another set of eyes followed the three girls.

A figure shrouded in darkness was on top of the city wall.

From that position, it had a straight line of vision through the erratically placed cargo boxes and into the space where a human, an elf, and an animal person were conversing.

Keeping breathing to a minimum, the figure studied the faces of each of the girls in turn until finally falling on the human knight.

—*Very strong.*

Watchful eyes narrowed.

"That complicates things," the observer whispered, looking at the saber at her waist and struggling to find a physical weakness on the blond-haired, golden-eyed girl.

The shadow observed them carefully until the animal girl opened her pouch and a crystal orb appeared.

A flame burned behind the irises that glared from afar. They were so focused on the fetus inside the green orb that they failed to see that the blond girl had collapsed.

They turned to look toward the crowded center of town before returning to the girl.

Finally, the figure reached underneath its chest plate and withdrew a reed pipe.

"—Come."

The high tones of a flute came forth from the figure's lips and pipe.

It spread far and wide, traveling through the air over the town.

"Are you feeling okay, Miss Aiz?"

"...Yes, just fine."

Her voice weak, Aiz started to slowly climb to her feet.

Lefiya was taken aback; she had never seen her idol struggle to stand before. Masking her concern, the elf looked down at the orb still in her hand.

A disgusting fetus protected by a green shell was reflected in her eyes. She, too, began to wonder what in the world the orb was as she looked back and forth between it and Aiz.

"A-are we gonna be okay...? W-was this thing too dangerous after all?"

Lulune was losing her cool once again.

Lefiya didn't have any answers. She took one more look at Aiz's face and made up her mind.

"I will carry it to our general."

While she had no idea why, she knew that the crystal orb had done something bizarre to Aiz. Perhaps it was because of their difference in race, but she felt no ill effects carrying the orb herself.

Of course, she wanted to be rid of the green sphere as soon as possible. She was determined to do anything she could to prevent Aiz from collapsing again, so there was no choice but to carry it.

After all, Lefiya had to help her fellow adventurer.

"Sorry, Lefiya..."

"Please do not apologize. At times like these I will do what I must...Miss Aiz, please stay back."

Trying to encourage her with a smile, Lefiya looked over to Lulune.

The dog girl gave a quick nod. The two of them quickly returned the orb to the small pouch and closed the drawstring. Returning it to the backpack, Lefiya swung the strap over her shoulder.

Collecting the staff that she had left propped up against a box, she turned to face Aiz and Lulune.

"Well then, shall we go—"

It happened just as the words came out of her mouth.

Off in the distance, they heard a chorus of roars *like broken bells.*

"?!"

The girls' eyes widened in shock before they raced out of the storage lot.

They zipped between the crystals and rocks that littered the dark path. Their breathing grew heavier as they picked up speed and finally emerged from the passageway.

They had arrived on some high ground that overlooked the entire Dungeon floor.

The three saw pillars of smoke rising from the town on the other side of the handrail the moment they set foot on the lookout point. Then…

"Those are…!"

The heads of countless man-eating plants rose high above the town.

"What do you mean 'monsters are breaking in'? What were the guards doing?!"

Bors's angry yell cut through the air.

The plant monsters were pouring over the city walls and making a beeline for Crystal Square. Their long bodies slithered forward as each of them howled into the night. The swarm was getting closer every second.

A scream, probably from one of the guards who'd seen a piece of the wall collapse, echoed into the night as tents and small shops were crushed under the monsters. Snaps of wood and groans of metal joined the ominous rumble of the howling onslaught.

"————————AAHHH!!"

Crystal pillars shattered, their fragments falling through the air like raindrops. The first wave of monsters had arrived. They blazed the trail for the rest of their kin to follow, flowing in like a tidal wave.

The sound of terrified screams rippled out through the town as the first adventurers caught a glimpse of the monsters and their seemingly limitless amount of whiplike tendrils.

"Tiona, Tione, protect them!"

The Amazonian twins rushed forward, following Finn's orders.

Bounding through the crowd with Urga and Kukri knives in their hand, the two girls launched themselves at the oncoming monsters with blades flashing in the night. Each slash sent heads and green appendages to the ground.

"The same things that were at the festival! Where are they all coming from?"

"Everyone, stay close! Don't run away!"

Unlike at the Monsterphilia, the two girls now had their favorite weapons at their disposal. What's more, they were strong enough to penetrate the monster's hide.

While the Amazons were busy taking down the beasts one after another, the mass of adventurers was in utter chaos. Attacked from every angle, some were knocked airborne by their snakelike bodies, and then snatched out of the sky by their fearsome jaws. Some of the adventurers were able to form groups and fight back, but the monsters held a clear advantage.

Once they knew they didn't stand a chance, Tiona's warning meant nothing as they split up and ran for cover.

They left Crystal Square, seeking safety in an all-out panic.

Tiona and Tione kept up the counterattack, doing their best to follow the fleeing adventurers and their ferocious pursuers.

"Riveria, these monsters respond to magic energy. Conjure up as much as you can to draw all of them back here! Bors, get everyone to form teams of five! It might be possible for one group to overpower one monster with that many members!"

"Understood."

"Y-you got it!"

Finn analyzed the battle, as much of it as he could see at once, and issued quick, precise orders.

A magic circle formed beneath Riveria's feet as Bors raced into the chaos yelling at the top of his lungs. The high elf's beautiful voice reached the monsters, and sure enough, they changed course back into the square. Spear in hand, Finn raced to the front lines and tore through every foe in his path.

His strategy was simple: kill them in one shot with a precise strike to the magic stone in the back of their throats. Other adventurers watched his bravery in awe, seeing the small prum jump into the air or run up the monsters' bodies to kill the beasts in one strike. He called out to them, voice gruff and dry, with encouragement and a call to battle. At long last, the remaining adventurers took formation.

The chaos under control, their counterattack was under way.

"Everything is too perfect...!"

Finn finally had time to analyze a situation now that the tidal wave of enemies was being held at bay. He frowned.

Even from where he was, the prum could tell that over fifty of the creatures were assailing the town. What's worse, more were arriving every second. Rivira was built on the side of the cliff in the middle of an island for protection. Even his ability to sense oncoming attacks didn't give him any warning this time. The fact that so many of these creatures had shown up here without any sign felt odd and very suspicious.

It was too *coordinated*.

Finn took off at a sprint, jumping on top of broken crystals and rock formations to leave the square, and raced through the town. He reached the side of the cliff in no time and leaned out over the guardrail.

"...?!"

What his blue eyes saw made him shiver in fear.

From his vantage point two hundred meders above, he could see the surface of the water dancing in the darkness as an unfathomable amount of the creatures emerged from the lake and started making their way up the cliff.

Monsters coming out of the lake—a lake in the middle of the safe point, no less? The impossibility made the wheels in Finn's mind spin into overdrive. Then the realization hit him like a magic-stone lamp switching on.

They had hidden their presence, lying in wait for the right time to attack.

That was something monsters could never do on their own. They required guidance.

It was unthinkable to lead so many of them at once, but that was the only explanation that made sense.

Finn's face contorted as the answer his brain had given him escaped from his lips.

"Could it be—a Tamer…?!"

CHAPTER 5

THE BATTLE OF RIVIRA

Гэта казка іншага сям'і.

RivuIpa Бітва

Lefiya stared out at the carnage unfolding before her eyes.

The town, normally beautiful at night with its scattered magic-stone lamps and sparkling crystals, was being destroyed.

It was impossible to miss the incredible number of plant monsters, their long bodies whipping from side to side as they charged forward. The river of slithering forms cleared the town wall moments after reaching it and scaled the cliff faces like fish jumping up a waterfall. There were enough of them already in town that Rivira itself looked yellowish-green in the dim light.

The onslaught crushed tent after tent and shop after shop, scattering their remains into the air along with the sea of tendrils.

Vibrant petals of the beasts' heads flashed as rocks, crystals, people, and anything else unfortunate enough to be in the town were trampled beneath the stampede.

Lefiya's dark blue eyes shook as they took in the pandemonium below, a shrieking chorus of screams and roars reaching her ears.

"Wh-what's going on, what's happening…?!"

"Monsters. They're attacking the town."

Lulune visibly shook with fear. Even Aiz couldn't hide her surprise.

The blond girl was known for being aloof, but now her gaze was sharp, her eyebrows low.

Upon further inspection, she could see that adventurers in Crystal Square were starting to fight back. The high vantage point here gave her a great view of a jade magic circle that had formed in the middle of the square. Monsters from all around were drawn to it like moths to a flame, and hundreds of adventurers broken into small battle parties were there waiting for them. More than likely, Finn was fighting alongside them.

The monsters farther away from Crystal Square ignored Riveria's magic energy and continued to rampage through the town. Some smashed their heads into the vending stalls and small shops, or thrust them into cave entrances, while others chased after the adventurers who were running away from the square. In the middle of the pandemonium, a flash of silver cut through one of the monsters' bodies every few seconds. Aiz guessed it was probably Tiona using Urga.

"Let's go back to the square and meet up with Finn."

No one disagreed with Aiz's decision.

A fierce battle might have been raging in the center of Rivira, but it was the safest place to be.

Lulune nodded up and down as though her life depended on it. Lefiya responded with a quick "Yes."

Readjusting the shoulder strap of the pouch, Lefiya left the high ground right behind the other girls. Just then...

"OOOOOooooOOOOOOOOooooooooooo!!"

"?!"

A howl like that of a broken bell echoed through the air as a plant creature crawled down in front of the girls.

It arrived with such vigor that it trailed a small landslide of rocks and debris in its wake as it slid down the cliff face and into their path. The girls came to a sudden halt, their eyes wide. Aiz reacted in a heartbeat and rushed forward with her sword drawn, leaving the still-awestruck Lefiya and Lulune behind.

The monster was cut down in an instant, but Lefiya's relief was short-lived, as a distant rumble strong enough to make her body shake came down from above. She looked up to find its source.

"More from over there, too...?!"

"You gotta be kidding!"

The three girls were still technically in the town, in the northwest corner close to the wall.

A swarm of the monsters appeared as they poured over the top of it.

Lefiya didn't wait for Lulune to finish screaming before running into another pathway, past the remains of the opponent Aiz just took down. The creature leading the charge came to a halt over its fallen kin's corpse before swinging the head of its long body toward the path as it continued its pursuit.

"Lefiya, get to the square!"

"Miss Aiz?!"

The pathway was a dead end; the girls were trapped. Aiz jumped out from the group, charging headlong into the oncoming horde.

She unleashed a storm of slashes. Aiz was able to hold the onslaught at bay, cutting down monster after monster without hesitation.

Lefiya stood in awe for a moment, watching Aiz's golden hair sway back and forth. Her first instinct was to try to help the girl who was facing numerous enemies alone. As much as it pained her, though, she contained the urge, grabbed Lulune's hand, and took off at a sprint.

She would only hold Aiz back if she stayed here. The monsters reacted to magic energy. So if she were to start conjuring magic, it would force Aiz to defend her rather than go on the offensive. Lefiya and Lulune might have been at Level 3, but the monsters were at least that powerful, if not more. Their hides would have been too tough for them to crack. The two of them alone wouldn't be able to defend themselves in battle, let alone counterattack.

But with saber in hand, this number of enemies wouldn't be a problem for Aiz.

She had to do what Aiz could not: deliver the crystal orb to Finn and escort Lulune to safety as soon as possible. There was a murderess on the loose in Rivira in addition to the monsters.

The elf repeated these facts to herself over and over, gritting her teeth as she ran with Lulune in tow. Her thin legs carried her as fast as they could, feet kicking hard against the ground with every stride.

The path led directly to Crystal Square. However, it was crawling with monsters, so they decided to take a detour through a northern pass that was far less overrun. They were careful to avoid the man-eating plants and took shortcuts in an effort to shave seconds off their arrival time.

Angry howls filling the air around them, the two girls emerged from the path into an area of the town that might as well be called a crystal forest.

Cluster Street.

Like Crystal Square, it was one of Rivira's famous locations.

It had earned its name from the clusters of large crystals that shot up from the ground like pillars. There were so many, in fact, that they created many intersecting paths that were about as wide as the backstreets aboveground. The crystals reflected anyone who walked through, making the whole area appear like a labyrinth of mirrors. This was also the only place in Rivira where the pathways had been paved with stone.

Two sets of feet echoed against the crystal walls. Lefiya's and Lulune's faces reflected off the many surfaces as they raced through.

"Whoa, damn! Was that an explosion?!"

"That was…Riveria's magic!"

A thunderous roar filled the air as a pillar of flames erupted from the middle of town.

Lulune's shoulders trembled as she watched the dim blue of "night" over Rivira give way to a flood of red-hot light. The crystals flashed around them. Even the ceiling itself looked crimson as sparks danced into the air.

"Whooaaaaaaa." The impressed voices of the adventurers in the square reached their ears. Lefiya knew immediately that many of the monsters had been incinerated by the most powerful fire magic in Orario.

"…?!"

A figure appeared in the midst of the flashes and shadows from the flames.

Sparks rained down around the being in the girls' path.

A male adventurer…?

Leg armor, gauntlets around the arms, and a breastplate.

The man was completely decked out in black armor.

A shabby rag was wrapped around his neck, and a helmet covered his head. The skin on the exposed half of his face was dark, the rest wrapped in a bandage. Lefiya could only see his right eye, and it was blankly staring at her.

The elf's eyebrows curved upward as she began to feel something was off. Meanwhile, the man started to walk toward Lefiya, not saying a word.

"S-stop right there!!"

Lefiya yelled out of reflex.

The man's ominous aura—not much different from that of a black beast from the bowels of the Dungeon—was overwhelming. Lefiya raised her staff.

However, the man took no heed. Step after step, the distance between them was steadily vanishing.

Lulune pulled her ears back, tail nervously swishing behind her while she growled at the approaching man. Her animal instincts were becoming more pronounced as the color drained from her face. Her eyes locked on the armor that covered the legs that were getting ever closer as he walked down the middle of the narrow five-meder path. Meanwhile, Lefiya's sweaty hands tightened their grip on her staff, her lips a heartbeat away from conjuring a spell.

Then, the moment he came within ten steps of their position—the man disappeared.

He was too fast for Lefiya to react.

His approach was so quick that he was in the elf's face before she had time to show surprise. In that same instant, he grabbed hold of her neck with one hand.

"Gah—!"

Her feet left the ground as the man picked her up, as if she was as light as a toothpick.

The gauntlet's cold grip wrapped all the way around her neck. The unrelenting metal pressed up against her skin, and a chilling fear overtook Lefiya. She lost her grip on her staff. It landed with a clatter on the stone pavement at her feet.

She grabbed the man's right arm with both hands in a panic, but his hold showed no signs of weakening, no matter how hard she pulled.

Each of the five fingers started to tighten, threatening to choke—no, crush—her throat. The man's strength was immense.

"Ugh-ugahhhhh!"

Lulune's body shook, her mind going blank as she charged forward. She dived headlong at the man, eyes flashing.

She whipped out her knife as she came to Lefiya's aid, but the man didn't even look at her, only swung his left arm in her direction. A moment later, she collided with the nearest crystal.

A large web of cracks appeared as her back slammed into it. The dog girl fell to the ground in a heap.

"Ah…! Ug, uh…?"

Lefiya gasped for breath as she began to lose her grasp on consciousness.

Her light golden hair meekly swayed back and forth as her kicking started to slow down. She could feel the strain on the bones in her neck through her entire body, each pop sending waves of pain down her spine.

Her mouth was wide open, gasping for air that couldn't get through. Tears were building up in her eyes. The man's grip had forced her to look upward, so she was unable to see the utter lack of emotion on his face.

Crick! Her thin neck started to contort.

The hands that had been desperately pulling against the gauntlet fell limp at her sides.

She heard the scythe of death itself coming down from above her.

—Miss Aiz.

The last of the crimson-shaded crystals on the ceiling blurring in her vision, one solitary tear rolled down Lefiya's cheek as she tried to whisper Aiz's name.

A moment later…

"OOOOOOOOoooooOOOOOOOOOOOOOOOOOOOOOOOOOO!"

Large clusters of crystals blew apart in small explosions as pieces of a plant monster's body plowed through them.

Shards of crystal scattered through the air, reflecting the creature's final moments. Lefiya's eyes opened as the dying cries reached her ears.

Eyes unblinking and full of resolve, the blond knight had arrived at the last possible second.

"‼"

As the man gazed at the girl who had appeared at his side, Aiz brought down her saber.

The armored man dropped Lefiya without a second thought and narrowly evaded a fatal blow. A long, sharp gash appeared in his breastplate.

Thump. Lefiya's limp body hit the stone pavement. The Sword Princess immediately jumped between her friend and the mysterious adventurer, standing in front of the crystal carnage created by the monster's dying body. The two warriors squared off against each other.

Aiz's saber whipped through the air under the "sky," which was glowing red with fire.

Cough, cough.

Aiz heard Lefiya coughing and gasping for breath behind her. However, all her attention was focused on the person standing before her.

A male adventurer covered in black armor. As far as she could tell, the only weapon he had was the longsword at his waist. Despite the amount of armor covering his body, it seemed only average in strength. None of it appeared to be extremely high quality.

His unnaturally deep left eye glared back at her, and he clicked his tongue.

"Lefiya, are you okay?"

"F-fine…"

Lefiya's breathing was slowly but surely returning to normal as she responded to Aiz. Still sitting on the ground, she used one hand to massage her neck while the other wiped the tears away from her eyes. Still, she didn't look away from the man.

The dying monster had slammed into part of the crystal wall behind the mysterious black figure. One of the pillars had collapsed, shutting off potential exits through Cluster Street. The man in black armor kept his distance. He'd waited for a chance to kill Lefiya as soon as she left Aiz's side.

The blond knight had used all her might to lay waste to the monster ambush and managed to catch up with the other girls before the man could succeed, but the timing was too perfect not to have been planned out in advance.

"…Are you the one who killed Hashana?"

Echoes of other adventurers fighting not too far away reached their ears as Aiz decided to use the momentary pause to try and get an answer.

All information thus far had said the killer was female. But Aiz just couldn't shake the feeling that this man was Hashana's true killer.

The two girls watched closely as the man spoke for the first time.

"What if I am?"

Both of the girls' eyes went round the moment they heard the voice.

It was high-pitched, unbefitting his appearance—*a woman's voice*.

"So, you are not male…?" Lefiya asked in confusion.

The elf couldn't take her eyes off the masculine body and clearly male face.

The face was nearly devoid of emotion, and half of it was wrapped up in a bandage, but there was no room for doubt. It definitely belonged to a dark-skinned, virile male. Nothing about his appearance was feminine.

The stone-faced figure drily explained:

"I just peeled it off."

"Eh…?"

"*I just peeled the face off the corpse.* Now I'm wearing it."

Words failed Lefiya.

Even Aiz was having difficulty believing what she had just heard.

"Injecting a dead body with 'Poison Vermis' prevents skin decay... Didn't you know?"

He—no, she—spoke in a perfect monotone, which only served to amplify the chill running down Aiz's and Lefiya's spines.

In other words, the person in front of them had stolen that face.

After breaking Hashana's neck, she literally cut his face off.

The reason the body was found without a head wasn't because of the temper tantrum.

—It was to conceal the fact that his face had been stolen.

"So you mean, that face belonged to Mr. Hashana...?"

Color that was finally returning to Lefiya's face drained away again with each word. Her hands covered her mouth in shock.

The woman wearing a mask of flesh neither confirmed nor denied her words. At this point, she didn't need to respond.

Aiz squinted, trying to get a better look at the figure's face. The purpose of the bandages wasn't to conceal identity or heal from injury, but to hide the parts that didn't line up with her real face.

"Ah, screw this, it's too frickin' tight."

The woman ignored the two girls staring at her and started roughly removing her armor in frustration.

She stuck her fingers into the gash in her breastplate and tore it off her body. As pieces of the armor fell to the ground, two breasts, still restrained by an inner shirt, burst forward toward freedom. Tearing away even more of the protective covering, the woman exposed the silky white skin on her neck, arms, and legs.

The powerful impression of the male face had thrown everyone off. She had created the mask in order to stay in Rivira and look for the item Hashana had been carrying. Since the investigation had focused solely on women, she'd found a way to remove herself from the list of suspects from the beginning.

It was a strange sight to behold, a man from the neck up but a woman from the shoulders down. Suddenly, *rip*.

The anti-deterioration agent must have worn off, because the mask started to flake off her face. White skin appeared around her left eye—a woman's skin.

At long last, the woman looked up with only her helmet, knee plates, and gauntlets still on her body.

"I'll be taking the seed now."

With that, the woman drew the longsword hanging from her waist and charged directly at Aiz.

"!"

"You're strong, just as I thought."

Aiz met her at full speed.

Desperate and her opponent's longsword clashed as Aiz took the fight as far away from Lefiya as possible.

Aiz moved at the same blinding speed as the woman. Eyes narrowing, the blond knight intensified her attack.

"...?!"

Lefiya was speechless as she watched the furious sword fight unfold.

The longsword swung down, and the saber cut to the side. Silver arcs carved through the air, each sword coming in for another pass only to be rejected and come back for more. The two women were a blur as they attacked each other from all possible angles. The narrow street between the pillars didn't allow much room to maneuver, but the two warriors changed positions constantly as they matched blow for blow.

What's more, their reflections in the many crystals made it appear as though entire armies were engaging in an all-out brawl in the middle of Cluster Street.

—*She's so strong!!*

Aiz was taken aback by her opponent's display.

The techniques that she polished through countless hours of training and combat weren't enough to match the woman's skills. The mysterious fighter didn't just rely on swordsmanship; she mixed in a flurry of punches and kicks, the likes of which Aiz had never seen. She was forced onto the defensive. Her arms were already covered in bruises from her opponent's gauntlets. Every impact from the longsword or one of her slicing kicks sent waves of pain through her entire body. Even though she was finding small windows to counterattack with her saber, her opponent's blade was coming close enough to cut strands of her blond hair every time she dodged.

She couldn't believe she didn't know the name of an adventurer with such skill and prowess.

Whose face was hidden behind the mask? Aiz kept trying to get a closer look.

"*—Unleashed pillar of light, limbs of the holy tree. You are the master archer.*"

Suddenly, the words of an enchantment filled the air from behind Aiz.

Lefiya had picked up her staff. There was no time for her to climb back to her feet. A golden magic circle appeared around her as she sat on the stone surface.

Ranged support was inbound. The mysterious woman's gaze fell on Lefiya. Aiz jumped in the way in an attempt to distract her.

"*Loose your arrows, fairy archers. Pierce, arrow of accuracy!*"

The amount of sparks from the fight drastically increased in that instant. Lefiya completed her trigger spell as quickly as possible.

Their opponent was unable to break away from the wall Aiz had created with her saber.

A beautiful yet powerful voice echoed through the air as a pillar of light erupted from the magic circle.

"Arcs Ray!"

An arrow of light barreled forward.

It was a single-target spell that was designed for speed. However, Lefiya had poured a large amount of Mind into the attack. Compounded with her high Magic ability, the spell looked less like an arrow and more like a beam.

Additionally, the light was like a homing missile. Once launched, the energy of the spell took on a life of its own and would not dissipate until it hit its target.

The brilliant light illuminated the crystals of Cluster Street. Aiz quickly sidestepped the oncoming spell as the female adventurer squinted her left eye—and stuck out her arm.

"Eh?!"

"?!"

Lefiya and Aiz watched on in disbelief as the woman stopped the beam with the palm of her hand.

Thunderous roars echoed through the street as a spray of light particles diffused from the main arrow. The gauntlet couldn't handle the energy and shattered, but the woman's skin was unaffected. Instead of backing down, she was pushing back.

Swinging her arm with all her might, she sent the beam off its course and hurtling into the wall diagonally in front of her.

"~~~~~~~~~~~?!"

Crystal debris rode the shock wave that blasted its way through Cluster Street.

Lefiya's scream and Lulune's unconscious body were swept up into it as well. At the same time, Lefiya lost her grip on the pouch in her hand and the cover flap fell open. The blue-green crystal orb rolled out onto the ground.

It took a moment for Aiz to recover her balance after the impact, and the woman saw her chance to attack.

"?!"

The longsword grazed the surface of Aiz's skin. The merciless attack signaled the start of the next round.

The knight's blond hair swished as she jumped back into combat. She couldn't believe it—her opponent was moving even faster than before. Her already immense power had increased exponentially, with a boost in speed, making Aiz's arms go numb every time Desperate collided with the longsword.

She couldn't see the depth of her opponent's strength.

The emotionless eye staring back at her made chills run down her spine.

"Keh—!"

She struggled to hold a downward swing at bay, her body bending backward underneath its force.

Aiz's face showed a trace of fear for the first time since the fight began. She knew she couldn't afford to hesitate. Lefiya and Lulune would be in danger if she didn't give her all immediately.

She had never used her magic in a fight against another person because she felt it was unfair to her opponent, too strong for a duel. It was time to abandon that way of thinking.

"Awaken, Tempest!!"

The trigger spell flowed from her lips.

"Airiel" was triggered by Aiz's call. Air currents enveloped her sword and body in the blink of an eye.

Aiz reengaged her opponent with the explosion of speed granted to her by her magic.

"Wha-?"

Genuine surprise appeared in the woman's left eye.

The impact nearly knocked the longsword from the killer's grasp, and it threw her opposite shoulder forward. Although she had managed to block the blade in time, she couldn't keep her feet and stumbled backward under the incredible force of Aiz's magically enhanced saber.

Wind roared through the battlefield on the next strike. The torrent of air was strong enough to knock the murderess's helmet off her head, taking most of the flesh mask with it. *Crack, crack, crack!* The stone pavement beneath her feet crumbled as the woman desperately tried to maintain her balance as the gale blew her backward. As soon as she came to a stop, the now-uncovered woman looked up.

Hair the color of blood danced in the breeze.

Most of the short, fine strands were held together in a small knot at the top of her neck. Her hair was cut roughly, as if it had been much longer before.

Her green eyes sparkled like gems.

Half of the woman's true face was visible beneath the heavily damaged bandages that managed to still cling to her head. Her pure white skin and symmetric features twisted as her long left eye went wide.

"That wind…So then, you must be Aria."

The blond knight's eyes widened at the mention of that word.

Ba-dum. Aiz's heart beat so hard it was almost deafening. The shock was so intense that she couldn't speak, the word "why" threatening to overload her mind.

Her thin neck quivered.

For one moment, both warriors stared at each other in shock. The silence was eerie.

"—AaaaaaaAAAHHHHHHHHHHHHHHHHHHHHHHHHHHHH HHHHHHHHHHHHHHHHHHH!!"

It came out of nowhere.

Inside the crystal orb on the ground—the female fetus screamed.

"?!"

Aiz spun around to find the source of the earsplitting pitch.

Of course, the red-haired woman heard it, too. But before she could react...

The fetus inside the orb started to thrash about, slamming its tiny hands and head with eyes much too big for his body size against the green shell until it cracked.

"AaaaAAAHHHH!!"

Aiz's magic seemed to have triggered this frenzy. It was unclear where its tiny body got the strength, but a moment later the creature launched the crystal orb, two or three times bigger than itself, flying through the air like a rogue cannonball.

Aiz could see the thing's unnervingly large eyes hurtling toward her as she quickly jumped out of the way. The orb kept flying through the air, leaking liquid on the way past.

It collided with the dead monster halfway buried in the crystal wall. The sphere shattered and the fetus *seeped into the monster's body like a parasite.*

"Wha—"

"OOOOooooooooOOOOOOOOOoOOOOOOOOOOOOOOOO OOO!!"

The should-have-been-dead monster behind Aiz and the red-haired woman howled.

The fetus was sealing itself into the monster's hide and causing other changes to its body in the process.

A series of red veins worked their way around its body like thick spiderwebs under its skin. The monster's howls coincided with each new blood vessel.

Thrash! The beast flinched as if it had been shot with electricity before rearing up.

Muscles pulsed.

Lefiya froze at the other end of Cluster Street. Every twist, every painful howl, every jolt the creature experienced as it slowly transformed was reflected in her dark blue eyes.

One transformation was leading to another.

It was an unnatural change, perhaps a sort of forced evolution.

The thing that had resided within the orb was changing the monster into something else. Was the sphere a kind of forbidden fruit, perhaps?

Aiz watched in horror as something started to emerge with an unbearable sound from the place where the fetus had sealed itself to the monster.

Something that looked human. Like a moth breaking free from a pupa, the shape was becoming more and more defined with each passing moment.

"——————————OOOOOoOHHHHH!"

The writhing monster, still in the middle of transformation, suddenly attacked without warning.

Aiz saw the creature coming, its thrashing body smashing its way toward her with no rhyme or reason. Picking up Lefiya and Lulune's unconscious body, she immediately started to retreat. She carried the injured girls away, as the monster repeatedly crashed its body into the crystalline path while it chased after them.

"Awww! This ruins everything...!"

The red-haired woman couldn't hide her frustration as she, too, withdrew from the scene.

The thick crimson veins had worked their way through the creature's entire body. However, it was focused solely on pursuing Aiz. Plowing through groups of crystals rather than going around them, it roared with such ferocity that each one was physically painful to the girls' ears. Aiz used a combination of dead sprints and leaping bounds to lead the creature on a wild chase through Cluster Street. She knew full well she couldn't fight like this and had decided to change course.

Meanwhile, the monster was nearing the end of its evolution when it happened to encounter other flowered beasts—and devoured them on sight.

A gruesome scene greeted Aiz's gaze when she looked over her shoulder. Bits and pieces of broken monsters were merging together.

The next thing that Aiz's golden eyes saw was—

—A human female shape emerging from the back of the parasite-infected monster, stretching its arms the same way a moth would spread its wings for the first time.

"What's that, an octopus?"

"Isn't that what we fought on floor fifty…?!"

Many battles raged throughout Rivira. Tiona and Tione paused to take note of the sudden appearance of the massive new foe.

Tiona's comparison was fairly accurate. The beast was transforming itself into something resembling an octopus. The main difference was that it had well over ten legs, each limb slithering and howling like it had a mind of its own and ending in the head of a flower monster. Above the area where the legs attached was a vibrantly colored, remarkably human female figure that was large enough to identify from a good distance away. It was very similar to the legendary half-human/half-octopus beast that was said to once roam the coastlines, Scylla.

It was that female shape that reminded Tione of the monster they had encountered on the fiftieth floor of the Dungeon not too long ago during their previous expedition. The one Aiz slew had had a lower body shape like a caterpillar, but the similarities were too obvious to ignore.

The figure on top of the monster finally stopped twisting and turning, settling down now that its metamorphosis was complete. Slowly, very slowly, its featureless head rose to its full height, and the beast started to move.

The monster set its course for the center of town, Crystal Square. Tiona and Tione gave chase.

"No one around here's under attack by monsters anymore, right?"

"Everyone that's safe should have been sent back to the square! We're going, now!"

Tiona called out to her older sister as she ran. Tione yelled back, kicking up loose rocks and crystal shards in her wake as she zipped by.

The carnage the Amazons left behind showed just how one-sided the battle had been. Decapitated monster heads littered the ground, and what was left of their bodies was embedded in the cliff face or in crystal pillars.

The girls made a beeline straight for Crystal Square, leaping and bounding over the remains of the tents and small shops that once lined the street.

"Where did they come from…is what I'd like to figure out…But finishing them off is more important."

"Yes, I completely agree."

"How the hell are the two of you so calm?! Get your asses moving!"

Riveria and Finn watched the monsters intently, studying their movements while Bors was on the verge of a breakdown beside them, yelling at the top of his lungs.

Aiz had arrived at Crystal Square, carrying Lefiya and Lulune over her shoulders. The many legs of the octopus monster followed close behind, each one of them howling and madly snapping in her direction. It was true that a great deal of the fiends in the square had been incinerated by Riveria's magic, but the adventurers were still busy contending with the survivors. Many of them forgot to breathe the moment the hideous creature came into their line of sight.

The man-eating flowers that made up its legs were nearly twice as thick as the rest of their kin. They moved like flexible tree trunks as they advanced deeper into the square. Crimson veins bulged out of their greenish-yellow bodies as they thrashed about like they were overcome with rage or had gone insane.

In sharp contrast to the many layers of howls erupting from its crazed lower body, the brilliantly colored upper body appeared rather tranquil. Its face lacked eyes and a nose, but featured a slightly open mouth that looked large enough to swallow a human being whole. Waves of green hair flowed from the back of its head all the way down to its waist. It was the one thing on the creature's body that could be considered beautiful.

The arms that emerged from its shoulders split into many tendrils at the elbow. They hung down loosely over the top of her numerous legs.

"Was another fetus responsible for creating that monster on the fiftieth floor…?" Lefiya whispered, her eyes glued to the beast as Aiz put her on the ground.

The creature was physically larger than the female-figured thing they'd encountered much deeper in the Dungeon because it had ingested several of the plant monsters. It was only about six meders tall, but thanks to its many legs, it took up an incredible amount of space. Even with its legs bent as it walked, the octopus monster was at least ten meders wide.

"We're back!"

"Eww, that thing's even more disgusting up close."

The Amazonian twins arrived from overhead, landing in the square.

The last of the sparks from Riveria's magic were fading away over the town. The octopus's eyeless gaze fell on the reunited battle party.

"!"

It made its move.

Whoosh! All the heads at the ends of its legs looked up like a pack of wild dogs. They all charged at Aiz as one, obliterating anything standing in their path.

The blond knight passed Lulune's unconscious body to Lefiya before running in the opposite direction. She was determined not to let the others gets dragged into the fight. Several pairs of fanged jaws clamped shut where she'd been standing a moment earlier. The creature continued its pursuit, destroying the twin crystals in the middle of the square in the process.

"It is focused on Aiz!"

"I wonder if it's because of the wind surrounding her body."

Riveria and Finn, staff and spear in hand respectively, analyzed the situation as they advanced.

However, Tiona and Tione got there first. Taking aim at two of the legs snapping at Aiz's heels, they jumped in.

"Hi-yahh—!!"

"OOOOOOOooooOOOOOOOOO!"

Tiona drove Urga straight through the neck of the nearest flowered leg. The silver blade flashed as the head let out a dying cry.

Tiona had been given the title of Amazon because of her desire to cut down her enemies. She lived up to her name in full as her beloved Urga severed the head in one clean stroke. It was the same as in the earlier battle, despite the creature's increasing girth. The end of the thick leg arced through the air.

"—!"

"That hurt!"

The now-headless limb was spewing blood high into the air, but that didn't stop it from launching Tiona straight back, hitting her like a thick whip.

Blocking the attack with the flat part of Urga's blade, Tiona rolled over her shoulder and jumped back to her feet.

"They're a heck of a lot stronger! And they don't die after losing their heads anymore!"

"They're nothing more than legs now! Of course they'd keep kicking!"

Tione took a different approach from her sister's wildly directed aggression, using calm, precise strikes. Her Kukri flashed as she turned another one of the creature's veiny extremities into cold cuts, yelled back to her sister, and dodged the other flailing limbs.

Tione saw that the leg she was working on had gone limp and used the window to press her advantage. However, the upper body also saw the opening and moved to defend.

Shifting its attention from Aiz, it launched its many tendrils toward the Amazonian warrior.

"Damn!"

Tione spun her body in midair, Kukri flashing as they deflected each of the stems one after the other. However, the next wave of vines came in from other angles, forcing Tione to retreat. She withdrew another knife from its sheath at her waist and flung it straight at the monster at point-blank range before jumping away.

The female figure raised a tendril to block the incoming white blade. She knocked it off course, but—*Shing!*—the tendril was lost.

"Riveria, I'm going ahead."

"Understood—You, over there! Lend me that bow!"

"Y-yes, my lady!"

Finn charged into battle, severing one of the creature's legs on his first pass. Riveria turned to an elf who happened to be among the adventurers still in Crystal Square.

No elf could refuse the order of a high elf. He carried a high-powered bow as a sub weapon, but surrendered it and his quiver of arrows to Riveria as soon as she rushed to his side.

Gracefully attaching the quiver to her belt, she withdrew one of the needlelike blue arrows in one swift motion. It was nocked and fired in the blink of an eye, followed quickly by a whole slew of them. Purposely burying them into the upper body's tendrils, she focused on drawing its attention away from Finn's attack, where the real damage was being inflicted.

Loki Familia's second-in-command had grown up as a high elf in her home forest. During that time, archery had been one of her few hobbies, and her skill showed. The figure atop the creature bent backward, the monstrous legs flinching every time one of the heavy arrows hit its mark.

"Bors, we need more help! See that we get it!"

Finn called back to the group in the square using the time given to him by Riveria's support. He moved as if he had eyes in the back of his head, avoiding the rain of arrows slicing into one leg after another. His small stature allowed him to weave through tight spaces as he removed several of the legs trying to catch up to Aiz.

Anytime one of the limbs came at them from above, he spun his spear like a hurricane to deflect it. Countless sparks flew from his weapon, lighting up his yellow hair as they fell around him.

"Ahh, I knew somethin' was wrong in their heads…!"

Bors hunched over in the middle of the square, shouting to no one in particular as the battles raged around him. He wasn't the only one left speechless by *Loki Familia*'s actions. Many of the adventurers fighting off the plants still in the square were dumbfounded that four people would face down an abomination like that on their own.

"…!"

Tiona, Tione, Riveria, and Finn launched their attacks in continuous waves, forcing the head to lose track of Aiz. The monster's frustration was apparent as it reluctantly turned its attention from the pursuit of the blond knight to intercepting the constant barrage of blades and arrows harassing it from all sides.

"Everyone…!"

Aiz had been dodging the jaws of the hungry appendages one after another as she led it away from Crystal Square. Naturally, she was curious as to where they had gone when she was momentarily freed from their pursuit. Turning around, she caught glimpses of all her allies putting themselves in harm's way.

She had to help them. Setting her feet, she was a heartbeat away from diving into the fray—when a shadow fell over her from behind.

"!"

Aiz evaded the incoming blade at the last possible second.

Spinning around to face the new threat, she saw the mysterious woman's red hair come into view.

"It's you and me. I can't go back like this...and I'm not letting you get away."

"...!"

Aiz raised her gaze to meet the woman's green left eye head-on.

Her opponent charged, attacking with such ferocity that it drove Aiz away from the square. Desperate in hand, Aiz matched her blow for blow.

She didn't have time to assist the others in battle; her foe wouldn't allow it. At the same time, there were many questions that still needed answering. This was her opportunity to get them.

"Aiz!"

She heard Tiona's voice from behind her, but paid no heed.

She accepted the woman's open invitation for a private duel and the pair left the square.

"Lefiya, do you remember the formation we practiced in our last session? Now is the time to use it."

"U-understood!"

Riveria spoke as she approached Lefiya, who responded with a nod.

The two elves immediately took off in different directions, one to the front of the octopus monster and the other to the back.

"_____!!"

Aiz left Crystal Square at the same time the battle against the extremely large monster was ramping up.

The female figure was focusing all its attention on Finn and the two sisters. At the same time, adventurers who'd finished off the plant monsters in their area summoned up their courage and came together to join the fight.

Magic users formed ranks a good distance away from the beast and stronger adventurers made a wall in front of them to block its attacks—but sheer numbers meant nothing in this battle.

The colossal creature spread out its healthy legs, still more than ten, and flipped adventurers out of the way like they were nothing more than ants. Everyone was knocked off their feet or into the air.

"UwahhHHHH! Holy shit, that thing'll kill us all!"

"Hey, get everyone on the edges out of here! We can't cover them all!"

Debris and adventurers flying left and right, Bors's yell barely made it through the typhoon of destruction. Tione yelled back to him to warn the other adventurers.

It had become a vortex.

Just like the currents that rage on the open seas, the many legs spun around and around, preventing anyone from getting into their surprisingly wide range. The moment any of them detected a hint of magical energy, it would lash out to attack the caster responsible. Any other adventurers who tried to protect the target magic user, including dwarves with their massive shields, were bowled over or tossed to the side.

Taking up position behind the creature didn't help, either. Each of the legs extending from the female figure's upper body acted independently, howling and lashing out in an unpredictable fashion. Even if a combatant made it past the leg's attack, the arms of the vibrantly colored upper body would either grab them or run them through. Finn and the Amazonian twins were the only ones who could get close enough to attack.

"We'll hack it away one piece at a time, eh?"

"GEHHHH!"

Urga flashed as Tiona severed yet another head from one of the monster's limbs. Its scream of pain cut short, the echoes traveled through the air long after the head hit the ground and stopped rolling.

Tiona carried, by far, the most powerful and destructive weapon on the battlefield. Urga's two blades had already claimed many heads. However, the only effect it was having on the titan was short-ening its appendages. That did nothing to stop the relentless attacks of the figure on top. A few acrobatic spins allowed Tiona to pull back.

"The magic stone has to be in its upper body. Aiming for it seems to be our only option at this point…"

Finn picked up a short spear—dropped by a different adventurer—and hurled it at the creature's upper body with all his strength. Unfortunately, the arms blocked it.

Finn watched the broken spear arc backward and sighed. The ten-drils acted not only as a weapon to take out targets that got too close but also as a defensive steel wall. Ranged weapons were practically useless against their overwhelming numbers.

He couldn't just charge in.

"Looks like we'll have to rely on the elves after all."

He glanced toward the other end of the square.

Riveria was standing with the lake behind her, magic staff in her grasp as she began to conjure.

"Proud warriors, marksmen of the forest."

An ever-widening magic circle appeared at her feet.

Then another, and another jade magic circle stacked on top of the first at Riveria's feet. Each one shone brilliantly, as if to make its presence known.

Other magic users watched in awe at the amount of magic energy.

"Take up your bows to face the marauders. Answer the call of your kin, and nock your arrows."

"!!"

Swish! The giant beast spun around.

It immediately changed course and rampaged through the square to the source of the magic energy. Even *Loki Familia*'s finest war-riors couldn't keep it at bay. The remaining adventurers dived out of its path, the wall they were trying to make completely disbanded.

Riveria narrowed her eyes as she watched the massive creature advance on her position, but she didn't stop casting.

"Bring forth the flames, torches of the forest. Release them, flaming arrows of the fairies."

"_____!!"

Each of the monstrous legs howled as they prepared to jump at their target.

Then, when the distance between them dropped to twenty meders—Riveria retreated.

Launching herself like an arrow, the elf disappeared from in front of the octopus monster. Of course, the magic circles immediately dissipated, along with all the energy that had created them.

She had stopped in the middle of conjuring her spell to escape from the oncoming attack.

The legs followed Riveria to the side, snapping at her heels. But the feminine shape looked from side to side in disbelief, her hair swishing back and forth.

—*"Fall like rain, burn the savages to ash."*

"?!"

The figure trembled.

A new, beautiful voice filled the air.

The octopus monster spun around and spotted a solitary shape on the west side of the square. It was an elf girl with a golden-yellow magic circle under her feet.

Riveria had been a decoy.

She had intentionally produced extra magic energy in order to mask Lefiya's presence from the monster. That had bought the younger elf time to conjure her own spell.

A bait-and-switch strategy perfectly executed by two powerful magic users.

Since one elf was able to distract the monster, her ally didn't need any support or defenders to conjure her spell. It was perfect teamwork.

Lefiya's majestic voice rode the wind on top of the last of Riveria's echoes and completed the enchantment.

"All forces, retreat!"

"Big one incomin'!"

Finn and Bors alerted the other adventurers to the danger and every one of them got out of the line of fire.

Lefiya took aim the moment that the only living thing left in the square was the monster itself and unleashed her Magic.

"Fusillade Fallarica!!"

"—————————————————————————AhhAAAHHHH!"

A hail of flaming arrows descended upon the octopus monster.

It was impossible to tell how many bolts were in each wave of the aerial inferno as the onslaught cut into the beast and its many now-headless legs. The upper body was being torn to shreds. Even its many tendrils were caught up in the explosions. The whole creature was being forced back, losing pieces of its body every moment.

The river of arrows continued to carve through the air for more than ten seconds. At least ten thousand of the magic projectiles turned the east end of the square, along with the monster, into a sea of flames. The sky over Rivira burned bright as spires of smoke rose above the island once again.

The female figure was trapped in a cage of fire as each of her legs ignited. An earsplitting scream filled the air as the ever-approaching inferno licked at its skin.

"Shall we press our advantage?"

"I will join you, General!"

"—Ready, set!!"

The moment Lefiya's barrage was over became their signal to attack. Three warriors charged headlong toward the female figure.

Finn with his spear, Tione with her Kukri, and Tiona with Urga spinning high above her head jumped into the air over the monster.

An incredibly fast strike and multiple flashes of silver light overlapped into one destructive attack that slammed into the creature's body.

But the assault didn't stop there. The three upper-class adventurers worked in tandem, zipping around the burning monster with the force of a hurricane, blades flashing as they dismantled the beast even further. Several of the flower monsters were completely severed from the upper body and sent hurtling away.

"AAAHHHhhAAAAAAAAAAAAAAAAAAAAAAAAAAAAAHH!" the female screamed out, its body writhing in pain. It leaned backward in a desperate attempt to get away from the attackers' blades.

A heartbeat later, the vibrantly colored body broke away from its lower half.

"It's running away!"

"Is that thing making a break for the lake?"

Already out of the main square, the fleeing creature tumbled its way down the sloping edge of the cliff.

Rivira had been constructed on the cliff face, and one of its sides ended abruptly in a sheer drop. If anything went off the ledge, it was a straight shot to the water below.

The abandoned lower body burned, forgotten in the middle of the square. The Amazonian twins leaned out over the railing that surrounded the square and watched the green hair of the vibrantly colored female figure thrash back and forth as it twisted and contorted its body to advance closer to the edge.

—*"Harbinger of the end, white snow. Gust before the twilight."*

The chant of a spell rang out.

Racing after the female figure down the cliff face was Riveria, her jade-green hair whipping out behind her in the wind. As she sprinted, an emerald-colored magic circle moved with her, always surrounding her feet.

"Fading light, freezing land."

Concurrent Casting.

Normally, mages stood still when casting spells to prevent them from failing or, worse, exploding. Performing an incantation at high speed was extremely difficult. For that reason, they required a great deal of protection while on the battlefield. But if they could master the technique of Concurrent Casting, they became a highly mobile destructive force.

However, Magic was a much harder horse to tame than any other weapon available to adventurers. Therefore, only the best of the best were able to obtain it, just a handful among thousands. It was similar to assembling a bomb with both hands while fighting an enemy, so it was only natural that very few adventurers were capable of it.

Riveria had ascended to a plane that Lefiya and the other mages could not yet reach. Manipulating her magic power with perfect precision, she chased after the tumbling monster at full speed.

What's more, the elf was faster than the smoldering female. Even without its lower body, the creature was still two meders long. It used its remaining appendages to force its way forward, crawling like an insect. Even still, it was making progress down the slant toward the edge of the cliff.

Small beads of light surrounded Riveria's jade hair as it whipped in the wind behind her during the chase. The distance between them was closing with each passing second.

"Blow with the power of the third harsh winter—my name is Alf!"

With that, the trigger spell was complete.

Riveria, casting in earnest this time, kicked off of a small boulder and jumped into the air as she thrust her staff forward.

"Wynn Fimbulvetr!!"

Three streams of arctic wind blasted forth.

Everything in range, including many of the destroyed shops and crystals that once stood around the square, were immediately encased in ice. The monster, in the middle of it all, was also enveloped in the blink of an eye.

"_____!"

The beast had difficulty screaming as its body began to freeze solid. But it could sense that its salvation was just within reach and whipped its arms forward with all its strength.

Tendrils slammed against rocks, breaking them apart as the creature swam through the air and made it over the cliff before its body turned into a block of ice.

Bits of the ice covering its body flaked off, looking like small comets as the beast descended. With nothing between it and the lake, a shade of relief passed through the female figure's lips.

"You take it on the left!"

"Gotcha!"

However—

A two-headed monster of a different sort jumped off the cliff after her.

"_____"

Tiona and Tione had raced past the left and right sides of Riveria and over the side without the slightest hesitation.

They kept running, their feet against the rock as they charged straight down.

From the monster's point of view, it was a nightmare come to life.

The wheat-skinned Amazons had chased it to the ends of the earth and off a cliff of despair.

"?!"

The feminine creature was falling headfirst toward the water. It whipped its arms up with the last bits of its strength.

The Amazonian sisters kicked off the cliff face in different directions the moment they saw the oncoming line of "spears" as if they had planned this in advance.

As the arms disappeared from her peripheral vision, Tione came in from the upper left of the monster, blades flashing.

"You're not getting away!"

Her Kukri arced through the air, slicing through the creature's limbs.

The monster had lost the last of its weapons. And now, flying in from the upper right came Tiona, ready to strike.

Bending her body backward, she lined up Urga's blade and poured strength into her muscles—a silver flash came straight down.

"Here I cooommmeee————!!"

A wide, arcing slash.

"_____"

Urga's overwhelming destructive power unleashed, the monster was sliced clean in two.

The pieces split from each other in midair before dissolving into ash amid brilliant purple flashes of light.

The body vanished into thin air, leaving no trace behind, while continuing to plummet toward the lake below.

"Hell, yeah!"

"Tiona, you idiot! Now the magic stone is gone!"

"Oh."

Tiona celebrated the victory until her sister pointed out they couldn't study it without a magic stone. The younger Amazon's face turned from jubilation to disappointment.

The two had reached terminal velocity, rocketing toward the water, and yet their descent had turned into a one-sided lecture and a continuous apology.

"…I hope Aiz and Lefiya are okay."

Tiona looked back up to the edge of the cliff, her back to the oncoming lake.

She could see crimson light cast on the ceiling of the Dungeon by the remnants of Lefiya's magic still lingering in Rivira. She didn't know all the details, but she could tell that redheaded woman fighting with Aiz was dangerous. She was obviously not normal, even at a distance.

Her hair flew above her head, pushed by the wind whistling in her ears. Tione could see her sister was worried about their friend and young ally, so she called out in an attempt to reassure her.

"Riveria's up there, and don't forget about the general. Of course they're fine."

"…You're right."

There was an element of pride, almost bragging, in Tione's voice. She wore a broad smile full of confidence on her face.

Seeing her, Tiona smiled, too. Both sisters cast their gaze up at the edge of the cliff.

Splash!

Two gouts of water erupted from the lake as they hit the surface.

The howls like broken bells had all but disappeared from the town.

While the last of the flower monsters were slain, the battle between Aiz and the red-haired woman raged in the west.

Fighting their way up the east-facing slope, the two women

emerged close to Rivira's western wall. This was the highest plateau inside the wall, but it had been turned into a wasteland of crushed boulders, broken wood, and crystal shards by the onslaught of monsters.

Far from the ceiling crystals that still flickered with crimson light, the area was shrouded in a bluish darkness. Places where the monsters had broken through the wall were visible all the way around the plateau. Aiz and the red-haired woman traded blows as they crossed paths while dashing through the remains of Rivira.

"!"

"That's a convenient wind."

The red-haired woman's expression didn't change as she commented on Aiz's Magic, Airiel. The wind-based enchantment not only increased her speed, but the power of her saber as well.

It effectively granted Aiz the strength of a ferocious beast. She was able to meet every strike of the longsword, no matter which direction it came from, and deflect it.

The sound of clashing blades spread out over the plateau as Aiz, with her wind assistance, repeatedly crossed swords with the red-haired woman.

Desperate arced through the air and collided with the enemy's longsword with such force that it knocked the woman backward. The two blades separated for the moment and both combatants took off running. *Tap tap tap tap!* Debris crunched beneath their feet as Aiz decided to venture a question.

"'Aria'—where did you hear that name?!"

The unrelenting emotions building up within Aiz had bubbled to the surface.

Her eyes burned with an unearthly rage, unblinking as she glared at her opponent.

Even Tiona and her other friends had never heard Aiz speak as loudly and forcefully as she just had. However, the woman running alongside her answered casually.

"I wonder...?"

"......!!"

Aiz's eyebrows shot straight down and she charged in for the next round of attacks.

Her silver blade was a blur, bearing down on her opponent faster than the eye could see. Striking ten times in less than a second, both blades bore the brunt of the exchange between the two warriors. The woman's remaining gauntlet became covered in several deep diagonal slashes, and strands of her red hair fell to the ground. Long red lines crisscrossed their way through the skin of both women.

Most likely, the redhead's longsword was a drop item from the Dungeon's Deep Levels, a monster fang that had been fitted with a handle and used as is. The lead-colored blade itself had an unaltered, almost wild aura to it. Dull flashes met silver streaks as the fang and Desperate collided once again.

—However, the enemy was overpowering Aiz and her wind.

Even with the enchantment's boost, the longsword was knocking Desperate off its path at incredible speed each time the two clashed. It even cut through Aiz's protection, making several deep cuts across her body.

Even Airiel at full power wasn't enough to gain the upper hand in this one-on-one duel. Aiz was able to keep her opponent from inflicting serious damage, but was still being overwhelmed. Her golden eyes were filled with surprise, but she didn't consider looking away.

The other woman knew something—she knew the name Aria.

Adrenaline flowed into her chest, seemingly into her very soul. Tightening her grip on the weapon in her hand, Aiz pushed her body to move even faster.

The expression on her face was fitting for someone with the nickname "Sword Princess Kenki." Her eyes only saw one thing, the enemy. Aiz struck forward once again.

"—And here I thought you had the face of a doll."

Then.

The red-haired woman noticed the sudden change in Aiz's rhythm, the passion burning in her heart.

Her green eye narrowed for an instant before her body almost disappeared.

Sidestepping Aiz's overhead strike, she moved with enough speed and power to cut through the wind.

An uppercut that started low and ended very high.

The woman's bare left hand traveled through the wind armor and buried itself deep into Aiz's stomach, launching the girl's thin body into the air.

"!"

The force of the blow knocked Aiz completely out of balance.

She tried to regain her center of gravity by manipulating the air swirling around her body, but before she could—

The woman stepped forward, bringing her blade high above her head and moving her bloodied left hand out of the way.

"___"

Jolt!

A cold spark raced up Aiz's spine.

Her enemy's green eye locked onto her; the sword came straight down.

Golden eyes as wide as they could go, Aiz rerouted Airiel's wind at the last moment to bring Desperate up at an unbelievable speed.

The moment held.

"___!"

A *clang* on par with an explosion rang out.

An arcing slice over the shoulder at blinding speed. The long-sword slammed into Desperate from the upper left and broke past the sword and through every single air current. The impact hit Aiz like a hammer.

The enemy disappeared from Aiz's sight as the girl flew backward and landed hard on a pile of debris.

"Ughh!"

Bits of wood, rock, and crystals blasted into the air around her body on impact.

All the air was forced from her lungs in an instant. Aiz's body went limp for a moment, refusing to listen to the commands from her brain.

Clang! Desperate bounced off the nearby boulder and rolled to a stop.

"Finally, this is over."

The longsword had shattered on impact. The red-haired woman discarded the handle and what was left of the shaft before rushing to where Aiz had landed.

The blond knight willed herself onto her knees. She glanced up in time to see her enemy charging, right arm drawn back behind her shoulder.

There was no escape.

The woman could see the expression of fear on the girl's face. The muscles in her gauntlet-covered fist tensed as she threw a punch—when suddenly…

"What?!"

The metallic echo reverberated through the plateau. Her fist had been stopped.

A long spear and staff crossed just in front of Aiz's surprised face. They'd come together at the last possible moment to block her opponent's attack.

The tips of each weapon were embedded in the ground. Aiz's neck swiveled left and right. A young prum man and an elegant elf lady were standing on either side of her.

Like knights protecting their princess, they had arrived just in time to shield her.

"Finn, Riveria…"

The two adventurers pushed the enemy back with their weapons as Aiz whispered their names.

The woman jumped away, clasping her right hand in her left. Finn adjusted his grip on the spear and charged forward.

"Miss Aiz!"

"Lefiya…?"

Aiz felt delicate hands supporting her chest and back.

A quick look to her right and she could see Lefiya was there propping her up.

"Lefiya, heal her, now!"

"Yes!"

Riveria issued the order as she turned to face the enemy. The battle between the red-haired woman and Finn was already well under way.

She swung her fists around like battle hammers, but Finn's small body proved to be a difficult target. Ducking low to the ground, the prum pressed in hard. He thrust his spear up from beneath her line of vision as a feint, then instead tried to sweep her legs out from under her with a low kick.

Frustration at her small target was written all over her face as the woman bent her upper body backward and jumped to avoid the attack. Eyes wide, she faced her opponent once again.

"Are you the Tamer who controlled those monsters?"

"…Confident enough to talk, I see."

"Not as much as you are."

The prum's normally friendly and warm expression had transformed into that of a determined warrior.

Sharp eyes studied his opponent as he struck from every angle, trying to find a blind spot, looking for a space between his opponent's limbs to move into after each strike. Sometimes, they showed him when to give distance or when to charge forward. Thanks to their perception, Finn was constantly moving to more and more advantageous positions.

His strategy was completely different from Aiz's straightforward combat style, and it frustrated the red-haired woman to no end. She was unarmed and forced to constantly match Finn's footwork to find opportunities to attack.

Her grip, strong enough to snap the neck of a man, closed on nothing but air. Even her kicks missed their mark. None of her attacks were connecting with her opponent's small frame.

She tried to grab the spear more than once, but each time Finn knocked her hands away with a series of upward thrusts, almost like he could see it coming.

A fresh cut on her cheek warped as a frown appeared on the woman's face.

"Don't—get cocky!"

"?!"

She kicked her left leg high above the prum and brought her heel down, slamming it into the ground with the force of a small explosion.

The rubble at the point of impact was launched into the air as a result of the extraordinarily strong blow. The shock wave knocked Finn off his feet, his clothing whipping around his body as debris pelted him.

Once he left the ground, his agility was gone.

Finn was a sitting duck as the woman twisted around for a back-handed blow.

"General!"

Lefiya's yell was masked by a gruesome snap—a piece of the long spear flew off into the air.

The weapon was broken, but the murderess's green eye was wide open in shock.

An uninjured Finn was upside down, looking up at her.

He had managed to jam the spear into the ground to use as lever-age, forcing his body just above the path of the backhand to avoid the attack.

As he flew literally head over heels in midair, the light in Finn's eyes disappeared for an instant as he withdrew a knife from the sheath in his belt.

Using his momentum from dodging the fist, he brought the white blade toward the red-haired woman, whose arm was still extended.

"Guh—!"

A spatter of blood shot through the air.

Finn's upward swing connected with the woman's chest, the blade cutting flesh.

The woman staggered backward—that was the window Riveria needed.

"Why, you…!"

The woman twisted her body to meet the new threat.

Her muscles burned as she whipped her fist forward like a wreck-ing ball.

Riveria only had one eye open as she adeptly avoided it, and then— *Tap.*

The gauntlet flashed right by her as her feet came to a complete stop. She had foreseen this reaction and had made sure the enemy's counterattack would fall harmlessly short.

But that was only the first part of her plan. The red-haired woman watched in horror as the elf swept the staff at her feet.

That light contact was enough to completely knock her off balance. The woman hit the ground.

"_____"

Next up:

Finn, round two.

"—Guah!"

His incoming fist landed square on her jaw, sending her flying backward.

Finn had used every muscle in his small frame, put every fiber of his being into that punch. The woman's body glided through the air and landed on the ground with a hard smack almost immediately. What's more, she kept rolling for another ten or twenty meders.

The golden combination of *Loki Familia*'s top two left Aiz and Lefiya speechless. It also served as a demonstration for why they should stay on their good side.

"…"

"Finn?"

"My finger's broken."

His face devoid of emotion or pain, Finn shook his right hand as Riveria's eyes opened in surprise.

Finn followed her line of sight.

"Gahhh…" The red-haired woman was climbing back to her feet, using her hands for support.

"First tier…Level Five—no, Six."

Blood flowed from her massively swollen left cheek and the fresh gash across her chest. A tone of deep hatred had taken over her voice, spitting out the words like poison.

Finn Deimne. Riveria Ljos Alf. Add in Gareth Landrock, and all three Level 6 adventurers made up *Loki Familia*'s top commanders as well as their strongest warriors.

Not only did they have more combat experience than Aiz, their knowledge of techniques and strategy made them much more powerful than their Statuses alone indicated. Finn and Riveria were pulling out all the stops to overwhelm the red-haired woman.

"The odds are not in my favor..." she mumbled to herself. Then she took off, running away without another glance at her opponents.

Aiz saw it all happen. Choosing to ignore the pain coursing through her body, she gave chase.

"Miss Aiz!"

Lefiya's call was far behind her. She practically flew past Finn and Riveria.

She was vaguely aware that they were following her, but Aiz had her sights set on her target.

"...!"

The woman passed through the gaping hole in the town wall, exiting Rivira.

Aiz wasn't far behind, chasing the woman west, down the trail of shattered rocks and crystal fragments. They were headed toward the center of the island. Aiz could hear Riveria and Finn telling her to stop, but she wouldn't let herself. Pushing Airiel even further, she started to close the distance, even though the woman was running at full speed.

Anyone who took one step out of Rivira knew that the rest of the island wasn't much more than a wasteland. The ground was covered with different sizes of rocks, making the footing unstable. Tall, wild grasses and small trees grew randomly here and there. Short crystals also sprouted from the surface, providing speckles of light in the darkness.

Aiz's Magic increased her speed exponentially, but just as her target was almost within striking distance, the woman made it to the other side of the wasteland and to the western edge of the island.

One green eye looked over her shoulder as she neared the cliff, then she jumped over the edge without a second thought.

Aiz ran to the drop-off, looking over with a deep frown. The red-haired woman was running down the rock face, combining her already incredible speed with gravity. By the time Finn and Riveria caught up to Aiz, the woman's silhouette was indistinguishable from the boulders at the bottom.

They heard a splash a few seconds later.

"Incredible..." whispered Riveria under her breath.

No matter where they looked, none of the adventurers saw the woman rise to the surface of the lake. Most likely, she was swimming underwater. If they lost track of her now, there'd be no way to pick up the pursuit.

The eighteenth floor of the Dungeon was that big. Vast plains, a wide marsh, and an expansive forest were all located on this level. There were places to hide around every corner. They could search all through the night and never find a trace.

Would she return to the surface or go deeper into the Dungeon, for the time being?

Whatever her decision, there was no way to follow her.

"...!"

Lefiya had finally arrived on the scene. Aiz was looking at where she saw the splash, lips shut tight. She willed her face into a calm expression, but her right fist was clenched and shaking.

She was experiencing a feeling she hadn't felt in a long time—emotional pain. It stabbed at her heart.

The powerless feeling from losing a battle wrapped itself around the girl.

Dim light from the crystals above made her golden hair sparkle fleetingly in the bluish darkness.

Healthy flames roared on top of four torches as their light wavered around the chamber.

Ouranos was silent, the flames illuminating the stone altar where he sat.

Elbows resting on the armrests, he fixed the blue eyes beneath his hood on the stairwell.

A few minutes had passed since Loki's departure.

Eventually, he opened the mouth that he had kept shut tight and spoke:

"Fels."

His heavy voice filled the room with echoes of the name.

He called to a dark corner of the chamber where no one should be present. However, there was a response.

"Yes, I'm here, Ouranos."

A figure in a black robe emerged from a darkness that the flaming torches could not reach.

The cloth covered the figure from head to foot; no skin was visible anywhere. No light reflected from beneath the hood, as if the being were formed of condensed shadows. Black gloves covered the hands at the ends of the robe's sleeves. A complex and intricate pattern was engraved on the back of them.

The new voice in the chamber was a middle pitch that had no characteristics at all. It was impossible to tell if the speaker was male or female.

"An unexpected visit from Loki...I was on pins and needles just watching."

"The whimsical actions of gods didn't start yesterday."

"Yes, but the reasoning was different this time. Drawing her attention is bad news, Ouranos."

The robed figure completely came out from the darkness at Ouranos's left and walked closer. He stepped up onto the base of the altar and came to a stop directly in front of the towering deity.

"Loki and Freya...It would be horrible for either of them to harbor any unnecessary suspicion. They must not become our enemy."

"I'm well aware of that."

Fels spoke as if he were trying to warn the deity. Ouranos seemed unconcerned, his expression stoic.

Apart from them, no one else was in the chamber. The roar of the flames was the only thing to fill the silence.

"What did you think of our conversation?"

"...Concerning the flowered beasts at the Monsterphilia?"

Ouranos's gaze shifted to the hooded figure.

The hood moved as if Fels was drawing in his chin at the question.

"Clearly there are beings who wish to destroy the peace and order of the city—no, of all Orario."

Fels's answer was clear.

"Ouranos, the 'whimsical actions of gods' might be connected to this incident. My own investigations have already confirmed seven types of unknown monsters lurking beneath Orario's streets."

"In that sewer system?"

"Yes. However they got there."

Fels added that he didn't know if a god was pulling a prank or if the monsters' presence was the result of more earthly hands.

"It could be the work of ones outside the city, or perhaps the group of deities that refer to themselves as 'wicked gods'...The remnants of the Evils."

"Ghosts of the past..."

A "familia" of deities who had once existed in Orario but who despised order and worked to spread chaos.

The familias in power now had conspired to destroy that group, with the Guild's permission and cooperation. Fels had suggested that some of these deities who still remained on Gekai could be working in the shadows.

"The fact that someone released monsters from Ganesha's holding cells might be a blessing in disguise. Thanks to that incident, adventurers were quick to take action...before the monsters could inflict too much damage."

"Indeed. It is safe to say that their plan ended in failure at the Monsterphilia."

The actions of a certain Goddess of Beauty had spurred Loki and several other gods to act alongside the Guild. By the time the plants had made their appearance, it was impossible to move freely about Orario.

Fels and Ouranos reflected on the surprisingly small numbers that were involved in the attack. Most likely, the mysterious beings behind the incident had sensed a great deal of activity on the surface and hastily removed the rest of the monsters from the sewers. They could be lamenting their failure at this very moment.

With Fels at his side, Ouranos looked forward once again.

"Someone who can manipulate the monsters in question...It appears there is a Tamer whose abilities surpass those of *Ganesha Familia*."

"Unbelievable...This is a nightmare."

Fels's head shook back and forth, his voice weak after hearing Ouranos's claim.

Someone was controlling the monsters; all their deliberation had led them to that answer. Fels sighed as if he didn't want to find out the truth. Ouranos glanced at the hooded figure out of the corner of his eye before looking forward once again.

Silence once again filled the chamber. Slowly, Fels looked up at the deity sitting at the altar.

"Ouranos, I also have sad news."

Fels began with a preface. His shoulders sank in sorrow before continuing.

"Hashana, the one who took up that quest, has been killed. A message from the town of Rivira reached me moments ago."

Ouranos closed his eyes.

He kept them closed for a few moments before looking down at Fels.

"What about the delivery girl?"

"I don't know. At the very least, she has yet to return to the surface."

"I see." Ouranos broke off eye contact.

There was pain in his eyes as the deity angled his chin ever so slightly skyward.

The ceiling of the chamber was so high that it was easy to forget that they were underground.

The four torches couldn't illuminate every corner. The darkness surrounding Ouranos and Fels hinted at the unseen dangers silently lurking in the near future.

The blue eyes narrowed.

"In that case…it was there after all."

Fels didn't ask for confirmation, only responded to Ouranos's statement with a firm "Yes."

"As much as I didn't believe it, it appears so."

Fels's robe lightly swished from side to side as he continued.

"A mysterious crystal orb that causes monsters to mutate…Something that we don't know about is happening in the Dungeon."

An Irregular that even Ouranos couldn't comprehend.

That…or the existence of something that *surpassed* monsters. Those were Fels's suggestions.

"Something is moving beneath the surface."

The sound of those words was absorbed by the four torches before fading into silence.

PARCHED SCREAM

Гэта казка іншага сям'і.

Сгу прагнуў

The woman was like the wind.

Pure, like a child, even more innocent than her own self as a toddler.

She knew nothing of people's dark side, and would never know.

She flowed like the blue sky above, swaying with the clouds.

Freer than anyone, she was like the wind.

As for herself,

She loved her—warm and kind like the breeze.

She loved the mother who smiled at her with no hidden agenda.

She remembered the feeling of her hand stroking her head.

Her cheeks still felt the warmth of her soft fingers' touch.

That beautiful voice still lingered in her ears.

The beautiful stories still replayed in her mind.

She was being held against her chest as one of the stories came to a close. She looked up and saw that innocent smile.

Cheeks blushing, she smiled back.

This woman could use magic; she believed it with all her heart.

Anyone who saw her smiled. She could make anyone smile.

She whispered, *"I want to be like you,"* in her young voice under the woman's affectionate gaze.

Become someone like the wind, someone like you.

"You are you. You know you can't be me?"

The woman's head tilted to the side as she responded in a voice exactly like hers.

"That's not what I meant," said the girl, puffing out her cheeks.

"Then what did you mean, roly-poly?" The woman laughed.

Still pouting, the girl couldn't help but be pulled in by that smile and eventually do the same.

Holding, being held, the two looked at each other in the eye and laughed together.

Soon, the girl looked the other way.

Looking over her shoulder, she saw a young man appear.

His light armor was accented by a black scarf and a silver long-sword tucked away in its sheath.

The moment the woman saw his face, she put the girl down. The woman stroked the girl's face one last time before slowly rising to her feet.

She smiled at the young man, but it was a different kind of smile. The man grinned back and nodded to her.

He felt the girl's lonely gaze and clumsily smiled at her, too.

"Sorry," her father said apologetically.

He turned on his heel, and called to her mother.

"We're going—Aria."

The two left her behind and walked arm in arm toward a bright light.

"…"

The dreamy fog started to slip away.

Her consciousness left a white forest, arriving at the darkness created by her closed eyelids. Time had bridged the gap between past and present.

Her shoulders shifted ever so slightly. The caress of cold air on her cheeks brought her fully awake.

Aiz slowly opened her eyes.

"Doing okay, Aiz?"

"…Yes."

A few heartbeats passed between Tiona's question and her response.

Looking up, she could feel the Amazon's gaze on the side of her face.

"Rest time is almost over. We'll be leaving any minute."

"Okay…"

A few images of her past lingered, still halfway between her dream and reality as Aiz answered. Tiona gave a crooked smile at the sight.

The blond girl lightly shook her head to get rid of the last remnants of sleep and looked around with clear eyes for the first time.

The first thing she noticed was the flickering light of a magic lantern, designed to be carried on long trips. It illuminated the faces of Finn, Riveria, Tione, Tiona, and lastly, herself. Everyone was sitting down, rummaging through backpacks and pouches to make sure weapons and items were in order. She was the only one who had been sleeping up until now.

They were all in a dim, dead-end room with off-white walls. Lefiya was at the other end of the room serving as a lookout, accompanied by one other member of their familia.

Aiz's battle party rested in a corner of the vast Dungeon.

Six days had already passed since the events in the town of Rivira.

Aiz and the rest of *Loki Familia* returned to the surface after the dust settled. At the same time, the girls who had been at the center of it all had to do many things.

The first was healing the injured and escorting them back to the surface for further treatment. After that, they each gave detailed reports of the incident to the Guild and Loki. As for the red-haired woman who assailed Rivira—the Guild considered letting the public know that she was a Tamer, at least until Loki told them to "Hold their horses." That piece of information remained secret, but *Ganesha Familia* insisted that she be known as Hashana's killer—and be blacklisted by the Guild.

Since only Aiz's battle party and Lulune had made direct contact with the woman, the monster's sudden appearance was recorded as an Irregular—the only other person who knew the truth about the Tamer was Bors, who had heard it directly from Finn. Only upper-class adventurers were privy to the knowledge of what had happened in Rivira, and that Hashana was murdered. The Guild believed that telling the many lower-class adventurers who couldn't make it into the middle levels would only spread unnecessary fear and confusion.

Lastly, the Guild demanded that every one of the innumerable brilliantly colored magic stones be turned over to them.

The fervor surrounding the incident died down as all evidence of it was swept under the rug.

"The town of Rivira is taking shape again. They really work fast."

"It's really amazing how motivated people get when there's that much money involved…Just to be clear, I'm not complaining."

Tiona and Tione struck up a conversation while everyone else was preparing to continue their Dungeon prowl by the light of the lantern.

Once they had finished everything that needed to be done on the surface, the group came back down to the eighteenth floor and found people hard at work—the town of Rivira was up and running again. Despite all the damage it had sustained, upper-class adventurers were already in the midst of reopening their businesses in the center of town.

Bors could be heard walking around town, spewing idealistic banter like, "This is an all-important forward base in the Dungeon! All of it goes to waste unless we bust our asses, got that?" He was very impassioned, tears even rolling down his cheeks. However, just as Tione had said, everyone there knew this performance was just for show. It was money they were after.

The long arms at the Guild couldn't reach the town of Rivira, which made it a paradise for those who didn't want to be found. It was a place where outlawed items like Status Thief could be bought and sold as residents and visitors saw fit, whenever they wanted. All morals aside, many adventurers needed a place like Rivira.

It wasn't known as the world's most beautiful rogue town for nothing.

Those who chose to do business there were some of the most bold and stubborn adventurers around.

"Those plant monsters and that Tamer have been keeping a remarkably low profile."

"Hmm, I doubt they can do much after pulling that stunt. Gods themselves have their eyes and ears open, so they can't do anything to draw attention to themselves. Also, it would be next to impossible to tame that many beasts overnight. I doubt we'll see anything like last week for quite a while."

"At least I hope there aren't many tamed monsters left," added Finn as he and Riveria joined the conversation.

There had been no reported sightings of any carnivorous flowers nor any trace of the red-haired woman since the incident.

The group had visited the Dungeon's thirtieth floor to investigate the quest Hashana had undertaken before his death. Unfortunately, there was nothing to be found. Where had he found the crystal orb? How did it get into his possession? They still didn't know. Lulune tried to contact her mysterious client after recovering, but had no luck.

"Well then, shall we be off? Lefiya, Rakuta, are you ready?"

"Ah, yes! Let's go!"

Now, Aiz and the others had returned to the Dungeon to complete their original objective: to earn money.

While on the surface, they had decided to add another supporter to their battle party, now seven strong.

At the moment, they were on floor thirty-seven.

That required passing through the lower levels and entering the Deep Levels.

Lefiya nodded as Finn gave the order to move out. The second supporter, a newly ranked-up Level 3 adventurer named Rakuta, looked very nervous. She'd been casually invited to join them in the Deep Levels to "study," and she looked very tense about it.

"Aiz, you were out like a light and didn't eat anything. You hungry? I've still got some of mine left."

"Thanks, Tiona…but I'm fine."

Aiz gently refused Tiona's kindness as the two of them stood up to gather weapons.

The previous leg of their journey had lasted more than half the day, so they had found an isolated room in the back corner of the thirty-seventh floor to have a long rest.

This wasn't a simple day trip into the Dungeon. Adventurers brought camping supplies when planning to stay underground for long periods of time. It was important for them to regain their strength and get some rest from time to time.

For that reason, many would choose to set up camp at safe points, but sometimes it would be too much work to go all the way back to the closest one. So, like Aiz's battle party, they would find a relatively safe place during their journey to recuperate.

The room they were in now only had one exit and wasn't very large. They'd sliced up the walls with their weapons upon arrival. Fragments still lay scattered around the floor.

Whenever the walls or the weaponized landforms were damaged, the Dungeon itself prioritized healing them. In other words, damaging their surroundings prevented monster ambushes.

Putting the last of their sleeping bags and the lamp into the supporters' backpacks, the battle party left the room.

"But it was a real surprise to find adamantite in those walls! A few slashes and something that valuable pops out? What luck!"

"That adamantite alone should get us quite a bit of money."

"For sure! That should put a dent in Urga's bill!"

Tiona had been in a great mood ever since they had prepared the room for camp because they'd found the rare metal just beneath the surface of the Dungeon wall. The Amazon excitedly exchanged words with Lefiya, but Aiz stayed quiet, very much in her own little world just beside them.

The word "Aria."

The Tamer's bloodred hair.

Each image stormed through her head one after another.

She was strong...

"Strong, she was so strong..."

Aiz whispered that to herself over and over, reliving the fight in her head time and again, remembering each overwhelming strike.

If only she could have done more, she might have learned something.

She might have been able to figure out how the woman knew the name "Aria."

If only I was stronger…

Weak.

Still weak.

Aiz Wallenstein, such a weakling.

Aiz mumbled under her breath, cursing herself. If she'd been stronger than that woman, if she'd had more power in her hands, if her mind and body hadn't been so weak…More words arose from the dark, muddy place in the back of her head.

She'd lost her edge at some point.

Her one and only desire had become nothing more than a memory.

Without realizing it, Aiz had let her motivation slip.

That forgotten scene now quietly burned with indignation within her soul.

"…Umm, Miss Aiz?"

It took all the courage Lefiya had to speak up.

Aiz's response didn't make it past her lips.

At that moment, a group of monsters appeared at the other end of the long pathway.

Aiz drew Desperate from its sheath and stepped forward with purpose.

This swarm of monsters knew the presence of the adventurers and moved to attack. Aiz strode out in front of the group and moved like the wind to engage them alone.

As the monster howls made her skin crawl, Aiz could feel Lefiya's gaze on her back.

However, the blond knight's expression seemed frozen as she whipped her blade through the air and kicked off the ground.

The thirty-seventh floor of the Dungeon was known as the White Palace.

That name was based on two things: the pale-white color of the walls and its extremely complex layout that made it a labyrinth in its own right. The scale was completely different from any of the floors leading down to it. All the rooms and hallways were spacious and wide. There were a few exceptions, like where Aiz's battle party had camped. However, most of the rooms exceeded ten meders in width.

The circular floor was like a fortress, standing five stories tall and wrapped in five massive round walls, with stairs leading to the next floor located at the very center. Adventurers needed to traverse many wide-open, exposed hallways as well as go up and down numerous stairwells in order to reach the center. Its size rivaled that of Orario itself. Although a route through the floor had been discovered and mapped, getting lost in this multileveled maze meant never seeing the light of day again.

The ceilings were so high that even top-class adventurers with their enhanced vision had difficulty seeing them. This gave the White Palace a gloomy atmosphere in every dimly lit hallway. The few lights present in the walls were barely strong enough to illuminate the adventurers' faces as they passed.

"You know, Aiz has been pretty scary since that day in Rivira. Just watching her is making my blood run cold. Was that Tamer woman really that strong?"

"Ngah~! No clue! But I'm going to the front, too!"

"Ah, hey! Take care of the ones around us first!"

Tiona swung Urga with all her might, forcing her way through the oncoming swarm of more than twenty monsters to catch up with Aiz on the front line. Tione kicked it into high gear, covering her sister while yelling at her back.

Apart from the expansive terrain, the thirty-seventh floor also had more types of enemies than some levels beyond the fortieth floor. What's worse, their respawning interval was extremely short. The one saving grace was that the same monsters consistently appeared at the same places. However, even a top-class adventurer would suffer the consequences if they decided to charge straight in unprepared.

Monsters kept barreling forward from the other end of the wide hallway. Tione, Finn, and Riveria worked in tandem to repel their attack and protect their two supporters.

"UUGGHHHHHOOOOOOOOOOOOOOOOOOOOOOOOOO OOO!!"

"!"

Aiz was already far out in front of the party, taking on a group by herself. A tall and thick creature called a barbarian swung a natural weapon at her, but she deftly avoided the attack and brought her saber forward. Her counter landed at the same moment the long club slammed into the ground. The barbarian dissolved into ash amid the echoes.

Many warrior-type monsters appeared on this floor: the barbarian, which boasted a body on par with a Minotaur; an upgraded form of the lizardman monster known as the lizardman elite, which first appeared on the nineteenth floor; a dark-black rock monster known as an obsidian soldier. Humanoid fiends filled the hallways of the White Palace.

Since all of them specialized in hand-to-hand combat, this floor was absolute torture for magic users. Without time to conjure their spells, they were extremely vulnerable to close-range attacks. Even worse was the fact that some of the monsters, especially the obsidian soldier, had natural protection against magic, thanks to the stones present in their bodies. A pure magic user like Lefiya could do little more than watch the battle unfold as Finn and Riveria set to work.

"HAAaaa!"

"!"

A barbarian opened its massive chin, lashing his long tongue through the air.

Spinning out of the path of the attack, Aiz slashed it into oblivion as it uttered its dying scream. Wasting no time, she charged forward to engage a stout obsidian soldier and sliced the animated pile of rocks in half.

Another corpse joined the pile building at her feet, ash falling in her wake. Every slash of her silver saber cut through multiple targets and sent streams of blood spurting into the air.

Desire burned in her golden eyes as they searched for the next enemy. Gaze focused, she cut through monsters coming at her from all directions, tracing circles with her feet as though she was a hurricane of saber slices.

A ring of dying breaths sounded in the hallway.

"Yeah, might want to keep a little bit of distance…Riveria, hasn't she told you anything? The pain of a single failure wouldn't drive someone this close to the deep end."

"She would not tell. She simply says, 'It's nothing,' and does not utter another word."

Finn looked uncomfortable, frowning. Riveria sighed, her frustration coming to the surface.

The monsters in their area slain, the two had nothing left to do but watch Aiz's battle from afar. Tiona had finally reached the blond-haired, golden-eyed girl, and the two of them wiped out the remaining monsters in no time flat.

"Looks like there's no point in trying to get to the bottom of this right now…Yeesh."

"Um, General, Lady Riveria…Is Miss Aiz all right?"

"Usually an empty stomach will slow her down when she gets like this…We know she has not eaten a thing, so we should offer some food. That might calm her."

"Y-yes."

A bead of sweat trickled down Lefiya's cheek as she was taken aback by Riveria's surprisingly knowledgeable tone.

Tiona, Tione, and Lefiya had watched Aiz with obvious concern over the past few days, but Finn and Riveria had told them to let her be. They seemed to know something the other girls didn't, so all three of them chose to put their faith in their leaders. After all, Finn and Riveria had spent more time with Aiz than they.

The two supporters quickly collected all the loot, and the party moved on. Traveling toward the center of the floor in a single-file line, they cleared the last wall and continued their journey in the innermost section of the White Palace.

There was a place on the thirty-seventh floor of the Dungeon where monsters consistently spawned at alarming rate; it was known as the Dungeon's Coliseum. Naturally, Aiz wanted to charge right in, but of course, her allies stopped her this time. They pressed on, encountering swarms at every turn.

While Aiz didn't stop her aggressive fighting style, she also didn't do anything that put her allies at risk. She never lost sight of the fact she was a member of the battle party and acted accordingly. Her aloof expression returned the moment each battle ended, and she even participated in the Amazonian twins' banter while giving clear answers to their questions.

Only when she drew her saber did she take on a different demeanor.

"We've already slain a ton of monsters, so it probably gets us a crap-ton of money, right? This is, what, our fifth day in the Dungeon?"

"Yeah, I guess……"

"I mean, if we took all this stuff back to the surface, we've got to have three million valis, easy. Lefiya, how much do we have in contracts?"

"Please wait a moment, I shall check…Just from the quests we took in Rivira, we have a little less than a million valis, I believe."

Looking for an interesting topic, Tiona engaged Aiz in conversation. The original reason that the two of them had come to the Dungeon in the first place was to repay the loan for Urga the Second and to replace the rapier Aiz had used while Desperate was being repaired. Remembering their earlier goal sent Aiz's mind in a different direction, bringing up images of the boy who reminded her of a white rabbit, and the fact she still had to apologize to him.

Aiz shook her head and chased the images away. She didn't have time for that. At the same time, the thought of standing before him, the way she was now…seemed like tarnishing a precious jewel. It was somehow scary.

Aiz looked away from Tiona. Meanwhile, Tione helped Lefiya get a better estimate on their loot.

Whenever the party couldn't carry any more stones or items, they would return to the town of Rivira and trade the items for deeds to make more room.

Since they could never get full price while still underground, they kept the truly valuable items to sell once they got back to the surface. They unloaded everything else in Rivira. Trading the items in for quests was much more efficient than dragging everything up to the surface and coming back down.

"Ah, this room."

Fighting their way through waves of level-three and level-four monsters, the battle party finally arrived at a room that was noticeably larger than the rest.

This is…

Aiz took time to study their surroundings even while engaged in combat with the cluster of enemies already inside the wide area.

The rooms in the White Palace steadily increased in length and width closer to the center. This particular room was overwhelmingly huge, so adventurers who had passed through the White Palace never forgot it. The blond knight's vigilance paid off when her gaze swept over the floor.

That's when she caught a glimpse of it.

Crack!

"You hear that? Where'd it come from?"

"Not the walls. The floor."

Several lizardman elites went flying, courtesy of Urga's blades, as Tiona sprang into action. Tione's Kukri were nothing more than silver flashes as she answered her sister's question.

The cracking echoes weren't coming from all around them, but from beneath their feet. The fissures spread out like a spiderweb in a matter of seconds. No less than ten monsters emerged from the floor in the blink of an eye.

Monsters with no muscles or skin, only bones.

Parts of their exposed skeletons were thicker to make sharp pieces of armor all around their bodies. Each one of them was born carrying a bone sword or bone ax in one hand and a bone shield in the other.

Spartoi.

Another warrior-class monster of the thirty-seventh floor, like the barbarian.

"Finn, I'm going."

"Wait, Aiz!"

Spartois were the most physically dangerous monsters on this floor.

Despite their appearance, they were extremely strong and fast. Wielding several different types of weapons, facing off against one of these was similar to fighting against a skilled adventurer.

Aiz jumped in front of the battle party to take her level-four-category opponents from the front; she left the rest to Tiona and the others. Desperate hummed as it came out of its sheath. The blond knight couldn't care less that she was outnumbered as she charged into the group of spartois.

"!"

"GAHH!"

The closest skeleton led with its shield, sword high above his head, ready to strike. Aiz took it head-on, sweeping her saber forward.

The shield couldn't repel Desperate, and Aiz charged through the collapsing skeleton to dodge an oncoming bone lance from the side. The lancer stepped past her as Aiz avoided a bone ax that came down right where her head had been a moment earlier and knocked a sword wielded by the largest monster of the bunch to the side. A flash of silver went through each enemy as she passed. Several severed torsos fell to the ground at her feet.

"OOO-OOHHH!"

"_____!!"

"...!"

Black, eyeless sockets focused on Aiz, and Aiz alone.

Bones rattled as the monsters quickly glanced at each other, setting up a plan like a pack of wolves hunting their prey.

Aiz glared back at the monsters, who had not only mastered their individual weapons but advanced teamwork as well. But that wasn't about to stop her. She charged forward, silver saber flashing.

Five minutes of intense combat passed in which Aiz couldn't overlook a single detail and even felt a little anxious in the middle of it all.

Now there was only one left, and Aiz went airborne with Desperate coming straight down.

"GROOOOOOOOOOOOOOOOOOOOOOOOOOOOOOOOOOO OOOOO!"

The blade sliced through the top of its head all the way down to the base of its hip. The monster's dying scream faded along with its broken magic stone as its body turned to ash.

Swish! All the spartois dispatched, Aiz whipped her blade through the air before pointing its cutting edge toward the ground.

It was impossible to count all the cleanly sliced bones scattered about the floor. The few stones that were intact sparkled inside their bony cages, dark purple speckles in the dim light.

The blond knight stood in the middle of the remains of at least ten monsters, letting the sounds of battle dissipate around her as the dust settled.

"…And she did it all herself."

"She'd be a lot cuter if she pretended to be in trouble every now and then…"

The Amazonian twins sighed, one criticizing and the other pointing out the irony of the situation. They watched as Aiz left the now-tranquil battlefield and headed back to the group.

She returned Desperate to its sheath and acknowledged Lefiya and the other supporter as they passed.

"…Very well done, Miss Aiz."

"Thanks…I leave the rest to you, Lefiya."

The elf smiled back at her, the muscles in her face relaxing, before she began to collect the loot still on the floor.

With a wave and a nod to the second supporter, Aiz watched Rakuta set to work as well.

"Nice, nice! Good work, Aiz! Need a potion? Or an elixir? How about one of your favorite sweet-bean-flavored potato puffs?"

"Why would she need a potion anyway? There isn't a scratch on her."

Tiona regained some of her usual cheer and walked out to greet Aiz with a big smile.

Ignoring the dig from her older sister, the Amazon knew that the perfect time to bring up Jyaga Maru Kun was when Aiz was tired and hungry after battle.

Aiz's soft voice was a little bit higher than usual when she responded.

"Thanks, Tiona. I'm fine...but I want the last one."

Grumble. Perhaps it was because she hadn't eaten anything since before they took the rest, but the noises from Aiz's stomach betrayed her.

However, the potato puff hadn't been preserved all that well in their traveling supplies and looked to be on the verge of going bad. Her shoulders sank in disappointment.

"In any case, the monsters have been taken care of...What should we do now, Finn?"

The difficult battle behind them, Riveria cast her gaze down at the prum.

While they might not have explored every nook and cranny of the thirty-seventh floor, they had reached the entrance to the next floor at its center. Pressing onward meant going down to the thirty-eighth.

Danger and the unknown increased with every floor in the Dungeon. Considering their unsteady supply of items and the weapons they had used up, she sought the leader's opinion.

"Hmm...Should we head home? This trip was more for fun anyway, so staying here long enough that we run out of food and have to go back home with empty stomachs would defeat the purpose. What are your thoughts, Riveria?"

She looked at him in agreement. The time to pull back had come.

The elf nodded when Finn continued by saying this was not an expedition with an overarching goal, so they had no reason to needlessly hang around.

"I will follow your orders, General…All of you, we're returning to the surface!"

""Coming!""

Tiona and Tione responded in unison, and both supporters chimed in with a "Yes, ma'am!" and "Understood!"

With orders to go back to the surface, everyone breathed a sigh of relief, knowing that they didn't have to worry about Aiz's unusual disposition for much longer.

Tiona wanted to lighten the mood—and have a little fun—so she changed the topic.

"But, you know, if Bete were here he'd be putting up quite a fuss right about now. He always tries to act like a big shot in front of Aiz!"

"After that night at the bar, we told him that Aiz flat-out rejected him once he sobered up. He was on the verge of tears, so depressed."

"Ohhh?! I would've loved to see that! Why didn't you tell me, Tione?!"

Tione had a serious look in her eyes for a moment as she looked to her younger sister, but she couldn't hold back a small grin.

The two of them started having a bit of fun at Bete's expense. On a side note, he hadn't been invited to join the second journey due to Tiona's cunning plan to keep him in the dark.

Tension was leaving the air around the battle party as the supporters collected the last of the loot.

But then, out of the blue…

"…Finn, Riveria. I'd like to stay behind, alone."

Aiz spoke up.

Tiona's and Tione's heads whipped around in surprise.

She could feel their gazes, but her aloof expression remained unchanged. The only exception: her eyes looked more determined with each passing moment.

Normally, Aiz went with the flow. But now she was asserting herself—much more strongly than any of her allies had anticipated. Finn quietly looked up at her.

As for Riveria, she closed one eye and narrowed the other as she studied the human girl's face.

"I don't need any rations. I don't want to cause problems for anyone. So, please."

Aiz's voice slowly but surely took on a pleading tone as she almost begged her allies to let her stay behind.

"H-hold on a sec! Aiz, you're causing us problems just by asking! If you stay behind, I'll be too worried to think straight!"

"I agree with Tiona. No matter how low-level these monsters are, I refuse to leave an ally alone down here. Too dangerous."

Tiona couldn't stay still after hearing Aiz's desire and rushed right up to her. Tione cocked an eyebrow and added her opinion to the mix. Their words showed just how much they cared for the blond girl.

Aiz couldn't say anything to alleviate the sisters' concern.

"Why do you want to fight so much?"

The human didn't have an answer for Tiona, who considered her a friend. All Aiz could do was quietly look at the floor the moment she saw Tiona's sad expression.

Tiona's concern was coming from the heart, and Aiz couldn't reject that. A long silence fell.

Tiona, figuring out that the girl wouldn't say anything, started stretching her body so that she could drag Aiz back to the surface by force if she had to. But first, she unloaded her thoughts like a verbal firing squad.

"It's such a waste, Aiz! You're so cute and lovely, why don't you try acting more like a lady? How can you be losing to me, an Amazon, in fashion sense?"

"I…don't care about that kind of thing."

"Why not? Don't you want a good, strong male…or at least some fellow you like, at least? Is that pretty face of yours only for show?"

"Stop telling others to do things that you don't do yourself."

Losing patience with her overreacting, Tione took another dig at her sister. Riveria sighed just a few paces away from them.

Then she turned back to Finn.

"Finn, I shall ask you as well. Please respect Aiz's wishes."

""Riveria?!""

The Amazonian twins couldn't believe their ears.

Even Aiz was surprised, although she didn't show it.

She had fully expected Riveria to refuse her request outright and possibly scold her for asking.

"Hmm…?"

Even Finn was intrigued by this turn of events and looked up at the elf's beautiful face.

"This girl hardly ever makes a selfish request. I would like you to consider it."

"The request of a parent looking after their child won't sway me, Riveria. Tiona and Tione are correct. As long as the safety of this battle party is in my hands, I won't allow it."

"I realize that I am spoiling her…Well, then."

Sighing again, Riveria turned to face Aiz.

She knew that the girl was making the others worry and couldn't say another word in her defense.

While she didn't know what was really unfolding in the human girl's heart, she let her shoulders and face relax as she beheld her.

"I shall remain as well."

The elf declared that she would serve as a supporter for Aiz.

Finn pretentiously put his hand to his chin as he stared deep into the elf's jade-green eyes and nodded.

"Okay, I'll allow it."

"Ehhh, Finn~. Talk some sense into her~."

Tiona was at a loss and objected.

Finn gave a half-smile before continuing.

"We won't have to worry about the unexpected as long as Riveria is with her. Actually, we're the ones that'll have to stay on our toes on the way back up."

"That's only because I can't attack and heal, General."

There was a bit of a prickling in Tione's tone, but she didn't attempt to go against orders. She didn't try to blame him, either; she just wasn't happy about the decision.

Finn shrugged it off. The matter was settled—Aiz and Riveria would stay on this floor.

Lefiya and Rakuta must have sensed that something unusual was happening and quickly returned to the group with their bags full of loot.

"Miss Aiz, you are not coming back with us?"

"Yes…Sorry for being so selfish, Lefiya."

"Then, um, ehh…I-I shall remain as well! I promise I will not hold you back! Please allow me to be your supporter!"

"Ah, in that case I'll stay, too! See, isn't that simple?"

"Didn't the general say we're low on food? Splitting with two people is doable, but splitting up enough food and water for four people? All of us will go hungry."

""Awhhhhhhhhhhhhh…""

Lefiya's and Tiona's heads drooped in disappointment the moment Tione pointed out that very important fact.

It would be difficult for three people to remain on this floor considering the amount of food and healing items still in their possession. Aiz's Desperate might still be in good shape, but the rest of their weapons had seen better days. It wouldn't be a surprise if one of the blades cracked in the next battle.

A tearful Lefiya and Tiona said their good-byes.

Riveria watched the three girls' conversation unfold from outside the group.

Finn slid up next to her.

"So, what was the real reason behind that suggestion?"

Riveria heard his quiet voice and glanced down to meet his gaze.

"You don't expect me to believe you meant exactly what you said?"

"…Even if we were to stop the girl now, it would only delay the inevitable. No matter what action we take, something will happen. If she's going to erupt one way or another…I'd rather have her explode under my supervision."

"Now I got you."

Finn laughed and closed his eyes for a moment. Upon reopening them, he looked sidelong at Riveria.

He seemed like he wanted to say something to the woman acting like a stern parent toward Aiz, but he just couldn't find the words.

"While I doubt that that Tamer will show up, please be careful. I'll leave all my magic potions with you…You're the one that agreed to Aiz's decision, so you're responsible for whatever happens just as much is she is."

"I am aware…And, my apologies. Thank you."

She held the position of second-in-command in their familia and was one of the most experienced members, as Finn had alluded to. She thanked him and gave a deep nod. The prum pulled several vials of red liquid from his pouch and handed them to Riveria before she walked over to Aiz.

The two women watched the others prepare to leave. The group stepped away from them after a few minutes.

There was only one entrance to this room. They stood in the off-white archway and saw the rest of the party off as Tiona and Lefiya repeatedly yelled words of encouragement to Aiz.

"…Thank you, Riveria."

Now alone in the room, Aiz spoke.

Riveria was standing next to the girl, but didn't look at her. Instead, she gave a short but impassioned lecture.

"I do hope this is the last time, but what is done is done. Allow me to just say this: Do not force me to do too much."

"…Sorry."

Aiz felt exposed on so many levels when in Riveria's presence.

It was completely different from how she felt in front of Finn or Loki, and also not the same as when she was with Tiona and the others. She couldn't hide anything, close to being naked.

The elf's small rebuke, as well as her own apology, made clear the bond between the two.

Although she couldn't put it into words, Aiz felt a warmth with her that was different from the trust and camaraderie she had with other members of the familia.

"..."

The two stood in the dim room, not doing much of anything in the heavy silence.

Even the roars of roaming monsters were distant. None of them seem to be getting closer. An eerie, unnatural stillness descended around Aiz and Riveria.

The air enveloping their light armor and battle cloth was brisk. With the dim lights far above on the thirty-seventh floor's high ceiling, the atmosphere was bone-chillingly cold.

The icy breath of the Dungeon swept past their necks.

"...?"

Thinking it strange that they were staying in one place, Riveria cast her jade eyes toward the human girl.

Aiz felt her gaze, but showed no signs of moving.

Just like before, the girl had no intention of exploring every corner of the thirty-seventh floor. Nor was she lying in wait for monsters to come to her.

She had a different reason for wanting to be in this room on this floor.

If she was right, then—

Aiz was deep in thought, breathing as slowly and quietly as possible. The time crawled by, with nothing happing, until...

A small, minute shake under the floor made its way through the soles of her boots.

—I knew it.

"It's here."

"What is?"

Aiz's eyebrows fell as she took a defensive stance and scanned the center of the room. Even though Riveria had asked for confirmation, she felt it, too.

The ground shook again and again, even stronger than before.

"It could not be..."

The floor dipped in the middle of the chamber the moment those words escaped Riveria's lips.

Then—*CRACK!*

The rock seemed to scream out in pain as a gigantic fissure opened in the floor.

The space shook even harder as the crevice expanded. New cracks shot out in all directions as far as they could see. A massive pitch-black body so large that they couldn't believe their eyes rose from the crevice and stretched far above their heads.

Pieces of rock fell off the body one after the other, crumbling down in an avalanche of dust and soil. The room wouldn't stop shaking. The noise was deafening, each echo a crushing blow to the ears until finally its emergence was complete.

Aiz watched the pitch-black monster rear back to face the ceiling hidden in darkness.

"—OOOOOOOOOOOOOOOOOOOOOOOOOOOOOOOOOOO OOOOOOOOOOOOO!!"

The enormous being, so big that even the female-figured monster that appeared in Rivira couldn't hold a candle to it, announced its birth with an equally tremendous roar. The overwhelmingly intimidating aura emanating from its body put that octopus-like creature to shame.

It could be nothing else but a floor boss.

The Monster Rex that resided on the thirty-seventh floor of the Dungeon.

Level Six, Udaeus.

"So then, three months have already passed..."

Monster Rex all had a predetermined respawn time. Once one of them was defeated, it would not reappear in the Dungeon until the allotted time had passed. At this moment, almost exactly three months ago, none other than *Loki Familia* had defeated this monster using its full combat strength. Now, Riveria looked up at it half in awe as the words slipped out of her mouth.

Physically, Udaeus was a skeleton monster, a spartoi that had just kept on growing. Every bone that composed its body was jet black. Just looking was enough to make an adventurer fear being sucked in. At the same time, they gave off an eerie and ominous sheen.

The beast itself was over ten meders tall despite its lower body remaining underground. The bones that made up its spine leaned forward, each of its many vertebrae swaying to and fro like they had a mind of their own. Its skull was adorned with two horns similar to an ogre's and small crimson flames flickering like eyes in deep sockets that were otherwise pitch black.

An unusually large and thick magic stone sat protected by its sternum and rib cage in the middle of its chest.

The dark purple crystal sparkled exactly were the heart should be, but there were no organs to be seen in this floor boss.

"Riveria, don't help me."

Aiz stared down the monster she had known would appear and withdrew Desperate from the sheath at her waist.

It was the perfect chance for her to advance to the next stage.

She'd hit a wall in her growth and needed a bigger "container" for her excelia. To do that, she needed to defeat a tough enemy like a Monster Rex alone. It would be a *grand accomplishment* the gods themselves couldn't ignore. Aiz would go beyond her own limit.

To become stronger, far stronger, so that she would never lose to anyone.

To leave her weak self in the past, to obtain even more power.

Aiz's golden eyes looked up to her opponent's face, overlapping her memories of the woman with bloodred hair onto the enemy before her.

"Aiz, do you seriously intend to do this by yourself?"

Riveria watched the girl advance and called out to her.

A vertical wave passed through Udaeus's many vertebrae and ended in another ear-crushing howl. However, Aiz was unfazed. She kept advancing with her silver saber shimmering quietly in the darkness.

"I'll be fine."

Then she said with absolute confidence:

"I'll end this quickly."

The mountainous skeleton started to waver.

The presence of an adventurer within its striking distance unleashed its killer instincts.

All its bones rasped against each other as the girl faced down her incredibly strong enemy on what would soon become their battlefield.

The knight kicked off the ground and charged headlong into the ill-advised battle.

Aiz dashed straight toward the enemy.

Desperate, a weapon that had seen her through too many battles to count, was firmly in the grip of her right hand. Her eyes focused on the spartoi's chest in a full-frontal attack.

"OOOOOOOOOOOOOOOOOOOOOOOOOOOOOOOOOOO OOOOOOOOOOOOOOOOO!!"

Udaeus's tremendous howl shook the chamber as she closed the distance in a flash.

Its burning, crimson eyes found the golden shadow. The long bones of its distorted left arm rose above its shoulder, preparing to bring them down on its foe.

The small shape was locked in its sights as it prepared to swipe her from the side.

"Awaken, Tempest!!"

Aiz activated the short trigger spell of her Magic with the monster's attack bearing down on her.

Air currents instantly surrounded her body and armor. Her speed now dramatically increased, Aiz extended her right leg and kicked off the ground, leaving a small explosion of stone shards in her wake.

Jumping forward, she twisted her body out of the way before Udaeus's arm could make contact and arrived at the creature's base.

Not only was she too close to be hit by another swing, she'd made it into her opponent's blind spot. The monster couldn't see her.

Aiz looked up at the hollow cavity just overhead and jumped straight up.

The floor boss's left flank was completely exposed with its arm still out of position. This was her chance. She leaped through the air with her saber ready to strike. Gathering wind around the blade, her magic increased its cutting power as well as its reach.

Twisting her back like a spring, she swung Desperate behind her left shoulder and saw the perfect opportunity to strike. Her blade tore through the air in a horizontal slash before the monster could react.

"UUUHH!"

"¡"

Her target was the large magic stone located in the middle of its ribs. Seeing her opening to attack between the exposed bones of its chest, she went for it. Unfortunately, the fifth rib shifted up and blocked just enough of her blade to skew the attack. The assault had gone directly for Udaeus's heart, and the spartois was swift to respond, focusing its attention on defense.

—So close.

Aiz glanced at the black bone that had blocked her attack with her usual aloof expression, genuinely surprised she hadn't cut it in half. In fact, there wasn't even a scratch on it. She lamented the lost chance under her breath.

If she'd been able to put even one crack into the stone, Udaeus's movements would have become clumsier. Chances like this didn't present themselves very often, but she couldn't afford not to take advantage of them.

Aiz's momentum carried her past Udaeus's rib cage and down to the floor behind it. A quick spin and she charged again.

There was nothing to protect the boss's spine, another opportunity—until…

A black, harpoon-like pillar shot out of the ground and forced Aiz to break stride.

"!"

It was just about to hit her chin, but she bent back at the waist in time to dodge it.

Her golden hair flung forward as the black column whizzed by her ear. Suddenly, another five pierced through the ground like halberds. Aiz quickly spun to the side to get out of the way.

The pillars shattered the floor on their way through, and pursued Aiz wherever she went with unyielding tenacity, attacking from beneath her line of sight.

—That was why.

Udaeus itself was a sitting duck, unable to dodge much of anything. This was the reason why even a large battle party couldn't charge onto this floor without a plan.

They wouldn't get close to it without finding a way to deal with the pikes that burst from the ground without warning. Anyone who threw caution to the wind would become an instant pincushion, falling victim to Udaeus's greatest attack and defense.

The Monster Rex didn't keep its lower body buried under the floor without reason. In truth, Udaeus didn't have a lower body to begin with.

Instead, its upper body stood like a massive tree with a vast network of roots spreading out onto the floor. In other words, there was a minefield of innumerable black spears just beneath the floor under Aiz's feet.

The entire room could be considered part of the monster's body at this point—the entire battlefield was within its range.

As soon as adventurers were forced back into Udaeus's line of vision, the black pillars would block their only route of escape. The king of the skeletons never allowed anything to leave its chamber until the massacre was over.

"RUOOOOOOOOOOOOOOOOOOOOOOOOOOOOOOOOOOOOO!"

"Kah!"

The incredibly fast and unpredictable attacks from below perfectly complemented the looming, lumbering, yet incredibly strong upper body as both relentlessly attacked their target: Aiz. She was already in danger of being surrounded by the line of harpoons.

But their appearances were coordinated, almost as if telling her "come this way" and restricting Aiz's freedom of movement. Forced to continuously dodge their relentless assault, Aiz had been led back in front of Udaeus before she realized it.

The flames burning deep in its eye sockets flashed menacingly as the floor boss unleashed the merciless onslaught, slamming both of its arms onto the floor over and over. Aiz was trapped in a pincer—the pikes from below and the bones from above. Her face distorted in distress as the air currents surrounding her body pushed her to safety by the narrowest of margins.

"Aiz!"

Riveria, whom Aiz had pleaded with to stay out of the battle, called out to her from the other side of the pillars.

The elf was still close to the entrance to the room. Udaeus had yet to notice her presence. Riveria's entire body was tense, her feet restless like the calm before the storm as she watched the battle unfold from afar.

Under normal circumstances, a battle party exceeding thirty upper-class adventurers would coordinate their attacks to slay this beast. Normally, the pikes would be distributed among the many targets, but Aiz was facing all of them on her own. Her Magic allowed her to move at a speed far beyond a normal human, but it was only a matter of time before they caught up to her.

Riveria had made up her mind. Staff in hand, she was a heartbeat away from stepping onto the battlefield. That's when she felt Aiz's gaze.

"*I'm fine,*" the human girl seemed to convey through her golden-eyed stare. Riveria grimaced, trying to impart her own thoughts through her expression.

"…!"

Aiz broke eye contact almost as quickly as she had made it, then faced forward just in time to dodge another spear from the floor under her chin.

The pikes came in different sizes. Some were only one meder or so long and meant to break her stride with their sharp points. Others were long, thick pillars over three meders tall and completely changed the landscape of the battlefield. The combinations of width and length were endless.

It went without saying that they hit hard. However, Udaeus's attacks from overhead were far more destructive. Everything that happened to be beneath one of it strikes was shattered on impact. Pikes became nothing but flat rubble in their wake. Aiz might be protected by wind armor, but even that couldn't absorb a direct hit. The female-figured monsters she had fought on the fiftieth and eighteenth floors seemed weak by comparison. This creature's strength and abilities made it worthy of being a floor boss.

Aiz was in danger of losing her footing. She sliced through each pike as she went past while keeping an eye on Udaeus's body.

Aim for the joints...!

Indeed, the massive skeleton looming overhead had several weak points to choose from. What's more, the spaces between its shoulders, elbows, and all the way down to the smaller joints flickered with a violet light similar to a magic stone's.

It was this power that allowed the skinless and muscle-less Udaeus to move in any direction it pleased. The Magic energy center between each of its bones also acted like the glue that kept the beast from falling apart. Spartois also had them—although they didn't glow anywhere near as bright—so a common strategy to cripple them was to strike those areas. The purple glow of Aiz's many possible targets flickered in the darkness.

Her opponent's stamina would never run out, so she had to land a decisive blow before hers reached its limit. Aiz shifted her battle strategy from defense and evasion to offense and attack.

Focusing her Mind, she yelled:

"Wind!"

Her spell was at full power.

The streams of air surrounding her body grew thicker and more intense, turning Aiz into the eye of a small hurricane. The aches and pains throughout her body screamed in protest as Aiz used the air currents to her advantage and achieved her fastest speed yet that day.

"?!"

The flaming pupils of Udaeus's eyes wavered as Aiz once again disappeared from its line of sight.

She approached the monster from the left, going around the outside toward its back. The crimson flames once again caught a glimpse of the blond shadow. Each of the vertebrae in his neck undulated into a deafening howl as more pikes erupted from the floor.

However, none of them found their target. Not even close.

They were too slow; Aiz was too fast.

Her movements were quick enough to surpass and overwhelm the attacks from below. She was already gone by the time each one burst from the floor, striking nothing but empty air. They traced Aiz's approach like a mountain range desperate to keep up with the sun.

The blond knight paid no attention to the "landmines" going off in her wake. Her gaze was locked on to one thing, the creature's spine, specifically the lowest joint in its back.

She rushed forward in a straight line, Desperate ready to strike. A thin tornado wrapped itself around the silver blade of her saber. Aiz then timed her swing perfectly as she dashed past the monster's base.

"GOHH!!"

Udaeus's entire upper body tilted right as the blow connected with incredible force just above the bone that served as its foundation. Aiz also appeared on the right side of the beast, its spine bending over her head. Slamming her feet into the ground and putting her left hand on the floor for balance, Aiz abruptly flipped the direction of the air coursing around her.

Centrifugal force wrecked its way through her body, but she managed to kill her momentum in the blink of an eye. The girl then kicked off the ground without missing a beat. She left a divot in the floor and a trail of debris in her wake as she shot toward Udaeus's spine like a bullet of wind,

The same attack, but from the other side—toward the now fully exposed joint in its lower back. Her saber sliced forward in a blur.

"OOOOOOOOOOOOOOOOOOOOOOOOOOOOOOOOOO!"

The vertebrae shattered. Its foundation gone, Udaeus lost his balance and fell facedown onto the floor.

It looked as though the floor boss was prostrating itself. Aiz was following the prevailing theory for adventurers when facing a Monster Rex or any other large beast: get them to the ground. She wasn't about to let this opportunity go to waste and looped around to attack.

"GUUUUOOOOOOoo!"

Udaeus flailed around to prevent her from getting close. Hundreds of pikes rose all around its body in a desperate attempt to keep its unseen enemy at bay.

But that didn't stop Aiz. She sliced her way through and made her way on top of the beast's right shoulder. The tip of her saber pointed down, she found an opening just above its shoulder blade and thrust Desperate straight into the violet glow beneath her feet.

The cutting edge of the blade hit something hard. It couldn't proceed any farther despite the incredible magic boost.

Aiz yelled.

"Rage, Tempest!"

The full power of Airiel rushed down the sword.

An additional blade of wind carved its way into the joint in the blink of an eye—and severed it.

"_____!"

An earsplitting roar blasted its way out from Udaeus's spine.

The explosion of wind separated the arm at the shoulder. The appendage drifted away as if in slow motion as the rest of the arm bones crashed to the floor in deafening impacts.

Udaeus had lost his entire right arm.

"What power…!"

Riveria could hardly believe her eyes. The words rolled off her tongue in disbelief.

It wasn't powerful Magic that had inflicted this much damage on the floor boss, but a single sword. The elf was shocked at Aiz's display of might.

"!"

The uncontrolled explosion of wind also knocked the girl into the air. Aiz quickly recovered, landing on her feet and continuing the assault.

She fully intended to repeat the process and take the monster apart piece by piece. Udaeus continued to howl in pain and anger as the floor boss glared in Aiz's direction with burning contempt.

The next series of pillars to burst forth from the ground weren't aimed at Aiz, but to protect its joints.

"!"

More and more pikes emerged, providing a layer of armor where there had been none before.

Her enemy wasn't stupid. Udaeus had figured out Aiz's strategy and quickly increased its defense. More than likely, it needed to buy time to recover.

It wouldn't take much time for her to divert the energy radiating from its core to revitalize its damaged lower back. However, no amount of magic would bring back its severed arm at this point.

Udaeus was attempting to pull its upper body upright by healing from its wounds.

Of course Aiz wasn't going to let that happen. She ran up the pikes, jumped, and aimed her blade at the closest joint. However...

"OOOOOOOOOOOOOOOOOOOOOOOOOOOOOOOOOOOOO OOOOOOOOOOOOOOOOOOO!!"

Udaeus, still facedown on the floor, roared once again.

This time, the howl was like a request to its mother, the Dungeon. Then a mass of spartois surfaced from the floor, like loyal knights come to protect their king.

"?!"

The white-boned warriors rushed into Aiz's path with weapons at the ready. Aiz tried to use her airborne momentum to fly past them, but they gathered to her like moths to a flame. Aiz was forced into battle.

At the same time, several more spartois appeared in front of Riveria.

"Keh?!"

A swarm of monsters approached the unprotected magic user, who was used to being in the rear of the battle formation.

Almost twenty of the monsters had been born. Cursing herself for allowing their ambush to make it this far, Riveria took evasive measures as she met the skeleton monsters in combat.

Despite not being suited to handle this type of battle, the elf combined defensive staff strikes with Concurrent Casting to buy herself enough time to conjure Magic.

"UUUOGH…"

With Aiz and Riveria occupied, Udaeus finished its recovery in no time flat.

The blond knight bit her lip and watched the beast shatter through its pike armor and "stand" tall once again.

Its eyes burned deep in their sockets as the floor boss loomed over the battlefield without its right arm. Without warning, it summoned the biggest shaft yet from beneath the floor at its base.

The joints of its black fingers curled around the tip of the black bone and yanked it free—a sword.

The weapon was at least six meders long.

From Aiz's point of view, it was a thick, jet-black longsword. And yet, it was not much more than a long dagger to Udaeus. Similar to the Nature Weapons used by other monsters in the Dungeon, but in the shape of a black greatsword.

The monster looked down at Aiz, the girl clutching Desperate in her right hand. It was as though the girl was looking up at an opponent armed with a harpoon, while all she carried was a toothpick.

—*What's this?*

Aiz, and even Riveria, were caught off guard by Udaeus's unexpected change in strategy. The floor boss armed itself similar to a spartoi, and slowly lifted the weapon in its left hand high into the air.

Aiz cleaned up the remaining monsters around her and kept an eye on this new form of attack. She was in the process of deciding whether to gain some distance or press the attack—when another surprise reflected in her golden eyes.

Shoulder, elbow, wrist.

Each of the monster's joints began to pulsate like shooting stars burning in the night sky. *Zip!* Seeing the ominous violet light emanating from Udaeus's left arm sent a jolt up Aiz's spine.

The towering monster froze for a moment, its left arm held high. Switching gears, Aiz ran with all her might to gain as much distance as possible.

The surviving spartois' attacks bouncing off her wind armor, the blond human forced every bit of strength out of her muscles to be anywhere but within the monster's range.

It was at that moment that Udaeus's arm became a blur.

"_____"

The black greatsword came down faster than the eye could see.

The violet light from the joints in its arm flashed as the floor boss moved with a speed that Monster Rexes weren't believed to possess.

Aiz could see a black shadow approaching out of the corner of her eye. An enormous blast of wind caught her the moment it was out of sight.

"—?!"

The pikes sticking out of the ground and the spartois were wiped out instantaneously.

Even Aiz, who had managed to get out of range, was overtaken by the shock wave and thrown into the air, hitting the ground with a hard thud.

The floor that absorbed the blow was burned to a crisp, smoke rising from a tremendous gash that cut right through it. Aiz couldn't hide the shock on her face as she quickly jumped to her feet, eyes focused on the floor boss.

She reasoned that it was a slicing technique that Udaeus made possible by charging the joints with extreme amounts of magic energy. Its incredible strength, combined with Magic, had produced an incredible explosion that destroyed everything around the black greatsword, with a force that even she couldn't completely escape despite the assistance of her wind magic.

The only good news was that the monster couldn't do it twice in a row. Her golden eyes narrowed as Udaeus held its left arm back and started to charge the attack once again.

Severing the monster's right arm must have hit a nerve. Against a large battle party, the floor boss had likely never had a chance to draw its weapon, but Aiz attacking by herself had given Udaeus the time it needed to summon the black greatsword. Using that much magic energy without a conduit like the sword would probably have blasted it into pieces.

Udaeus's ace in the hole—a trump card that had never been seen before.

Revealing a hidden power like this was like a piece of a mask flaking off to reveal its wearer's true identity.

Warning bells were blaring in Aiz's mind; beads of sweat rolled down her face.

"Aiz, fall back! The weapon is useless if it cannot reach you!"

An arctic wind swirled at the entrance to the room. Riveria's words rode the cool breeze out to Aiz.

The elf's voice was finally free from her incantation and she shouted a warning to her ally, but the human had no intention of obeying.

Gripping the hilt of her saber with even more force, Aiz's body tensed as she charged toward Udaeus.

"You fool…!"

Aiz could hear Riveria chastising her as she chose to go on the offensive.

The monster was already aware of the elf, sending some pikes to bar her path and even more spartois in her direction. Physically separated from Riveria, Aiz engaged Udaeus head-on.

The greatsword came down at an angle.

She could tell by the position of the sword and the monster's stance where the attack was coming from and quickly moved to evade, but she was still caught in its wake, the sharp air biting at her skin. She winced in pain. The weapon made contact with the ground at that same moment, showering her with debris and filling her ears with a deafening *BOOM*.

Every time she charged closer, a new wave of pikes barred her path. They weren't intended to attack her directly, but to create a five-meder wall to cut off her offense. Aiz couldn't break through the many rows with only one slash, and she was forced to break off each of her assaults as well as dodge Udaeus's follow-ups. Wind whistled by her ears as the floor boss destroyed the pillars in its attempts to hit Aiz with its overwhelming power.

The enemy could attack with pikes and explosions of magic energy. Saying it was difficult to overcome would be an understatement.

Aiz moved all around as fast as the wind would allow, managing to get behind Udaeus many times, but the obstacles and newly spawned spartois wouldn't allow her to get as close as before. The beast's black bones bore many scars inflicted by her saber, but it wouldn't allow her to get close enough to strike its joints or any other vital areas. In fact, it gave up defending everywhere else altogether.

Udaeus swung again; Aiz had lost count of how many she'd dodged. All that mattered was she keep moving at full speed.

Finally, she found a window of attack and moved in to strike.

Crick!

She heard the muscles in her body physically give out.

"_____"

She'd been using Airiel at full power for too long.

However, it wasn't her Mind that broke under the incredible strain, it was her body that had reached its limit first.

A red pain flooded her entire body in an instant, setting off even more alarms in her head. Strength left her body like the cut strings of a puppet. Her movements became meek, visibly losing their edge and vitality.

Udaeus saw its chance and brought another wave of columns out of the ground with ferocity.

"!"

One, sharp and thin like a black spear, was aimed for her temple. Though she twisted away at the last moment, the strike disrupted the air current protecting her.

Another round of pikes ascended at Aiz in succession. They came from left and right, front and back, each cutting deeper into the wind armor, and delivering blow after blow directly to her body.

Off balance, Aiz had no way to escape from the onslaught. In the midst of her desperate flips and spins—her golden eyes saw it.

Udaeus, with its left arm high in the air.

Shoulder, elbow, wrist. All three joints glowing violet, and the arm about to come down.

Aiz was easily within range. Her blood ran cold as the crimson flames mercilessly stared down at her.

Her mind went blank. She didn't even feel the strikes pelting her body.

Then she summoned everything she had left and jumped into the air using sheer willpower.

A moment later…

"OOOOOOOOOOOOOOOOOOOOOOOOOOOOOOOOOOO OOOOOOOOO!"

"Ugh!"

It connected.

The last traces of her wind armor shattered as the blade slid past her body. Even though she had avoided a direct hit by jumping wildly into the air, it had left her wide open to a shock wave that accompanied the impact. That was more than enough to launch her into the air.

The angle was shallow, so she hit the ground rather quickly. However, Aiz kept rolling for dozens of meders, bouncing off of shattered pillars and debris as if caught in raging rapids. Wind armor long since broken, the last traces of Airiel came to an abrupt end.

Her smoking body finally came to a stop, leaving her on her back. She was in too much pain to fully comprehend the extent of her injuries, but even so, she forced her eyes open.

Her vision was tinted deep red.

"Aiz!"

Riveria's scream.

The girl's body shook softly as she tried to sit up. Riveria's face contorted, seeing her in so much pain.

"—MOVE!!"

"Geh?!"

Riveria wildly swung her staff forward, knocking the spartoi out of her path and putting a major dent in its head in the process.

The last of the monsters that had surrounded her dispatched, the elf started to run toward her battered and bloodied friend.

"OOOOOOOOOooooooo!!"

"!"

However, new columns rose at her feet. Riveria acrobatically dodged the threat and looked up toward the monster. Udaeus was a great distance away, but she could tell that the two crimson flames deep in his eye sockets were focused directly on her.

It must have identified her as the greater threat. Riveria's eyes narrowed as she dodged another round of the black pikes.

Harbinger of the end, white snow. Gust with the wind before twilight.

She would blast the thing into oblivion.

The mage's beautiful face took on the extremely rare expression of rage as she ran at full speed while Concurrent Casting. Her jade eyes were burning in their own right as she glared back at Udaeus. The one-hundred-meder distance between the two didn't mean a thing. More and more pikes burst from the floor as a magic circle appeared under Riveria's feet.

The monster could sense an unusually large amount of energy gathering; its shoulders started to tremble. As for Aiz…

Her eyes wide open, she shouted at the top of her lungs:

"Riveria!!"

The girl's voice broke Riveria's concentration and the magic circle disappeared.

"Don't interfere...!"

Sitting up, the girl grabbed Desperate from the spot where it lay at her side and used it as a cane to pull herself up.

The cut on her cheek still leaking fresh blood, she sounded as if she was about to cry.

"Please, don't...!"

Drip, drip. The wound on her face showed no signs of clotting as red trickled down her chin.

Aiz climbed back to her feet while standing in pools of her own blood.

Riveria stared at her in disbelief as Aiz cried out her trigger spell:

"Awaken, Tempest...!"

Air currents enveloped her body.

She once again turned to face the monster with the blessings of the wind assisting her movements.

The crimson flames shook once again, this time in disbelief that the girl still had the will to fight.

"AAAAAAAAAAAAAAAAAAAAAAAAAAAAAAAAAAAAAA AAAAAAAAAAAAAAAAAAAA!!"

"!!"

She kicked off the ground at the same moment the monster howled into the air.

She ignored her body's groans of pain and forced it forward out of sheer willpower, pouring all her Mind into the wind.

She didn't care about later. The only thing that mattered to her now was settling the score with Udaeus once and for all. She charged forward, saber at the ready.

"Aiz...?"

Riveria stood in awe of what she was seeing.

All spartois in the girl's path fell by a single stroke; all the pikes missed her in her up-tempo dance. The silver blade left deep gashes in the floor boss's black bones.

The wind howled as Aiz put her life on the line.

More...More!

Each strike, each movement was filled with passion, desire.

Each kick off the ground was filled with the yearning to be faster than anything else.

Her heart screamed out, placing all her faith in the wind that embraced her.

I want more!!

Each limb was heavy as lead; her throat was parched and lungs were dry; streams of red blood flowed down her cheeks.

She burned with anger at the body they wanted to collapse to its knees. *Why are you so frail, so fleeting?*

How could she turn this mind and body...

...Turn this mind and body into something like the sword in her grasp—a sword that would never break, a sword that could become as fast as the wind? How?

More—I need more power! I have to be stronger!!

Her vision flared white before becoming black.

Her consciousness left the battlefield, all while her body fought against the gigantic monster, finding its blind spots.

Into her soul, into the very deepest parts of her being.

Down, down even farther.

More, I want—!!

She couldn't, she couldn't, she couldn't.

Aiz couldn't allow this weakness.

More than anyone else, she refused to let this frail girl exist.

I will—

Aiz knew too well.

Up to this point, and from this point on...

She knew that the path she walked would always be littered with the corpses of countless monsters.

Slice, cut, and slash.

She would climb the mountain of bones to go even farther beyond.

And toward what waited for her there.

On that distant height—

—I will take it back!!

Her desire.

Her craving.

Her earnest wish.

"—UUAAAAHHHHHHHHHHHHHHHHHHHHHHHHHHHH
HHHHHHHHHHHHHHHHH!!"

Noise escaped from the throat that had forgotten how to express emotion.

The parched scream led her hands, feet, entire body past their limits.

Faster, sharper, more instantaneous strikes overwhelmed Udaeus, breaking its bones.

And where their two weapons collided, the cutting edge of the black sword started to crack.

"GUUUuuuuu!"

Udaeus felt a twinge of fear.

Fear of the girl. Fear of the superior knight of wind.

Fear of the figure charging this way, slashing down all the spartois in the blink of an eye and weaving her way through the pikes.

Losing blood, her bones on the verge of cracking, her body was as stable as a candle's flame in a strong breeze. But all that paled in comparison to the rage that consumed her, increasing her strength further still. The Kenki's mighty strikes were terrifying.

Her still-pristine silver saber flashed as if it was expressing the power of her will—a power that went beyond the floor boss's ability to suppress.

"—OOOOOOOOOOOOOOOOOOOOOOOOOOOOOOOOO
OOOOOOOOO!"

Udaeus howled in an attempt to purge its trembling black body of the fear threatening to take hold.

Aiz's craving for more had driven her speed to godly levels. The monster tried to charge its magic for another slash, but Aiz attacked its joints like a divine wind. Udaeus had no choice but to cease charging and defend itself. Now that they were both at the upper limits of their power, the decision Udaeus had to reach was clear. No matter what obstacles it sent in Aiz's direction, sharp spears or high walls, she saw them coming, dodged, and landed a hit that was too

© Kiyotaka Haimura

strong for the beast to repel. Spartois were being struck down faster than they could be born from the Dungeon floor.

But above all, her strikes were heavy.

Her blows were cracking its ribs, instilling fear in its core, and even its sturdiest component, the black greatsword, had been damaged.

There was no limit to the power of the wind.

"UUUUUUUUUUUUUUUUUUUUUUUUUUUU!"

"!"

Udaeus had to take a chance.

Looking out over the vast field of broken bones in front of it, the floor boss summoned row upon row of extremely large pikes only in front of itself.

Thousands of sharp points weren't aimed at a single target, but instead at everything on the surface of the floor that it could see. Aiz was forced to break off her attack and gain some distance.

Then, Udaeus used the last of its pillars to form a circular barrier around and behind the girl while pumping energy into its joints.

"!"

The spikes were humongous, jutting ten meders into the air and standing so close together that there was no space between them, a perfect wall. Aiz was caught in the middle of a crescent moon.

The only way open to her was forward, trapped in a cul-de-sac of death.

The beast had prevented her from getting close, forced her to retreat, and still managed to trap her within striking distance. Udaeus had run out of pikes, so it raised the damaged black greatsword high into the air. Rotating his shoulders, it got into position to unleash a strike that combined all its destructive power and speed at once.

The only direction that Aiz could go was toward the beast, and the sword would come down long before she could escape from the ring.

Shoulder, elbow, and finally wrist. Aiz looked on as violet light emanated from the joints of the monster's left arm—and made her decision, frowning.

She squatted low to the ground, gathering as much power into her knees as possible, before jumping and flipping backward high into the air.

Higher and higher she went, until she reached the top of the crescent-moon wall at the end of the cul-de-sac and *landed on her feet.*

She made eye contact with the crimson flames that were shaking in surprise before launching her painful and protesting body into a full-blast air current.

Udaeus's howl accompanied a flash of magic as it brought the black greatsword straight down.

By contrast, Aiz focused her divine wind on a singular point.

"Lil Rafaga!!"

The massive black blade collided with the spiraling arrow of wind.

Finishing move versus finishing move in a head-to-head test of strength. Udaeus's three joints pulsed like supernovas of violet light. The gale whipping around Aiz cut through the air faster than any natural storm could hope to achieve.

Wave upon wave of air fought against the purple glow, like two rivals trying to determine which was ultimately strongest.

"Wind, wind, wind!!"

Her voice was heard and the wind pushed itself even faster in response.

Udaeus's burning eyes flickered as it felt the force against its blade. It howled even louder, forcing more energy into its joints. The violet glow grew into a blinding light, and this time it was Aiz who grimaced as the rival met her challenge.

Each increase in the wind speed brought her body closer to the verge of being ripped apart. With each passing moment, there was a feeling that the two great powers would destroy each other. Footsteps of impending doom crept up in the back of her mind—when suddenly…

"Gather, breath of the earth—my name is Alf!"

The tones of the radiant voice reached Aiz's ears.

"Veil Breath!"

A jade light descended onto the girl's body, its warmth enveloping her like a glove.

Glancing to the side, she could clearly see Riveria standing relatively close to the area between her and Udaeus with her staff raised.

Veil Breath was Riveria's support magic.

It took the form of a deep green light that sat on a single target like cloth, adding a layer of protection from both physical and magical attacks. Similar to an enchantment, its effects continued for a set amount of time, and also, however slightly, healed the recipient.

Riveria's assistance granted Aiz's body a small amount of relief, giving it a chance to reclaim some of its strength. The elf's sharp, jade eyes met the human's golden ones, wordlessly conveying, *"At least allow me to do this much!"* They only maintained eye contact for a few fleeting seconds before the human turned her head forward, back toward her enemy.

Thanks to the layer of light surrounding her body, the pressure of the boss's blade felt lighter. *With this*—Aiz thought to herself as she gathered energy in her revitalized muscles and unleashed Airiel's full power.

"_____!!"

In that moment, the shaft of the black greatsword fractured as Aiz's arrow of wind claimed victory.

The blade of Desperate carved its way to the crumbling sword, breaking it down to half its original size. Aiz emerged from the falling rubble and tore through the air toward her opponent.

The torrent of wind wrapped itself around Udaeus's left arm, and tore it apart at the joints.

"_____!"

The pieces of Udaeus's left arm fell to the ground with thundering crashes.

Aiz could hear the beast howling behind her after taking his other arm off at the shoulder. But her body had reached its limit, every bit of strength leaving her muscles as her magic faded.

She fell out of the air, hitting the ground with a dull thud.

"Ah...!"

She lay on the ground like a masterless puppet.

She closed her eyes for a moment, the red spots in her vision turning to black. However, they were open again in a flash.

From the vibrations reaching her through the floor, she knew the monster was in pain. Despite being covered with wounds from head to toe, Aiz slowly climbed to her feet, the green glow still enveloping her body.

...I'm fine.

Riveria's magic was still with her.

So.

One more time, she could squeeze out more strength.

Just a little more, and she would use the last of her power.

To defeat the enemy. To surpass it.

To become strong.

To rid herself of weakness forever.

"*...Awaken, Tempest.*"

Her voice might have been weak, but her words were clear and determined.

Wind armor returning, she looked over her shoulder toward the enemy behind her.

She watched the armless floor boss howl and wail for a moment, and she tightened her grip on the hilt of her saber.

Aiz took a step forward.

The fight continued for close to an hour after that.

Riveria took care of the spartois while keeping a close eye on the battle. The two combatants took turns inflicting damage on each other, with neither able to claim a clear advantage as their duel showed no signs of slowing down.

Then.

One silver arc sliced through the air and connected with its target. Aiz inflicted a decisive blow.

"OOOOOooooooooooooooooo————..."

A broken lower jaw, many fractured bones, part of its head crushed.

Udaeus was already riddled with gashes all over its body. A weakening roar escaped from the exposed bones inside of its mouth and echoed throughout the room at the same time the beast's body fell to the floor.

Its lower back had been sliced clean through, causing Udaeus to fall backward. Puffs of smoke ballooned into the air as each of its remaining bones hit the ground.

"..."

Dried blood covering her face, Aiz approached her fallen enemy with the silent calm of a still night.

Without its connection to the ground, it was impossible for Udaeus to summon any more pikes. Pieces of its black bones stuck out of the ground like grave markers given to the countless white-boned warriors that had been slain during the ferocious battle. Aiz wove her way through all of them before jumping on top of the monster's chest.

Without its arms, all Udaeus could do was eye Aiz with the weakly flickering crimson flames in its eye sockets. They watched powerlessly as the girl walked onto its sternum. The solid bones beneath her feet were already breaking apart, the brilliant sheen of the magic stone beneath her a distant memory. The faint light emerging from it was so weak that it seemed it could be snuffed out at any moment.

Aiz said nothing as she lifted Desperate with both hands, the blade pointed toward the heavens.

She whirled around with the saber, then she sliced straight down from high above her head to her feet, making nary a sound.

"_____"

The crumbling bones fell apart as the wind blade connected with the magic stone.

A web of fissures raced across the stone surface. A high-pitched *crack!* filled the air.

Udaeus's entire body collapsed inward a moment later with a *whoosh*. The black bones dissolved into ash and diffused into the remaining wind.

The black gravestones dissipated along with them, echoes whirling around the room as they crumbled.

"…"

Aiz stood in the middle of the quiet battlefield, saber hanging loosely in the limp grip of her right hand. It was all over.

Her blond hair faintly twinkled in the dim light; the still-pristine silver saber glinted at her feet.

A mountain of ash and monster corpses beneath her, she slowly looked up.

Blood still dripped from the open wound on her cheek and ran down onto an already bloodied breastplate.

There were no words. She simply looked up at the ceiling as though her soul was being drawn out of her body under the cover of darkness.

"…"

"…Riveria."

Sheathing her saber and walking down to the floor, Aiz caught a glimpse of her companion walking toward her.

The human girl's shoulders shrank like a child expecting to be scolded by her parents. Riveria came to a stop right in front of her and placed the palm of her hand on the girl's bloody cheek without saying a word.

"Be still."

Aiz had been on the verge of breaking the silence, but Riveria placed a finger over her lips and began casting.

It was full-fledged healing magic this time. Warm green light emerged from the palm of her hand on the girl's face and worked its way around her body, healing her wounds as it went. Aiz closed her eyes, feeling the touch of Riveria's fingers and the warmth of her magic.

Once all Aiz's wounds had closed, Riveria ripped off a piece of her own top-class battle cloth and wiped the blood off of Aiz's skin, like a mother wiping dirt off her child.

Likewise, Aiz wasn't happy about having the extremely expensive, and abrasive, cloth rubbed against her skin. She closed an eye and bore it as her plump cheeks got pushed from side to side.

"…"

"…"

The girl's face clean, Riveria lowered the cloth and looked her in the eyes.

Aiz stayed silent and looked up to meet the gaze of the elf who stood taller than she did.

"What is troubling you?"

Not a scolding, not a criticism, but a simple question. The girl's golden eyes went wide.

Riveria looked as though she were trying to say something in her clear gaze. The muscles in Aiz's chest tightened as her gaze fell to her feet before she worked up the courage to start talking.

She started with the incident in the town of Rivira, and what she had refused to divulge.

The red-haired Tamer. Everything.

"She…she called me…Aria."

Riveria's eyes opened as wide as they could go the moment those words escaped Aiz's lips.

Words failed her. Covering her mouth with her hand to hide her surprise, she clearly understood the meaning.

A few moments passed and Riveria put her hand down. At last she knew what had driven Aiz to such a degree of recklessness, and she quietly sighed.

She cast her gaze on the girl once again.

"Aiz, will you not rely on me?"

"!"

The girl's face shot up. Riveria took another step forward and stroked Aiz's blond hair.

The two made eye contact, Aiz basking in Riveria's motherly gaze and warmth. But she couldn't take it and looked away.

"I…and Tiona, and Lefiya, and everyone else…we consider you to be a member of our own family."

Her warmth seeped its way all the way into Aiz's heart.

It penetrated the wall that she had put up around herself and embraced her soul. The black flames that had been burning within her finally started to die out.

The fingers that stroked her hair tapped her breastplate.

"You are not alone anymore. Do not forget that."

"…Yes."

Touched by something close to love in Riveria's words, Aiz hid her eyes behind her bangs and nodded.

Blushing, the girl finally looked up again.

"Riveria…"

"What is it?"

"…I'm sorry."

She saw the elf's cheeks pull back. Riveria was smiling.

"Huh?" mumbled Aiz, using both hands to support her tilted head.

Riveria had scolded her many times, and raised her with an iron fist. Never once had Aiz seen this woman do this in her life.

Eyes widening, Riveria couldn't help but smile again.

"Not only are there many magic stones, but there is also a large number of items to collect. Aiz, give me a hand."

"…Understood."

Aiz followed Riveria toward the shimmering rocks buried under the ashes of Udaeus.

It took a lot of effort, but the two of them collected all the loot and put it into the backpacks that Lefiya and Rakuta had left for them.

Riveria swung the bags over her shoulders, and the two of them left the room behind.

Two women, jade and blond hair waving from side to side as they walked.

Moving side by side like mother and daughter, the two returned to the surface.

AN UNEXPECTED REUNION

Гэта казка іншага сям'і.

Рэюньён раптам

It took Aiz and Riveria three days to return to the Dungeon's upper levels after Udaeus fell in battle.

Normally, passing through the lower and middle levels could take much longer, but they chose the shortest route, with Riveria handling most of the encounters to give Aiz a chance to recuperate. They even spent some time resting in the town of Rivira on the eighteenth floor, so the two adventurers showed little signs of fatigue.

"Aiz, are you certain it was a good idea to leave that drop item with him?" Riveria asked.

"Yes…I don't really use greatswords," Aiz answered.

The two of them were discussing the drop item she'd chosen to leave behind in Rivira: Udaeus's Black Sword.

There were many items left after they had slain the small army of spartois as well as Udaeus itself. Among them was the weapon that had given Aiz so much trouble; the black greatsword hadn't turned to ash with the rest of the monster. Of course, it had taken a great deal of damage during the battle, but the remains were just the right size for an adventurer to retrieve it.

Carrying this amazing trophy into the town of Rivira had caused quite a stir. The news spread from shop to shop like wildfire: A never-before-seen drop item from the floor boss Udaeus—one that could only be acquired by challenging the beast with a small party—had come to town.

In the not-too-distant past, Bors had dreamed of becoming a smith. One look at the drop item, with its razor-sharp edge that could have easily passed for the work of the High Smiths, brought tears of joy to his eyes.

Bors had become quite the weapons expert during his time in Rivira and had convinced Aiz to leave the sword with him for safekeeping in exchange for shaping it into a grand weapon that would be ready the next time she ventured this far down into the Dungeon.

"And we don't know when the Tamer will attack again…Having a strong weapon is reassuring."

"That man's choice of words is incredible…"

Riveria sighed. She could still hear Bors saying, "It'll come back to ya one way or another," in the back of her mind.

What's worse, she could imagine the look on his face as he ran his hands down the blade and laughed out of pure enjoyment right about now.

"…?"

"What is wrong, Aiz?"

The two had made it to about halfway through the fifth floor.

Aiz had been lost in thought for a while, when she suddenly spotted another adventurer in the middle of a room.

"There's someone on the ground."

"Did a monster get him?"

Riveria's eyebrows sank as she surveyed the scene. Aiz walked up to his side. He was on his stomach in the middle of the wide room with its light green walls.

The closer the blond girl got to him, the more her eyes shook.

The light armor of a lower-class adventurer…a thin body that wasn't done growing…and hair the color of white virgin snow.

The adventurer was none other than the rabbit-like boy Aiz had been wanting to see again.

"No visible wounds, healing and detox appear to be unnecessary…Looks like a classic case of Mind Down."

Riveria knelt beside the boy and made her diagnosis. She seemed rather disinterested when she reached the conclusion.

Aiz was right behind her, eyes glued to the boy in shock. Words came out of her mouth before she could stop them.

"This boy…"

"What, do you know him, Aiz?"

"Not really. We've never spoken directly…He's, um, the boy I told you about. The Minotaur…"

"…I see. This is the one that idiot insulted."

Riveria had been informed about the real reason Aiz ran out of the bar the night after their last expedition.

She lamented over Bete's actions for a moment before returning her gaze to the boy with a little bit more understanding in her eyes.

As for Aiz, the one she'd been wanting to apologize to was now right in front of her. Her chest tightening, she said the first words that came to her mind.

"Riveria, I want to compensate him."

"…There are other ways to say that."

Riveria had asked what she would like to do, and the girl's response had been clear, if a little bit too formal. She sighed again.

"Huh?" Aiz blinked a few times.

"Well, helping someone at a time like this is common courtesy…"

Aiz vigorously nodded her head as the two women once again looked down at the young adventurer.

A thought came to the elf's mind, and she glanced at the girl beside her out of the corner of her eye.

"…Aiz, do for this boy exactly what I tell you. For compensation, that should be enough."

"What?"

Aiz looked at her in confusion and she responded casually.

"Allow him to sleep with his head in your lap until he awakens."

Aiz blinked again.

"…Is that enough?"

"Well, I am not certain. But you must protect this spot, even if there is no reason to go above and beyond that…Besides, there is no man alive who would not be happy to receive that from you."

Aiz's confusion only increased. She decided to tell Riveria exactly how she felt.

"I don't understand…"

"You do not need to."

Riveria chuckled quietly to herself, her face relaxing as she made eye contact with the girl. Aiz was still wondering if it was okay to do such a thing. However, the things Riveria told her were almost always right on the money.

"Mmm," mumbled Aiz, her face aloof. Riveria stood up.

"I shall return to the surface. Remaining here would only get in your way. The two of you must be alone to reach an understanding."

"Yes. Thank you, Riveria."

"Ah."

Riveria gave an affirmative nod and left them behind.

They were in the upper levels. She knew that nothing around here posed any kind of threat to Aiz, so she wasn't worried in the slightest about leaving her alone.

Aiz watched her leave before looking back down at the boy's white head. She knelt close to him.

Slowly, very slowly, she sat down.

Now then, how will this turn out…?

Backpack over her shoulder and staff in her right hand, Riveria thought about the look on Aiz's face when she left her alone with the boy as she made her way through the Dungeon.

A frog shooter monster tried to bar her path, but she struck it down in the blink of an eye.

Nothing would make me happier than a good outcome, but…

Riveria was well aware of Aiz's state of mind.

The girl's heart and body had been out of balance ever since she'd fought the red-haired Tamer. The pain inside her had driven her to try challenging a floor boss on her own.

While most of the remnants of that pain had been expelled, the elf still felt a little bit uneasy. Aiz was not quite back to normal just yet.

Considering all of this, Riveria was hoping that small amount of physical contact with the boy would distract her from the inner turmoil for a short while.

"That and…"

Riveria had noticed a very slight change within Aiz when the two of them were together.

She genuinely hoped that the girl might become a little bit less blind.

"…Well, it won't turn out for the worse."

It's not as though the boy would run away, she mused to herself.

"…"

There was something refreshing about the weight on her thin thighs.

Aiz silently looked down at the boy with his head in her lap, his eyes closed as though he were sleeping on a pillow.

…This is a little embarrassing.

She felt rather awkward after lifting his head and sliding beneath him.

Cheeks blushing, she very carefully adjusted her position to match him. She didn't want to wake the white rabbit, so her every movement was slow and gentle.

"…"

The two humans in the middle of the room were discovered by one monster after another, but one flick of Aiz's wrist was enough to dispatch them without disturbing the boy.

She continued to protect him, looking down at his peaceful face whenever she wasn't taking care of any would-be attackers.

"…You've been working very hard."

His armor had changed since the last time she saw him.

It might have been new, but it was already covered with scratches and dents. She could tell it had been used, a lot. There was no doubt in her mind he had been fighting monsters in the Dungeon every day.

It was heartwarming to see this much effort. He was a pure young man with an untainted spirit.

Innocent, so very innocent.

Completely different from her. The purity emanating from his spirit

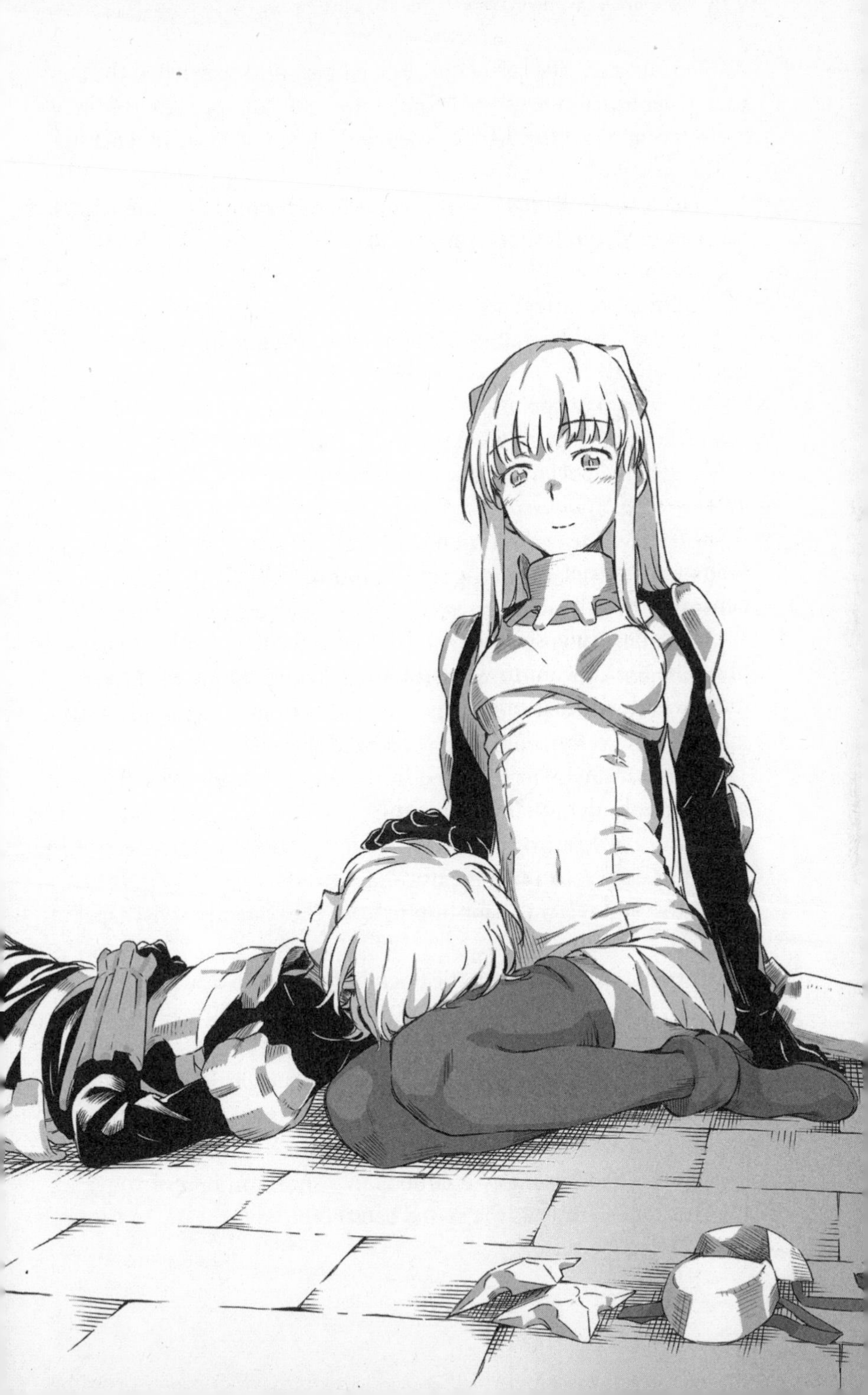

calmed her own. The last of the black flames still flickering in the bottom of her heart were washed clean until finally disappearing entirely.

A smile appeared on Aiz's lips before she knew what was happening.

The pure white rabbit soothed her.

An urge to stroke his hair overcame her. Her fingers drifted down and caressed his cheeks from time to time.

"...Mom?"

The boy spoke after a few minutes.

A quiver ran through Aiz's shoulders, caught off guard by the boy's sleep talk.

...Is yours gone, too?

She thought to herself, but the words didn't come out.

Her golden eyes looked away for a moment.

We are...a lot alike...

She felt a sudden connection with him that she knew she shouldn't hold on to, as well as a twinge of loneliness.

Aiz brushed the white bangs out of the boy's face and apologized.

"Sorry. I'm not your mother..."

A moment later, two groggy ruby-red eyes opened beneath her.

They became clearer every moment as the boy woke up. His gaze locked onto hers the moment he realized she was there.

The boy seemed lost, trapped in the moment their eyes met. Aiz started stroking his hair once again.

The tips of her fingers ran past his eyelashes before he slowly pulled himself into a sitting position.

She thought it a waste for him to leave the warmth of her lap, but gave up.

The boy stayed sitting on the floor, but turned to face her.

"...An illusion?"

"Not an illusion."

The boy's drowsy face suddenly froze, his right hand in midair. Eyebrows slanting outward, he wore a rather unusual expression.

It might even have been a little rude.

Aiz, who had felt many emotions in a short amount of time, felt her lips pout slightly as she stared back at the boy.

...H-huh?

Ruby-red and golden eyes stared at each other. The boy didn't budge, but Aiz started to get flustered.

Had she done something wrong? Although her face didn't show it, the young spirit dwelling within her was racking her brain, desperately running around and looking for an answer. The white rabbit only looked at her, frozen like a statue with his white hair sticking up like ears, waving back and forth.

—That's right, I need to apologize.

Aiz started to open her mouth the moment the thought hit her.

Then she saw the boy getting redder and redder from the neck up by the second. By the time she fully noticed, his head was roughly the color of an overripe apple.

His beautiful red eyes were in bad shape, twitching almost like there were worms crawling under the surface.

Now she knew for sure something was wrong. She frantically prepared to ask him what—when the boy jumped to his feet.

Then...

"GAAAAAAAAAHHHHHHHHHHHHHHHHHHHHHHH-HHHHHHHHHHHHHHHHHHHHHHHHHHHHHHHHHHHH-HHHHHHHHHHHHHHHHHHHHH!"

He ran away from Aiz at full speed.

"..."

Bounding and leaping like a panicked critter, the boy disappeared from the room.

Still sitting on her knees in the middle of the floor, Aiz couldn't move at all.

"Geh-geh-geh." She thought she heard some monster laughing in the distance.

"...Why do you always...run away?" Aiz mumbled to herself, on the verge of tears.

Lefiya · Viridis

BELONGS TO:	*Loki Familia*
RACE:	elf
JOB:	adventurer
DUNGEON RANGE:	fifty-first floor
WEAPON:	staff
CURRENT WORTH:	910,000 valis

Skill   Lv.5

STRENGTH:	I 79	**DEFENSE:**	H 107
DEXTERITY:	H 184	**AGILITY:**	G 226
MAGIC:	C 688	**CONJURE:**	H
IMMUNITY:	I		

MAGIC:	Arcs Ray	• Single-target Magic • Hones in on designated target
	Fusillade Fallarica	• Wide-range attack Magic • Fire element
	Elf Ring	• Summoning Magic (Summon Burst) • Only Elvish magic can be summoned. • Trigger spell and spell's effect must be known. • Mind is expended for this Magic and summoned Magic.
SKILLS:	Fairy Cannon	• Increases Magic power • Strengthens only offensive Magic
EQUIPMENT:	Forest Teardrop	• Only for magic users, strengthens magic power • Next to useless as a physical weapon • Crystals on its head respond to user's magic, glowing bright blue. • 37,800,000 valis
	Silver Barrette	• Metallic hairband, light • Provides almost no physical defensive boost • Accessory that provides predictive power for adventurers, prevents paralysis

LEFIYA VIRIDIS

Afterword

This is the second volume of the spinoff series—but the number of characters has already exploded. The headache I've gotten from giving characters who will appear in the main story a flying start has informed me just how difficult it is to write a gaiden—a side story.

I know it's stealing entrances from characters later on, but it would make me happy if these new men and women were welcomed with open arms when they appear in the main storyline.

On a different topic, one of my editors and I had a very entertaining conversation about zombies in the second installment of a certain action-adventure horror game when we met to discuss this volume. While not much of a gamer myself, I spent countless hours watching my friends play and going through guidebooks. I remember being very knowledgeable about the storylines.

In that specific game, there's a "Side A Storyline" with the male hero of the story and a "Side B Storyline" with the heroine that you could switch between during a play-through. There are some weapons and items that only the hero can use, and others only available to the heroine, a sort of backward restriction...At least I think that's how it works.

There is a male hero in the main story, and a female hero in this gaiden. They share the same world, so that led us to experiment with a few things and have some fun. "What if we have him use a weapon in the main story that she couldn't use here?" Both of us got really excited and talked for hours about the endless possibilities. This was after it had been decided that Volume 5 and Gaiden 2 would be released in a two-month span.

Reading this book right after finishing Volume 5, or reading Volume 5 right after this one, might just bring a smile to your face.

While acknowledging the fact that the main series can't continue while I'm having you read the gaiden, from time to time I will casually work these in from here on out.

And now to show my gratitude.

First to my editors, Mr. Kotaki and Mr. Takahashi, for your assistance and advice during the creation of this book. I can see and feel the influence of your words from cover to cover every time I read it. Next, for the beautiful illustrations from Mr. Kiyota Haimura that have given this book a unique charm that went beyond my expectations. Thank you so much. Lastly, I want to say thank you to everyone involved in the creation of this work and to the readers who make it all possible. Words cannot express how grateful I am.

Thank you for your continued support.

Until the next installment.

Fujino Omori

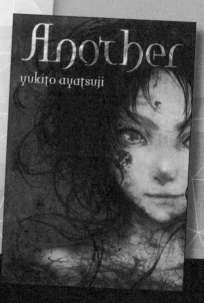

CONTENTS

© Kiyotaka Haimura

The town, the sky, everything was cast in a fiery crimson glow. As shards of flames poured down on the crystal path, a single shadow emerged.

Is it WRONG to TRY to PICK UP GIRLS in A DUNGEON? ON THE SIDE

Sword Oratoria

FUJINO OMORI

ILLUSTRATION BY
KIYOTAKA HAIMURA

CHARACTER DESIGN BY
SUZUHITO YASUDA

© Kiyotaka Haimura

FINN DEIMNE:
Charismatic field general of *Loki Familia*. Prum.

"Those perverts have their eyes set on the general...!!"

TIONE HIRYUTE:
The older Amazonian twin.
Has a crush on the familia's leader, Finn.